"Like the books of the late Stieg Larsson, Thompson's reflect the gray cold of Nordic winters . . . But Thompson's books move more quickly (and violently) than Larsson's." —*St. Louis Post-Dispatch*

Praise for

HELSINKI BLOOD

"*Helsinki Blood* is as dark and bracing as a Nordic winter . . . Kari Vaara blasts other maverick cops out of the (icy) water."
>—M. J. McGrath, author of *The Boy in the Snow*

"Finnish noir is the current tone of Thompson's series . . . Readers who are already invested in this character ache to see him succeed. Just the fact that Thompson can make the situation believable and make us care is evidence of his talent." —*Library Journal*

"I can't get enough of this author. No one writes noir better, Nordic or otherwise." —Leighton Gage, author of *Blood of the Wicked*

"Inspector Kari Vaara's latest nightmare barrels along at a breakneck pace as he faces enemies on his doorstep as well as his own demons within. James Thompson's spare, no-frills action is straight to the point. *Helsinki Blood* is as raw as it gets, it doesn't pause for breath and it takes no prisoners."
>—Quentin Bates, author of *Frozen Assets* and *Cold Comfort*

"Compelling . . . Thompson draws on his long residence in Finland to convincingly portray a grungy northern underworld."
>—*Publishers Weekly*

"Kentucky native Thompson has created in Kari a hero as dyspeptic as Kurt Wallander and as prone to vigilante justice as Harry Hole."
>—*Kirkus Reviews*

continued . . .

Praise for the Inspector Vaara novels

"Thompson's style is on the dark end of the 'Nordic Noir' spectrum. The genre—with its stark and often violent police procedurals—has proved wildly successful . . . The marquee names have come from Sweden—think Stieg Larsson's *Girl with the Dragon Tattoo,* or Henning Mankell's Wallander series—but Norway's Jo Nesbø, and Iceland's Arnaldur Indriđason and Yrsa Sigurđardóttir have also made their mark with international readers. Thompson stands out from that crowd by writing in English and telling Vaara's gritty narrative in the first person." —*The New York Times*

"A must read for fans of Stieg Larsson and Henning Mankell." —*Booklist*

"Mr. Thompson's ability to craft complex plot/subplots with such powerful prose makes him unique in the family of modern-day crime writers. Startlingly original and instantly cinematic, *Lucifer's Tears* unfolds in page-turning addictiveness until it delivers shock after shock in its denouement of police corruption and condemnation for those trying to rewrite history. It's going to be tough for other crime writers to beat this as Thriller of the Year. Grab yourself a copy now and see why." —*New York Journal of Books*

"In his dozen years of living in Finland . . . Thompson has absorbed enough cold, dark atmosphere for a spot on the roster of top Nordic crime writers—Mankell, Nesbø, Indriđason and the like." —*New York Post*

"The narrative is exquisitely quick . . . Hard to put down." —*Houston Chronicle*

"Don't miss this one." —*USA Today*

"Thompson, an American who has lived in Finland for years, writes vividly of a place he clearly knows and loves." —*The Seattle Times*

ALSO BY JAMES THOMPSON

Helsinki White

Lucifer's Tears

Snow Angels

James Thompson

HELSINKI BLOOD

BERKLEY PRIME CRIME, NEW YORK

THE BERKLEY PUBLISHING GROUP
Published by the Penguin Group
Penguin Group (USA) LLC
375 Hudson Street, New York, New York 10014

USA • Canada • UK • Ireland • Australia • New Zealand • India • South Africa • China

penguin.com

A Penguin Random House Company

HELSINKI BLOOD

Berkley Prime Crime Books are published by The Berkley Publishing Group.
BERKLEY® PRIME CRIME and the PRIME CRIME logo are trademarks of Penguin Group (USA) LLC.

Berkley Prime Crime trade paperback ISBN: 978-0-425-26461-4

The Library of Congress has catalogued the G. P. Putnam's hardcover edition as follows:

Thompson, James, date.
Helsinki blood / James Thompson.
p.   cm.
ISBN 978-0-399-15888-9
1. Police—Finland—Fiction.   2. Homicide investigation—Fiction.
3. Helsinki (Finland)—Fiction.   I. Title.
PS3620.H675H43   2013   2012039842
813'.6—dc23

PUBLISHING HISTORY
G. P. Putnam's Sons hardcover edition / March 2013
Berkley Prime Crime trade paperback edition / March 2014

PRINTED IN THE UNITED STATES OF AMERICA

10 9 8 7 6 5 4 3 2 1

Cover design by Daniel Rembert.

This novel is dedicated to the team at G. P. Putnam's Sons. They've worked tremendously hard to make the Inspector Vaara series a success, are an extraordinarily talented group, and they have my profound thanks, both for their efforts on my behalf and for sharing their knowledge and seeing to my education in the publishing industry. Here, I cite only the people I work most closely with at Putnam, but there are employees who have moved on or changed jobs within the company, and many others are behind the scenes, too many to list. They know who they are. Special thanks to editor Sara Minnich, marketing manager Lydia Hirt, and senior publicist Victoria Comella. And also to president Ivan Held, because he has done me some good turns.

And, as always, for Annukka.

Prologue

July eleventh. A hot summer Sunday. All I want is some goddamned peace and quiet. Now my house is under siege, I have an infant to both care for and protect, and I'm forced to do the last thing I wanted to do: call Sweetness and Milo, my colleagues and subordinates, or accomplices—the definition of their role in my life depends on one's worldview—and ask them for help.

I'm shot to pieces. Bullets to my knee and jaw—places I've been shot before—have left me a wreck. Only cortisone shots and dope for pain enable me to get around with a cane, speak and eat without wanting to scream. I'm still recovering from a brain tumor removal six months ago. The operation was a success but had a serious side effect that left me flat, emotionless.

My feelings are returning as the empty space where once a tumor existed fills in with new tissue, but I only feel love for my wife and child, and intermittent like for one or two others. My normal state and reaction toward others is now irritability. My wife, Kate, suffers from post-traumatic stress disorder and has run away from home, out of control of her own emotions, and abandoned me.

These combined problems, any one of which would drive a person to distraction under the best of circumstances, cloud my judgment and affect my behavior. My judgment and behavior were already clouded. I feel so certain it will all end badly that it seems more a portent than an emotion. Auguries and omens of catastrophe seem all around me, just out of sight, but every time I turn to face them, they disappear like apparitions.

1

June had come to an end. I seldom went out, mostly because mobility was so difficult, but it had been such a bad day—Kate had been gone for around two weeks. I was depressed and in awful pain—that I thought fresh air and sunshine might be good for me, help me gain some perspective. Mental health care workers often recommend just getting out and about to raise spirits. Dumbfucks.

I hadn't had a haircut in a couple months, went to the barber around the corner and got it cropped military short, as it's been for more than thirty years. It revealed the scar that runs four inches across the left center of my head to the hairline over my eye. The ugly gunshot wound on my face was no longer bandaged but not healed. Looking in the barber's mirror, I thought of my severe limp and knew all I needed was a long black leather trench coat to look like a cliché Gestapo torturer in a B movie.

Afterward, I went a little way down the street to Hilpeä Hauki, my favorite bar. I believed it might be therapeutic for me. It's a cozy, quiet place—they don't even play music—that specializes in imported beers, and the same faces appear almost daily. Conversations went on around me, but speaking wasn't required. People often just have a beer and browse through the daily newspapers or sit in silence if they don't feel chatty.

The patrons almost all know me, or at least of me, and wouldn't ask questions about my injuries, so I felt comfortable being there. I sat in "the dogs' corner," so called because customers are allowed to sit in the squared-off area near the L-shaped bar with their pets. A water bowl was under a side table next to the door. The staff even keeps dog treats handy. I ordered a beer and a *kossu*—the colloquial for Koskenkorva, a kind of Finnish vodka—and sat on a stool at the bar.

A young drunk guy came in. He was loud, attention-seeking. The bartender, a half Finn, half Brit named Mike, refused him service. He called Mike a *vittu pää*—a cunt head. Mike is a big guy and used to dealing with such behavior, but I stuck my nose in anyway. "Shut the fuck up," I said, "or I'll come over there and beat you to death."

The asshole was four paces away from me. He checked

me out and laughed. "Listen, crip, the only thing you're going to beat me in is an ugly contest."

I felt myself seething. Mike leaned over the bar, looked at me, shook his head no. I saw that I had reached down and was going for my backup piece, a Colt .45 with a three-inch barrel in an ankle holster. I didn't realize I was doing it.

"Bad day?" Mike asked.

I came to my senses and pulled the cuff of my jeans back down over my .45. "Yeah, I guess so."

"Why don't you come back on a day when you feel better." It wasn't a question, I was being kicked out. "I'll buy you a beer the next time I see you." He said it in a caring way, I couldn't be mad about it. And besides, he was right.

I got up to leave.

Without deigning to look at me, Asshole said, "See ya, Frankenstein."

I stepped toward the door as if leaving, but turned and swung my cane two-handed like a bat. Scored a perfect kidney shot with the back of the gold lion's head handle. Asshole went down like a rock, screamed and curled up into a ball. I gave the folks in the dogs' corner a small salute, wished them pleasant evenings and hobbled home.

On the way, I decided that in my current emotional state I was dangerous, not fit company for other humans. I decided to go into self-imposed isolation. It didn't last long.

Six thirty p.m. Pizza delivered, waiting for hunger to build. Check. Tranquilizers, pain medication and muscle relaxants ingested, so that I could work up to eating it. Check. Half tumbler of *kossu* on the side table beside my armchair, to amplify the effects of the dope. Bottle on floor beside me. Check.

Only an idiot pays attention to the warnings on medication stating that it shouldn't be taken with alcohol. Any fool knows tranks and dope work better with booze. The dope wasn't that strong, just tablets with thirty milligrams of codeine and some Tylenol, max eight a day. I eschewed stronger painkillers because they guaranteed addiction and detox, the last thing I needed to add to my list of problems. Tranks are addictive, but were necessary to relax my jaw enough to eat or speak. As the doctors taught me, I had to balance functionality versus nonfunctionality.

By that point in my life, I was expert at pain management. The buzz and pain relief the alcohol generated was enough to get me by. I'd gone to the manufacturers' websites of all the medications and worked out how many I could take of each per day, in conjunction with alcohol, without destroying my vital organs. I discovered double-checking medical advice was a necessity after once going to *terveyskeskus,* the public health clinic, also known as *arvauskeskus*—the guessing center—with a simple flu. Had I taken the medication as directed, I would have required a liver transplant.

Katt, my cat, was fed, watered and litter box cleaned, in case I passed out. Check. I was ready to settle in for another stoned evening of introspection. For some reason, I felt a desire to tour my self-imposed luxury prison first.

Behind the living room in our fourth-floor apartment, a low dais next to the kitchen, our dining area, has a big oak table that seats ten, so we can have dinner parties. The kitchen has brushed-stainless-steel fixtures. The refrigerator and induction stovetop are state-of-the-art. Not the best money can buy, but not far from it. The bathroom is a tad small, but bigger than is common in apartments in Helsinki. It has a small electric sauna in it, and like many people, we use it more for drying clothes than sweating in steam heat.

We have two bedrooms, one for Kate and me, with an over-sized and almost too comfortable bed—I sometimes have to force myself out of it to face the new day—and one for our daughter, Anu.

In front of the dais is a long couch that faces an entertainment center. When you're sitting on the couch, a bank of windows makes up the wall to my left. Floor-to-ceiling bookcases—which I built myself—make up the right side of the room. They're chock-full, overloaded with books and music. My CD collection numbers over five hundred now, and my vinyl records number near a thousand. My man's chair sits to the side and in front of the couch, near a large window, angled toward the forty-two-inch flat-screen television and stereo in our entertainment center. In summer, this is poor placement for the chair. The window faces east and gets the full blast of morning sun until the building across from me blots it out. The sun penetrates the drawn, thick red curtains, makes them glare like the front window of an Amsterdam whorehouse, and the light beating through them makes me swelter.

Most people love summer. It's so short that it's like a flower that blooms and quickly dies. People make such a huge deal out of it. *We must have as much fun as possible while we can. Celebrate. Celebrate. Celebrate!* Socially, it's pressuring. If people don't want to go to a summer cottage, pick berries and barbecue—or, if they stay in the city, don't sit on the patios and drink fourteen hours a day—they're considered deranged. And the whole country shuts down in June and July while people vacation. No work gets done. Fuck summer. If I were a flower, I'd be a lily. They only open at night.

When we moved here from Kittilä, my hometown in the Arctic Circle, we got rid of all our old furnishings as a way of symbolizing a fresh start. It had all been collected by me over the years. Almost everything here is sparkling and new, chosen by Kate and me together, to make it ours instead of mine.

My tour of our home was some sort of self-punishment, an emotional self-flagellation. A re-enforcement of the knowledge that this is a home meant for a family, not for a man living alone, estranged from his wife.

I sat down in my oversized crushed blue velvet armchair. I more or less lived in it. I clenched my teeth to keep from grunting out loud from the coming blast of pain, and pulled my bad leg up onto the matching footrest in front of it. Being shot in the same knee for a second time did it no good at all. I already had a bad limp from when I was shot the first time, almost twenty years ago. The same went for my face. A second gunshot wound in the same jaw—the first a couple winters ago—created the current need to drink the *kossu with meds*. This latest wound tapped a bundle of nerves in my face, and because of the pain, I couldn't manage to chew without it—even speaking was difficult—and tolerating soup for every meal was insufferable.

This was my second week of self-imposed isolation, except for dragging myself out to buy basic provisions. I had tried the company of others. I went to my brother's midsummer party, but felt lonelier there among the revelers than I would have here at home by myself.

I had thrown away my crutches because they rendered me unable to carry anything. And also because of vanity. I despise the appearance of weakness. Everything I needed was close by. I had a granny shopping cart with two wheels. I gimped around with my cane in my left hand and pulled the cart with my right.

I checked to make sure my silenced .45 Colt was within easy reach, tucked under my seat cushion, the handle jutting out. After having been shot a total of four times, I vowed to never go unarmed again and to teach myself to be a crack shot, even though I have no interest in guns or marksmanship. However, only a reckless dumbass cop is stupid enough to have eaten this many bullets. I had no faith that I would become any wiser, so I needed to protect myself.

I hadn't spoken to another soul for days, other than to say thank you to the store checkout clerks and delivery people. My wife, Kate, hadn't answered my calls or text messages for a week, despite my right to see our daughter. My two protégés in our three-man crime unit—a euphemistic wordplay in our case, because as policemen, we've used Machiavellian rationalizations about the end justifying the means—inundated me with calls and text messages after we closed our last case.

Soon after, Kate left me and took Anu with her. I wasn't angry, just frightened. Detective Sergeant Milo Nieminen and Sweetness, real name Sulo Polvinen, officially a translator but in truth my assistant and strong-arm man in the National Bureau of Investigation, were concerned about me being alone in my current state: shot to pieces, less than functional and, they left unsaid, distraught about my family situation.

I ignored them for a time, and finally sent texts telling them I was fine, asked them to please fuck off, and saying that I would contact them when I was ready. Milo respected that. He had problems of his own. A bullet shattered the carpal tunnel and severed the radial nerve in his right wrist, causing paralysis of his hand. He has very limited motion in it now, including his all-important trigger finger.

He would have called it his gun hand, as he considered himself a self-described pistoleer before the bullet put an end to that delusion. I think he envisioned himself a Wild West anti-hero, a Finnish Wyatt Earp. Plus, Adrien Moreau, who Kate blew in half with a sawed-off shotgun, lopped off his ear and it was sewn back on. It doesn't hang quite right and he already had self-image problems, so I imagine looking in the mirror is difficult for him, let alone the automatic double-take people make when they see a disfigurement, no matter how small. I know all about that.

Sweetness came out unscathed. He's a natural killer, and had just dumped two clips of .45 caliber hollow-point rounds in our perp, at near-point-blank range, while neither Milo nor myself managed to even hurt anyone, let alone defend ourselves when we received our injuries.

Sweetness is rich from money we've stolen—as are Milo

and myself—and has absolutely no conscience but a heart as big as his six-foot-three, two-hundred-sixty-five-pound frame. Sweetness ignored my text and showed up at my door with three cases of beer and a carton of Koskenkorva bottles, a dopey grin on his baby face. I hired him because he took some hard knocks and I felt sorry for him, but also because of his innocence and honesty, his capacity for violence, and because I was drunk at the time. I've never regretted the decision.

Sweetness places great faith in the saying "If the alcohol, tar and sauna won't cure you, you're already dead." Neither of us knows what the tar is for, or what you're supposed to do with it to use it as a curative. We sat together for a while, had a couple shots and beers, talked about nothing. I promised him that if he gave me some space, I would call him if I needed something, and if I needed nothing, I would call him when I was ready for company. He agreed.

When I shut the door behind him, I realized how much I envied him his contentment, his happiness, his simplicity. Many people mistake his simplicity for stupidity because of his size and childlike face, and treat him as a Lennie Small, from Steinbeck's *Of Mice and Men*. He is, in fact, astute and observant, and speaks five languages fluently. Despite our agreement and my refusal to respond, he texted three times daily, "just to make sure." I was uncertain what he wanted to be sure of.

Sweetness looked up to me as a father figure. When I met him, he seemed lost. His brother had been killed by two bouncers. An accidental death, although better judgment on their parts would have prevented it. Sweetness's father put him up to murdering the bouncers, and he tried to stab them to death with a box cutter. He managed only to disfigure them, and his father, a worthless piece of human garbage, finished the job as they lay in their hospital beds. He's now serving a long prison jolt for the double homicide.

Sweetness's true nature is a combatant, his calling a killer. He's my friend, I don't judge him for it. I did, however, insist as a pre-condition to hiring him that he get a higher, university or polytechnic-level education, because life in an illegal covert operation couldn't go on forever.

I wanted only one thing for myself, to get my wife and child back and restore balance to our home. Kate was staying at Hotel Kämp, where she's general manager, although currently on maternity leave. My last case went bad and had a devastating effect on her. She witnessed the horror and, having no choice, even took part in it, and the result was the severe psychological damage that she now suffers. And it was my fault, because of a glaring error in judgment.

She was emotionally disturbed and had no business being on her own. I feared she would do herself harm. I was afraid she would take Anu and flee home to the States, maybe to Aspen, where she grew up. I spent much of my days concocting schemes to tempt her to come home. None of them were feasible.

My glass was almost empty. I contemplated whether to have more *kossu* or eat. I opened and closed my mouth. The pain was still riveting. More *kossu*.

A crash and sudden pain scared the living shit out of me. Broken glass showered the room. A half brick shattered the big window, flew across the room, struck the bookcase, and came to rest on the floor. Because my chair sits near the window, only good luck prevented me from being skewered by a large shard, but smaller fragments cut me in over a dozen places. My cat likes to sit on top of the chair, near my head. If he'd been there, he might have been killed.

I forced myself to stand up, to keep from getting blood on the chair, hobbled with my cane over to the foyer and put some sneakers on. I worried about Katt cutting his paws and locked him in the bedroom. I looked around, at a loss. Broken glass requires meticulous cleaning, which entails bending and squatting to the floor, and those movements were near impossible in my condition. No way I could get it all up.

I picked up the brick. "There are ten million ways you could die" was written on it with a black felt-tip marker. A reference to the ten million euros Milo, Sweetness and I had liberated from a faked blackmail scheme involving everyone from a psychotic billionaire to people in the highest levels of government.

I did the best I could, got a waste can from the kitchen, pushed the big shards into a pile with my good foot and put them in it. Because of my knee's limited range of motion, I had to lie on one side, propped up on an elbow, and pick them up with one hand.

Then I took out the vacuum cleaner and made some awkward attempts at pushing it around. I used the attachment designed for such things and vacuumed my chair with thoroughness. After bungling long enough, although I still saw the glint of tiny fragments, almost all the glass was cleaned up, and I felt I'd done the best I could for the evening. I redid the floors with parquet when we bought the apartment. The glass left deep scars in it. That irritated me more than anything.

My cuts were all superficial and stopped bleeding on their own. Still, I covered the chair with an old blanket in case they opened up again. Exhausted, I got a beer and poured another *kossu*. I sat down and thought it through, narrowed down the suspects of who might be harassing me. There were too many to even make an educated guess.

Cleaning up the mess caused me to mistime the drug-alcohol combination. I fell asleep in my chair with the pizza uneaten.

3

Katt's favorite spot, when I was in my armchair and in a reclining position, was to lie with his ass in my lap and his torso sprawled on my chest, staring up at me. He wanted to be petted, or for me to at least keep a hand on his back. He hated it when I slept. It interfered with his receiving attention. When he could no longer stand the boredom, he woke me each morning by climbing to the top of the chair and used the back of my head and neck as a scratching post. I looked like a pack of small, angry rodents had mauled me. That morning was no different.

When he was convinced I was awake, he grew content

and took up his second-favorite position. From atop the chair, he placed his front paws so that they hung over my shoulders, as if to choke me, nuzzled his head against my neck and napped. I considered teaching him to stop scratching me by doing what he hates worst, squirting him with a spray bottle of water, but couldn't do it. After all, he's my best friend. Besides, he's too stupid and obstinate to learn much of anything.

I let Katt snooze for a few minutes, then got up, limped to the kitchen with the aid of my cane and made coffee. Then hobbled back the way I had come, went out to the balcony and smoked a couple cigarettes while I drank a cup. I wanted to maintain some semblance of dignity and refused to smoke inside and stink up my home, so I tended to chain-smoke when I went to the trouble of making it outside. I came back in and looked around. Tufts of cat fur and glass fragments were in corners and under furniture. The place needed a thorough cleaning. I couldn't push the vacuum cleaner around well enough to get under furniture, in corners, against baseboards, the places where most of the dirt collects.

I needed to make a call and get the window replaced. I promised myself I would call a cleaning service and get the place back into shape again, too.

I turned the radio on and one of the big hits of the summer was playing. "Selvä Päivä"—"Sober Day"—by Petri Nygård. The song celebrates the rapture of being shit drunk. Aggravated, I put on Johnny Cash, *American Recordings*.

I took my morning dope. It knocked the edge off my pain

and made my muscles relax, and moving my jaw hurt less. I sucked down a protein drink for breakfast. I was trying not to drop any more weight. Katt sprawled across me while I browsed the daily newspaper. A key turned in the lock of the front door. I took my .45 Colt from under the seat cushion.

Most wives, after abandoning their husbands, would call before visiting and ring the door buzzer when they arrived. In strolled Kate, without warning, to find a pistol trained on her.

I put my Colt back in its customary place under the seat cushion. Kate pointed at it. "Are you out of your mind?" The look in her eyes was one unfamiliar to me.

"Events of late have made me cautious," I said.

Kate killed a man out of necessity. She saved all our lives. The trauma of what she'd done, though, threw her into a dissociative stupor.

I never should have let Kate leave, but how was I to stop her? Maybe I could have requested that her psychiatrist institutionalize her for a time. Leaving home soon after a psychological breakdown might have warranted it, but the shock of watching her walk out the door rendered me incapable of action. Afterward, for a while, she was distant, uncommunicative, but seemed stable enough. I often asked her to come home. She never refused, just said she wasn't ready for that, needed some time alone to think. I could accept that, it was reasonable.

When she started sliding downhill, I didn't see it for what it was: a headlong plunge into post-traumatic stress disorder. She started calling, often late at night. Sometimes she would scream at me for ruining her life. Sometimes she cried and begged forgiveness. Either way, I told her I loved her and asked her to come home. And she did, every third or fourth day, so I could see Anu. The first couple times she sat, often wordless, for an hour or two, while I doted on our child. The third time, she was unresponsive when I spoke to her. She put her arms around me and cried for a long time before she left.

The fourth time was bad. When you know someone really well, they don't have to speak or even move. Their eyes will tell you everything. The look in Kate's eyes told me she was in trouble. She had called the night before, at two in the morning. She didn't speak when I tried to get her to explain why she was so upset. She seemed unable to articulate words other than "I'm sorry." I listened to her bawl for over an hour, and then she hung up without saying good-bye or good night. This scared me. I tried to call her back. Her phone was switched off. When she showed up the next day, she had found her voice again.

Anu was in her pram. Kate parked it in front of me, placed an overstuffed bag of her things beside it, then gave our apartment an inspection walk-through, as I would a crime scene. The *kossu* and beer I hadn't finished before I fell asleep the night before were on the table beside my chair. As luck would have it, the song "Delia's Gone," about murdering a lover, was playing at low volume. The booze and music didn't make a good setting.

She nodded toward the beer and Koskenkorva. "You're drinking in the morning," she said, distress in her voice. "Are you drunk now?"

"I'm not drinking. They're unfinished leftovers from last night."

This, of course, gave the impression that I'd passed out in a drunken stupor. She looked at the shattered window. It disturbed me that she hadn't noticed it as soon as she walked in the door. This spoke of some kind of impairment of her powers of observation. Her tone jumped from distress to alarm. "What have you done? Did you break it while you were drunk? You have cuts. Have you harmed yourself?"

"Clearly," I said, "I did nothing stupid, or the glass would be outside on the pavement, not here on our floor."

She didn't seem to process this obvious truth. Her eyes narrowed, disbelieving, and then she switched topics as if the window was forgotten. "You're Anu's father and have a right to see her. This is your visitation time. Are you mobile enough for that?"

"Yes."

"You look awful." It was only a statement. I couldn't read her emotions from her voice.

She didn't wait for an answer. "You can't live in here, and it's not safe for our child."

"Someone threw a brick through the window. I'm not able to clean well. I'm not mobile enough."

She took out the vacuum cleaner and made the floor spotless in fifteen minutes, did a far better job than I did in over an hour the night before. She put it away and sat on the stool in front of me.

"What kind of condition are you in?" she asked.

I didn't understand why she asked me this. I had explained my condition and prognosis to her during previous visits. I repeated them to placate her.

"I'll recover. My limp will be worse, and I have some nerve damage in my face. It's impossible to say whether the nerves will heal or how well, if further surgery will be required, and if so, whether it will help. My main problem at the moment is that I'm in a lot of pain. I feel like I'm getting worse instead of better. I think it's my imagination, just the pain wearing me down."

"I'm sorry to hear that." She looked like she meant it, but she wasn't sorry enough to come home and help me when I needed her the most. But I wasn't worried about myself for the moment. Grave concern about her mental health took precedence.

"Have you been to see Torsten lately?" I asked.

Torsten Holmqvist, her psychotherapist. One of the best in the business. I was also once one of his patients.

"What passes between my therapist and myself isn't your business."

"I agree," I said. "I only asked if you've been seeing him."

"Yes, your crazy fucked-up wife has been a good girl and attended her therapy regularly. Are you satisfied?"

Now sarcasm. She was sprinting through a gamut of emotions so fast that it was impossible for me to keep up with them. I could think of a thousand reasons, but I wanted to know specifically what had caused her feelings toward me to become so harsh, and why it happened so quickly. "Kate, why are you so furious with me? Why won't you come home?"

She smiled and slowly shook her head, as if I were an idiot and failed to understand the most simple and evident truth. "You're the detective, why don't you figure it out?"

I ignored that. "Do you remember the island and the events that led up to you becoming ill?"

"I don't want to discuss it."

I didn't think she remembered, or at best, her memories were fragmented, or she wouldn't question why I sat with a pistol at hand. I didn't push it.

"Did I ever tell you how much I hate Finnish windows?" she asked. "What the hell kind of windows are hinged at the side and only open to forty-five-degree angles?"

"The kind where life revolves around winter and you need triple-glazed glass."

"Except for the one big window," she said, "which opens wide, but can't be left open because it sits so low to the floor that someone would tumble out of it."

"Because it gathers all the light possible in a place where there's precious little of it much of the year, and if it didn't open wide, you couldn't clean it."

"You have an answer for everything."

"No. Just for some practicalities."

"Windows are supposed to open upward and wide, so you can safely air out the goddamned house."

"I'll speak to the building commission about it."

She seemed not to hear me. "I have some errands to run. Are you able to care for Anu for a few hours?"

A sarcastic tone had crept into my voice. I replaced it with an affectionate one. "Yes, darling, I am."

The use of an endearment threw her off kilter and she didn't know how to respond. It sometimes seemed she wanted me to be angry, as if she needed my anger to validate her own. But I wasn't angry, only frightened and sad. She paused to regroup, and when she finally spoke, her tone had changed. Reason, perhaps even some affection, had crept into it. "Please get someone in here to clean the place."

"I'll call someone today and have it cleaned so that it's presentable when you and Anu come back next time. I would like it if I could have regular times with Anu, maybe two or three times a week, instead of this system of you just showing up with her."

She ignored what I thought a reasonable request. "There are eleven pizza boxes in the kitchen. I didn't count the beer cans. You have a right to see Anu, but this isn't a proper environment for a child."

"I'm doing the best I can."

"That's the problem. Your best is bad because of your injuries. I'm concerned that you're not up to taking care of her."

"I'm capable," I say.

"Do I have your word about that?"

"Yes. You have no cause for worry."

"Let's try it now and see how things go," she said. "I've brought all her necessities."

An odd thing to do for a short visit. And, of course, Anu had a lot of things here as well.

I wanted to ask her questions. *Do you still love me? Do you want a divorce?* I felt, though, that her current emotional state might cause her to answer in the affirmative, and if I waited until she was further along in her therapy, she might feel differently. I wanted to tell her how much I love her and that I wanted her to come home, but thought she might spit the sentiments back in my face. So I let it go and didn't try to connect with her.

"That's great," I said. "Thank you."

She said nothing. She stood, did an about-face with military precision. Her heels clicked on the floor as she marched out. I got up, went to the balcony to smoke and watch her walk away, down the street toward the tram stop. My intuition told me something was drastically wrong, but I couldn't put my finger on what it was. Kate loves candles. I lit one, put it on the dining room table and promised myself I would keep one lit until she came home for good. I had an ominous feeling of foreboding, certain that I was going to burn up many more candles before my family situation was resolved. If it ever would be.

I tried to decipher the subtext of our conversation, could think of little else, but I was clueless. I called Torsten to ensure she had told me the truth about attending therapy. He said that she had. Patient-doctor privilege precluded further discussion, but he asked me why I was checking up on her. I said her condition worried me. After a thoughtful silence, he thanked me for calling and rang off.

I was powerless to do more. I had the window replaced and the house cleaned, fretted, and watched Animal Planet with Anu and Katt.

4

My intuitive fear proved correct. Kate didn't return for Anu. She, Katt and I slept in my armchair together. I was equally thrilled to be reunited with my daughter and frightened about the well-being of my wife.

Anu woke me in the middle of the night. I went to the kitchen to warm some formula for her. I looked at my wristwatch. It had stopped. The battery was probably dead. It was a TAG Heuer that Kate gave me for an anniversary present. I took it off, laid it on the counter, removed a meat hammer from a drawer and pounded the shit out of it. Tiny gears and springs zinged and sproinged around the kitchen. I decided it was properly tenderized and tossed it in the garbage.

The banging scared Anu and made her cry. I took her the bottle, comforted her, quelled her tears and fed her. I needed to work on the anger issues I kept telling myself I didn't have. I realized that I didn't know what Anu should be eating at six months. I wasn't sleepy and checked Wikipedia. It was time she began with some solid food. I would buy some baby food, or, with so much time on my hands, maybe make it for her myself.

In the morning, I changed Anu, had coffee and cigarettes. I was worried sick about Kate. Was she putting me through some sort of test? Was she safe? I thought about calling the hotel, about hunting for her, but this might be a failure of the test, if it was one. I promised myself I would wait a few hours, then do whatever it took to find her.

As I had for weeks, I turned the course of events that led up to this family disaster over in my mind, tried to pinpoint the moments where I went wrong and set this debacle in motion.

My thoughts were always random and scattered. Kate and I had faced many trials in the two years of our life together, not the least of which was the discovery of my brain tumor. It caused a personality change graphically illustrated by my complete and utter disregard of the law in organized-crime fashion. These choices suggested a man not in complete control of his faculties. Had I now regained control? I didn't know. Perhaps partially. Pain prevented calm and rational thought.

The facts, as best as I understood them, still exposed little to me about where and how I went wrong. I recognized, though, that there were two poignant reasons for this. One, I was too emotionally distraught to analyze much of anything. Two, I'm not a fucking psychiatrist. I understood a couple things. My experiences and actions, even though they were the result of brain trauma, had changed me.

I would, for instance, kill without hesitation for my family. Arvid Lahtinen, Second World War mass murderer, expert in such matters, good friends with my grandpa, also a mass murderer, and myself as well, told me killing was in my family blood. That to kill I only needed a sufficient pretense to preserve my self-image as a protector of people. I saw now that I would have made many of the same choices presurgery that I made post-surgery, but would have constructed a pretext to defend my actions. Post-surgery, I no longer needed a pretext.

Anu and Katt had both been quiet while I thought. Damned courteous of them. Katt had some kind of sixth sense about Anu. He kneaded me with his claws and purred with enjoyment while he scratched and tormented me, but never did so with her. The smell emanating from Anu told me it was time for a diaper change. I decided to give her a bath as well, after which I would search for her mother. Anu hated baths, screamed bloody murder when I wet her head. I heard myself sigh. The process of struggling with her in the bath would be difficult in my state. I had to admit, I was nearly an invalid.

I picked up my bad leg with both hands from the stool and lowered my foot to the floor. Bending the knee sucked. I slipped her carryall over my neck and slid her into it, then with care forced myself to a standing position. I took my cane and we headed off to her bedroom for changing. Katt followed us. The crash of glass scared the hell out of us. I left Anu howling in her crib and hurried to investigate.

The new window had exploded inward and the object that broke it was spewing mist beside my chair. I recognized it for what it was: a tear gas grenade. It would be screaming hot. I held my breath, whipped off my T-shirt, reached over, snatched it up with the cloth, and flung it back out the broken window onto the street below. I glanced down at the street and sidewalk. They were empty. No innocents were being poisoned.

Given my condition, I had dealt with it fast, before it permeated the apartment. I closed Anu's bedroom door, then opened the balcony door and all the windows in the house. We had gone from bricks to tear gas in a couple days. I wondered what the hell would be next.

I went to the bathroom and, when I was done choking and crying, ripped all the bandages off my knee and took a shower so I could touch Anu without getting tear gas on her. Then I went to the living room to assess the damage. Being left alone in her crib again angered Anu and she shouted. She has a real pair of lungs for a tyke, and it grated on me.

Once again, the large window was shattered and slivers of glass were everywhere, including in and on my armchair. A big shard shaped like a butcher knife skewered the top of the chair, where Katt took naps, at a forty-five-degree angle. If we hadn't gotten up, Katt would be dead. Closer to the window, as Anu was on my right side, I would have taken the brunt of the glass, but she would have been cut God knows how badly. Tear gas would have shredded her tiny fragile lungs.

Aware that my judgment was bad, I did my best to bear it in mind when deciding how to handle this. The decisions I had to make now were critical and I had no margin for error. I needed help. It was time to call in the cavalry.

5

T ear gas leaves an oily mist that would have made my home a health hazard for months if not removed with thoroughness. I called a service that specializes in crime scene cleanup. It charges exorbitant prices. Scraping shotgunned brains off ceilings and suchlike messes warrants a good wage. I paid double for instant service.

I wanted to think this through, narrow down the suspects, figure out who was turning my home into a war zone. I guessed the brick through the window was just the first shot off the bow—the note written on it combined with this escalation made that clear.

Letting these questions gnaw at me, like a dog worrying a bone, had to wait. The living room was a glass-covered danger zone in an apartment with a gimp, an infant and a cat living in it. Sweetness said to call when I needed him. I did.

He answered. "So the hermit reemerges."

I was shaken, at a loss for words, and took a second to collect myself.

He knows me. "What happened and what can I do?"

I sighed. "I need you to stay here with me."

He laughed. "You're lonely and you miss me?"

I explained about the broken window, what was written on the brick, and about the tear gas assault. "This is about the ten million we took, so we could all be in danger. We should talk. And I have Anu with me. I need protection."

"Where is Kate?" he asked.

"I don't know."

He got it then that I was living a train wreck in progress. "Sit tight," he said, "I'll be there soon."

"No," I said, "wait. The house is toxic. I'll take Anu and Katt to the park and call you when it's safe."

Next, I tried to call Milo. His cell phone was turned off. Milo and I are well-known figures because of the cases of international interest we've solved, a school shooting we ended—we were called saviors of children, but in truth it was little more than an execution when Milo put a bullet into the assailant's brain—and, to a lesser extent, because we've killed more men and been shot more times than any policemen in modern Finnish history.

Anu and I went out. I used the time to order new windows. I own a second house, in Porvoo. My old friend Arvid left it to me, and it fell into my possession when he committed suicide not long ago. I asked them to install bulletproof glass in both my apartment and the house, and air conditioners as well, in case the thick glass made the places airtight, like living in bubbles, and left us sweltering. They had never done such a thing, had no idea what it would cost. "It costs what it costs," I said, "and I'll pay you double if you can get it done in three days." This provided sufficient motivation to get an instant affirmative.

When the cleaners called and said they were done, I called Sweetness back.

Sweetness showed up with his girlfriend, Jenna. She's sixteen, a teen beauty, five foot nothing, has lush white-blond hair that hangs to her ample bottom, and is brick shithouse built, like a miniature Brigitte Bardot with more curves. She's also his third cousin once removed. Jenna follows him puppy-dog style wherever he goes. He doesn't appreciate Jerry Lee Lewis jokes about their relationship.

She has pale white skin, cherry red lips, and large breasts that look almost comically out of place on such a tiny woman. I wished he hadn't brought her. Pain and worry hadn't lessened my attraction to women, and she was a potential distraction.

Sweetness is only twenty-two, a happy-go-lucky giant of a man—his size would frighten children like an ogre if not for his baby face—but he's an alcoholic and a dangerous sociopath. Jenna and Sweetness: Beauty and the Beast.

They brought enough food, beer and booze for an army. Jenna emptied the bags and started filling the fridge. All the food was meat and eggs.

"Jenna goes where I go," Sweetness said. "And with Anu in the house, Jenna can help take care of her. I don't know anything about babies. Jenna insisted."

I thanked her. "What's with the food? You feeding wolves?"

"We're on a solid-protein diet," she said. "No carbs. Except for alcohol, of course."

"Of course," I said.

The traditional Finnish breakfast is rye bread with cheese. Maybe with some lunch meat, cucumbers and tomatoes on it. Nowadays breakfast is often bacon and eggs. This fad is driving bread companies out of business. No one seems to get that most between-meal snacks are solid carbs—cookies, chips, et cetera—and they lose weight on protein diets because they cut the snacks out, not because meat causes lean, healthy bodies. I didn't care. I could eat eggs and burgers.

"You look like shit," Jenna told me.

I said nothing, just shrugged.

She's spent plenty of time here and made herself at home. I heard her talking on the phone.

Sweetness took a flask from the pocket on the leg of his cargo pants, had a slug from it and offered it to me. I shook my head no. He put it away. In sealing the deal for his relationship with Jenna, he promised to quit carrying it and stop drinking all day long. He's in love with her. He's in love with booze as well. He was too young to see he couldn't have both and would have to choose between them.

Jenna noticed the look on my face when I examined the slash the shard had made in the top of my armchair. She knows how fond I am of it. "I can mend it," she said. "You'll never even know it was there."

I wanted to get on the phone and start looking for Kate, but decided to wait and chat with Jenna and Sweetness for a bit. It had been a while, and especially given all they were doing for me, it only seemed polite to do some catching up. The door buzzer rang. Sweetness answered it. Mirjami, object of my desire, was in the hallway. She looked at me and her face sagged. I must have looked so awful that it frightened her.

"Jenna called me and told me you're in trouble. Invite me in," she said.

"Do you need an invitation?"

"When I left, I told you to call me if you want me. You haven't called. The devil is on the doorstep. You have to invite her in before she can cross the threshold."

It got a laugh out of me. "Come in."

Mirjami is Milo's cousin, and stunning. They sometimes went out together, as friends. She thought it was cool because they never waited in lines at nightclubs or events. He flashed his police card for special treatment at every opportunity. He theorized that beautiful women competed, and if they saw him with Mirjami, it would make them want to take him away from her. He told me he would fuck her, cousin or not, if she would let him. "That's why God made birth control," he said. As a group, we're a tight-knit, incestuous bunch. I view it as a good thing. We can trust each other.

Mirjami coming here evoked mixed feelings in me. She's a registered nurse, a born nurturer, and she cared for Kate, Anu and me after the fiasco on the island in Åland that led to all our misery. She loved me—I didn't know why or if that still held true—and, despite my refusal to have sex with her, insisted on sleeping in the same bed with me.

I asked her to stop more than once. I was too doped and too injured after getting shot up in Åland to do anything about it. In my condition, I didn't care where she slept or who slept beside me. She would wait until I was asleep before crawling into the bed with me, and get up before either Kate or I woke.

Kate was in her dissociative stupor and, as far as I know, had no clue Mirjami was trying to steal her husband. Not long before Kate came back to herself, I told Mirjami in gentle but no uncertain terms that I was married and intended to remain faithful to my wife, that she was wasting her time. If anything, it made her love me more. "Unrequited love is sad and beautiful," she said.

She entered and sat on the armrest of the chair, looked me upand down with a speculative eye. "You're not getting better, are you?"

I looked up at her. "No."

Beautiful Mirjami. Tall, thin and lithe. Long russet hair pulled back. Lovely, coffee-colored, almond-shaped eyes and a dark golden-brown tan. Because I felt no emotions during the short time she lived here, I didn't realize that I missed her until she showed up on my doorstep again. I still didn't feel anything for many people, but she sparked something. Lovely though she is, it was her humor, playfulness and kindness that I missed.

"How bad is it?" she asked.

"Bad enough so bending my knee at all is excruciating, and the bullet in my face tapped some nerves. It makes it hard to eat or talk." I pointed at the medicine bottles and boxes on the end table beside my chair. "This shit helps. And *kossu*."

She pulled up my pants leg, careful not to hurt me. I hadn't rebandaged it yet. "It looks like it's healing properly. It's just that the wound was so bad. And I can't see what it looks like inside. You need to have a specialist get in there and have another look, see what can be done. The same goes for your jaw." She went through my meds. "You should take stronger painkillers."

"No, thanks." But the mention reminded me to take my afternoon dope.

"Then call your doctors and make appointments. If you're in so much pain, there may be problems."

"They've done all they can."

"If you don't, I'll call an ambulance."

"You win. I'll do it later."

"You'll do it now."

Fuck. I called my neurologist brother, Jari. My problems weren't neurological, but it would placate her. I explained my situation. He said he would look at my X-rays, speak with my doctors, and come over later to check me out himself. I reported. Mirjami nodded satisfaction and went off to check on Anu.

Sweetness took out the trash, and I looked around. The place was clean and tidy, and except for the broken window, hadn't been this nice in weeks. The window was no big deal, it was warm outside. The drug combo kicked in and I drifted off to sleep in my chair.

6

The door buzzer rang. I woke up and looked at my wrist to check the time, then remembered I had reduced my watch to tiny expensive fragments. I checked my cell phone instead. It was six forty-five in the evening. Mirjami had scooted into the chair beside me and had Anu in her arms. It seemed, as far as our relationship went, or rather lack of one, nothing had changed for her. For me, it was just one more problem and irritation to deal with.

My Colt was under her legs. I asked her to answer the door. She got up. I took the pistol and leveled it. She looked at the gun, showed no surprise and opened the door. Jari stood there. He registered shock at the sight of the .45 pointed at him. I tucked it back in its place under the seat cushion. He looked at the broken window. He didn't ask about either it or the pistol, just took a seat on the couch and set a black doctor's bag beside him. I didn't know physicians used them anymore.

Sweetness and Jenna had disappeared into Anu's bedroom. I could tell what they were up to by the sound of the spare bed squeaking and the headboard banging against the wall. It made Jari laugh. Mirjami put Anu in her stroller and offered to make coffee. Jari asked if he could have a beer instead. She brought three, one for each of us, sat beside him on the couch and introduced herself.

Jari looked at me, asked without speaking if I wanted our talk to be private.

"It's OK," I say. "She's a nurse and was looking after me in the days after I got shot. She'll just ask me to repeat what was said anyway, so she might as well get it from the horse's mouth."

"How much pain are you in?" Jari asked.

"A lot."

"Are you functional, or incapacitated to the point that you're nonfunctional?"

This was hard to admit, even to myself. "I'm nonfunctional."

"I'll give it to you straight," Jari said. "First, your knee. It's stuck to the rest of your leg with the medical equivalent of rubber bands, paper clips and chewing gum. You came within a hair of losing it. You're in such bad pain because the thing is trashed. As to your jaw," he paused and swigged beer, "you know when you watch boxing, and a punch to the jaw that didn't look like much is a knockout?"

"Yeah."

"It's not the force behind the punch that causes it. It's the twisting motion of the fist as it makes contact with the bundle of nerves located there that turns the lights out. Damage from the gunshot has impinged some nerves in that bundle—swelling, some small bone fragments and so on—and that's what causes you such misery."

"Can you take it away?"

"Pain exists for a reason. It's often a warning signal that movement is causing further damage. Your knee is a prime example of this."

"That's all well and good," I said, "but I have a baby to care for."

He looked around. "Where is Kate?"

"Missing in action."

He got it that my life had gone awry in every way and grimaced, but continued to refrain from comment. "Where are your crutches?"

"I threw them away."

"Why in the name of fucking God would you do something that stupid?"

"Because I've been alone and need at least one hand to use." I held up my cane. "This suffices."

"No, it doesn't."

I wanted to say something caustic, but I didn't. I was just cranky, as usual these days, and he was trying to be a good doctor.

"We have two options," he said. "We can increase your dosages of Oxapam and Norflex—the tranquilizers and muscle relaxants—and start you on Temgesic, a stronger painkiller."

"So then I'm basically a drug-addicted zombie who still has a wasted knee."

"It's not quite as bad as you describe it, but, yeah, it's a lot of drugs. Option two. I shoot your knee and jaw full of cortisone. It will deaden the pain for a few weeks. I've spoken to your doctors. It's not likely, but possible, that another prosthesis might work in your knee. It would give you a greater range of motion eventually, after a long bout of physical therapy, during which your body might reject the prosthesis and leave you back where you are now. I'm hesitant to treat your knee with cortisone, since you refuse to take care of it properly."

"I'm a nurse," Mirjami reminded him. "I can wrap it tightly enough so he can't move it much but won't cut off his circulation, then put a knee brace over top so he's not able to damage himself further without working really hard at it."

Jari nodded assent. "Are you going to be around for a while to do that?"

She looked at me, inquiring. I didn't let my expression answer her.

"If I'm needed and Kari wants me here," she said.

Obviously, Jari was curious about my relationship with her, but he's good at keeping his thoughts to himself.

"About your jaw," he said. "I think a surgeon needs to get in there and repair as much damage as possible. It might leave you with partial paralysis of the right side of your face and mouth."

"Every word I utter hurts like hell. I don't think I have much choice. Shoot me up."

"We need ample bandages and the brace."

Mirjami got her purse. "There's a pharmacy just a few minutes' walk from here. I'll be right back." She walked out.

"Things clearly suck for you in a multitude of ways," Jari said. "Anything you want to talk about while we have privacy?"

I shook my head. "Thanks, but no."

"Then let's take off your pants," Jari said. He knelt in front of me and helped me wriggle out of them, so I didn't have to move too much. "This is going to hurt," he said.

It already hurt. "Proceed."

He jammed a needle like a railroad spike into my left knee. I gritted my teeth. He wasn't exaggerating about the pain. He pulled it out, stuck it in again. Repeated the process a couple more times. Then took out a smaller needle. After finding out how much it hurt, I had a hard time not anticipating, wincing and keeping my head still. He injected more cortisone in my face, then told me to open wide, pushed the syringe deep into my mouth and jabbed the thing into my gum.

"There," he said, "that wasn't so bad, was it?"

"Let me stick you with the goddamned needles and you tell me."

He laughed. "I always say that. It's a little doctor's joke. I know it hurt like screaming hell. I could have given you an anesthetic first, but I figured you're a big boy. Also, about what you can expect: Your injuries will hurt worse for a couple days, then improve. This isn't a miracle drug, especially not for your knee. The cortisone will help some aspects of your wounds, others it won't. You'll still be in pain, but hopefully less of it."

I noticed the fucking noises from the bedroom had stopped.

"Don't stop taking the drugs," Jari said. "Cut down slowly if you don't need them as badly, but don't stop cold turkey or you'll have vicious withdrawal that will make those needles I stuck in you feel like a vacation."

Mirjami returned. He watched her wrap and brace my knee to make sure she did it to his satisfaction.

"Nice job," he said.

She smiled. "I practice."

Jari finished off his beer, took his bag and went to the foyer to put his shoes on. "If you have any problems," he said, "or just want to talk, call me."

"Thank you for this," I said.

"De nada." He shut the door behind him.

7

Next step, locate my wife. Sweetness and Jenna came back from the bedroom. "Thanks for everything," I said, "but I'll be OK now. You don't have to hang around."

Anu was awake, Mirjami was feeding her, sitting beside me again. "You don't need to stay either," I said. "If you can stop by every day or two so you can rewrap my knee after I shower, I would be grateful."

Sweetness shook his head. "We're not going anywhere. Milo and I liberated that ten million with you. That brick was a message to all of us. It's time to circle the wagons.

And speaking of Milo, you need to call and tell him what happened."

"The girls should leave anyway."

Jenna set beers, a Koskenkorva bottle and shot glasses for everyone on the dining room table. "I ain't goin' nowhere without Sweetness."

Even she calls him by the nickname Sulo hates. Kate hung it on him by accident, through a language snafu. It got a chuckle out of me. And then I realized Jenna knew about the ten million euros. Mirjami didn't flinch at its mention, so she knew too, which meant she'd been talking to Jenna, which meant they had become good enough friends to share secrets. They just met three months ago. I wondered if Mirjami had cultivated their friendship as a way of staying close to me. I'd noticed her calculating and devious side before. She knew how to get what she wanted.

"Hurting the girls is a potential way of getting at us," Sweetness said. "They're safer here."

He was right, it hadn't occurred to me. My fear because of Kate's absence multiplied.

"And have you looked in the mirror lately?" Mirjami asked. "You need care. And help with Anu."

"Don't you have a job?" I asked her.

"Haven't you read about the shortage of health care workers? I can quit my job tomorrow and have a new one within a week when I want to go back to work. In fact, I think I'll do just that."

I didn't have the strength or will to argue. I grabbed my

cell phone and pushed myself out of my chair. "I need to make some phone calls."

I noticed that Jari forgot the empty hypodermics. They struck me as something that might be useful. For what, I didn't know. I took my phone and laptop, went to the kitchen for quiet and privacy, then put the needles in the cupboard and sat at a little table for two that we usually use to prep food on.

Jenna called out, "Come and have a *kossu* with us."

"Later," I answered.

The stereo fired up. Portishead came on. I yelled for them to turn it down.

I called Hotel Kämp and asked for Kate's room. The receptionist informed me that she had checked out. I asked for Aino, Kate's assistant and acting hotel manager while Kate was on maternity leave. Good luck. Aino was working late. Bad luck. She hadn't seen Kate for a couple days, and didn't even know she was no longer staying at the hotel.

For a second, I was stymied, then told myself to be a cop. Kate and I share a bank account as well as having private ones. We have separate credit cards, but also one that accesses a shared account, and we have copies of each other's online banking codes, in case one of us should misplace them. I had all the financial stuff in the bookcase. I grabbed it, went back to the kitchen and got online.

It just took a few minutes for me to work it out. Kate withdrew five thousand euros from the bank. Then Mirjami walked in and laid a sealed envelope on the table. "Kari" was written on it in Kate's handwriting. "I found this in Anu's diaper bag," Mirjami said. She walked away so I could read it in privacy.

I tore open the edge of the envelope and pulled out a letter written on Hotel Kämp stationery.

Dear Kari,

I'm so sorry for the way I've treated you. I left you alone when you needed me the most. It was selfish and unconscionable. The things I've done have made me a failure as a wife and a human being. I'm certain that, given time, I will fail as a mother as well. I won't be back and please don't look for me. I promise that you and Anu will be better off without me. Heal, forget about me, and find someone who will make you happy and be a good mother to our daughter. I will always love you.

She signed it as she has always signed notes to me, with a lipstick kiss.

Everything clicked into place. Her odd behavior yesterday. The call in the middle of the night. Her uncontrolled weeping. It was because of remorse. She had been planning this. She had called on impulse, overwhelmed by guilt, to say without saying it—good-bye.

I was calm at first, approached the situation with a cop mentality. I called MasterCard, told them I wasn't certain if my card had been stolen or if I'd only misplaced it, and asked if they could check the latest purchases made with it. After some wrangling, I ascertained that Kate charged a flight to Finnair, bought a one-way ticket to Miami and left yesterday evening.

At first I was too stunned to move or speak. Then something like bats were flapping around in my head. My chest hurt and my vision went black. I stood up with my cane. I didn't know where I was going. I started swinging the cane. I broke the cupboard doors to kindling and heard myself screaming, raging. No words, just bellowing. I kept swinging and shouting. The plates shattered, the glasses smashed.

I reared back for another swing and the cane disappeared from my hands. I felt myself lifted off my feet and laid on the floor. Sweetness sat on my chest and pinned my arms down with his knees. Mirjami held my nose to force my mouth open. She dropped a fistful of pills in it. I tried to spit them out, but Jenna stuck the neck of the *kossu* bottle between my teeth, so I couldn't close my mouth. I choked and gagged on booze, had to swallow I don't know how many gulps.

I felt my body floating, like an astronaut in a gravity-free atmosphere, and I knew no more.

8

I wasn't hungover in the morning, I didn't ingest enough poisons for that, but was groggy from the dope and booze they knocked me out with. I was naked. Someone had undressed me. Katt was sleeping on my chest. Mirjami wasn't in bed with me, but she had been earlier. I smelled her scent on the pillows. The memories drifted back. My wife absconded to Florida. I destroyed much of the kitchen. I had to get Kate back. Now. But how? Kate kept her private things in the nightstand on her side of the bed or in her jewelry box.

Jari was right, my knee and face hurt even worse than

before the cortisone shots. I rolled and scooted to the other side of the bed and rifled through the little drawer in the nightstand. At the bottom of assorted papers and mementos was a packet of letters bound with a rubber band, from her brother, John. The return address was in Miami, Florida. John is human flotsam and jetsam. He destroyed his life with booze and drugs. The last I knew, he lived in New York. Best guess: he got in too deep with drug dealers, had no hope of paying them, and scarpered to the other side of the country before they killed him.

Now Kate was there with him. Kate was emotionally ill, not in control of herself. Kate could fall under John's drug-addled spell. Kate could take up his bad habits. I pulled on sweatpants and a T-shirt. My cane was beside the bed. I tottered into the living room. Mirjami was in my armchair with Anu. Sweetness and Jenna were still in bed. I got the impression that they did little except booze, fuck and sleep.

Mirjami had showered. Her long, dark hair was damp and hung over her shoulders. Anu pulled at it. Mirjami wore Kate's bathrobe. It disconcerted me.

"I looked at your web browser history," she said.

"I didn't smash the computer?"

"It's about the only thing you didn't destroy."

That was something anyway.

"I take it Kate has abandoned you and Anu," she said.

"Kate isn't well, as you know. 'Abandon' is too strong a word for what she's done. I think she just panicked and ran away."

Mirjami kept her face blank. "Maybe. What are you going to do?"

"I don't know." It came to me. I needed to speak to her therapist. And I needed to sit down. My phone was on the table next to my armchair. Mirjami brought me coffee and sat down beside me again. It's the ultimate gigantic man's chair, a gift to myself. The fit might be a little tight, but another person of average size could comfortably sit with us.

I called Torsten Holmqvist. "There's a problem with Kate," I said. "I need your help."

"You know the rules about doctor-patient privilege," he said. "However, she missed her therapy session yesterday. Would you happen to know why?"

"Because she left the country to stay with her drug-fiend brother."

"Oh dear," he said. "That is a bit of a predicament."

It was a fucking catastrophe. I wanted to choke him to death. "What should I do?"

"Where is your child?"

"With me. She dropped Anu off before she left, lied, and told me she would be back within hours."

"Are you in contact with Kate?"

"No."

"Well, I can't treat her if she isn't here. Is it possible to use your child as a carrot on a stick to entice her to come home?"

"Maybe you're not hearing me. I—am—not—in—touch—with—her. She—abandoned—her—child."

"Then I suggest you find a way to get in touch with her.

Given the extraordinary circumstances, I'll tell you what I feel I can without breaking her confidence."

I sighed. He was wasting precious time. "I would be grateful for that."

"Kate has related a number of experiences to me that border on the unbelievable. I'm uncertain whether they're fact or fantasy. Should I enumerate some of them?"

I wasn't sure and said nothing, uncertain what to reveal and what to hold back.

"When she first came to see me," he said, "she believed Icarus had flown too close to the sun, his wings had melted, he fell to the earth engulfed in flame and died at her feet. Now she claims she shot him to death."

He needed at least some truths to do his job and help her. "She shot him."

"Let me assure you, if you've committed crimes in the past, I feel no obligation to report them, and they will stay with me. You were also my patient, and that further complicates matters. If I felt failure to report a planned crime would result in the loss of human life, my obligation would sway toward a potential victim. Is that helpful to you in speaking about these issues?"

"The man in question was a former French Legionnaire. He had paratrooper wings tattooed on the side of his head. And yes, his clothing caught fire, so it's understandable that she associated him with Icarus. In fact, he referred to his tattoos as the wings of Icarus. Whatever Kate told you is most likely true," I said, "or at least based in truth. There may be some things she doesn't know about and so filled in the gaps herself, believing the worst, when it may not have been the case. What might be most helpful for you to know is that she had no choice in killing the man."

"I see."

God, I hate when he says that.

"Kate caused a death," he said, "a most gruesome one, I'm given to understand, and she now accepts that she caused it. She deplores violence. Killing another person violated everything she believed in and destroyed her self-image of who she thought she was. This caused acute stress disorder, which led her to fall into her previous dissociative state. Basically, her mind was protecting itself from an event so traumatic that she was unable to process it."

"I understand that much," I said.

"Over the past few weeks, her condition has evolved, or perhaps devolved would be more accurate. Rather than re-associate and come to grips with the events of that day, she has developed full-blown post-traumatic stress disorder."

"Which means?"

"That she is reliving that event over and over again in her mind, to the near exclusion of all else, and the truth of what she did torments her constantly, even in her dreams. That might be why she left. She may have felt unable to take adequate care of your child in her present state, yet another source of guilt. Or perhaps she feels unworthy of a child, which she regards as a blessing."

This all made excellent sense. "Can you tell me anything more?"

"No, I can't. I will say only this. She sees what she views as her own mistakes and inadequacies reflected in you, like a mirror into her own soul. However, if you can return her to my care, I'll encourage her to tell you this herself."

"What should I do?" I asked.

"I don't know. As I said, I can't treat her if she isn't here. If she were, I believe her therapy would be short term and she would return to a semblance of emotional normality within a few months."

"Thank you for being so forthright," I said.

"Please keep me informed," he said, and rang off.

I WENT out to the balcony, smoked a couple cigarettes and thought things through, then came back and sat down again. Katt took his place atop the chair, front paws to the sides of my neck. Talking hurt like hell, but I tried Milo again. This time, his phone was switched on. "Where are you?" I asked.

"I'm fishing in a sailboat near my summer cottage, about to fire up a bowl of dope."

"I didn't know you had a summer cottage, a sailboat, or that you smoked pot."

"Well, now you know. The cottage is on Nauvo, near Turku, has been in my family for generations, and I smoke all the pot I can get. You always comment on my bloodshot eyes and the dark circles around them. They're bloodshot from the pot, and the dark circles are because sleeping bores me. Any other personal details you would like me to share with you?"

"No. I need your help." I was so upset that for a minute I couldn't continue.

"Care to elaborate?"

I pulled it together. "Kate has done a runner. She's emotionally ill, suffering from post-traumatic stress disorder because of what happened on the island. She left Anu here with me. I checked her accounts. She's in Miami, Florida. Her brother, John, is there. I'm sure she's with him. I have his address. My physical condition is too bad for me to do this myself. I need you to go to Miami and bring her home. Please."

"What if she won't come?"

"Do whatever it takes. Don't give her a choice. And there's more you need to know." I told him about the shattered window, what the brick said about ten million ways to die, and the tear gas. "We shouldn't have stolen that money," I said.

I heard waves break, him suck on a pipe, and the crackle of burning marijuana.

"Do you have any idea how goddamned hard it is to sail and fish with only one good hand? We didn't steal it, we earned it. If we hadn't taken it, the national chief of police and the interior minister would have, and then blamed us for it anyway. We were fucked if we did or fucked if we didn't. We might as well be rich."

He was right. "We have to think of our families," I said.

"They could hurt them to get at us. I'm thinking about your mother."

He muttered "Fuck," then went silent for a minute. "Mom is here, I can't think of anywhere safer, unless I send her out of the country. You know, Vaara, you're a real fucking buzzkill."

"Yeah, I know."

"I'll be back in Helsinki in about four hours," he said. "And don't worry. I promise I'll bring Kate home to you."

"Thank you," I said, and we rang off.

9

Sweetness and Jenna watched TV, disappeared occasionally for fuck sessions, sipped beers. Mirjami continued the rôle of Anu's nanny. Changed her, fed her, played with her. I gave her a couple hundred euros for grocery and household money. The keys to Kate's Audi hung on a nail by the front door. I told her to use it if she liked. She went home and got clothes, makeup, the things she needed for an extended stay, and grocery shopped.

We still hadn't discussed how long she should stay. I didn't mention it. It was clear that Sweetness, my Luca Brasi, would stay until these crises had passed. As such, Jenna would also be a permanent member of the household until then. I supposed Mirjami had the same in mind. I hid my exasperation with unwanted houseguests. It wasn't their fault that I wanted to be alone. I thanked Mirjami for being such a great help to me, especially now, when I needed it the worst. My gratitude was sincere. I said I could never possibly repay her. This gladdened her. She said her twenty-third birthday was two days away, for me to do something nice for her.

I sat with Anu, Katt and a crime novel, *Rööperi*, by Harri Nykänen. Anu was in the first stages of learning to talk. *"Äi-äit-äi-äit."* Mirjami wanted to believe Anu was calling her *äiti*—mother—but that was wishful thinking. Anu was just babbling, as children her age are wont to do. Men came to replace my windows with bulletproof glass. At about six by eight feet, the one that had been shattered was a big job. I took us all down the street to Hilpeä Hauki to sip beers until they were done.

HILPEÄ HAUKI—the Happy Pike—is unassuming, furnished with simple dark wood, polished brass bar fixtures and beer taps. Sofas and padded chairs surround low tables in the corners. Most patrons were outside on the patio. It was vacation season and the sun was shining, they could drink the day away. The bar's front window is made of several glass panels. They can be pushed and folded to collapse together on one side and create an open-air bar. Conversations and a gentle breeze wafted inside. I texted Milo and told him where we were.

Mike came over and greeted us.

"Seems like you're living in here," I said. "Don't any other bartenders feel like coming to work?"

"They're mostly on vacation, so I'm working open to close by myself most days."

"Sounds like no fun."

"The paychecks are fun. Can we have a word?"

"Sure. You can say whatever you need to in front of these folks, though."

"Are the girls old enough to drink?"

Jenna isn't. Not legally, but she drinks like a fish, so on a social level, she's well beyond her years with booze. And being so well-endowed makes her look older than she is. I lied for her. "Yeah."

He leaned over and put his hands flat on the table. Full-sleeve tattoos showed below the rolled-up cuffs of his shirt. He lowered his voice so other customers couldn't hear. "Are you carrying a gun?" he asked.

Just to tease him, I pulled the .45 from the holster clipped to my belt at the small of my back and plunked it onto the table. "Want to hang it behind the bar while I drink?"

He grimaced. "Put that fucking thing away. That's why I want to talk to you. That kind of shit scares people. That guy you hit with your cane coughed up blood."

I didn't care, said nothing.

"You're a police inspector, and I respect that," he said, "but I'm sheriff in this bar. I don't want or need help."

I saw that I'd really upset him. "I apologize. I know I screwed up when I opened my mouth and threatened that asshole, but when he insulted me, I just lost it for a minute. Like I told you when you asked me then, it was a bad day."

He scrutinized me. "Is today a bad day?"

I had to laugh a little. "Worse."

"I'm sorry, but you know where I'm going with this, right?"

"Yeah, I do. If I keep frightening the good citizens, you're going to have no choice but to ban me from the bar."

He nodded.

"Don't worry," I said, "I'll behave. This crew I'm with saves me from myself in my darker moments. I'm sorry I put you in an awkward position."

He stood upright and put a hand on my shoulder. "Thanks for understanding. I promised to buy you a beer the next time I saw you. What will it be?"

"A Young's Double Chocolate Stout. To sweeten my disposition."

"And for the rest of you?"

Jenna got a pilsner. Sweetness took a lager and three shots of *kossu*. Mirjami got a mineral water. She sat next to me, Anu in her stroller between us. Mirjami reached over and gave my hand a squeeze. "The little one has to be taken care of," she said, "and I think a few drinks would do you some good."

She had a way of making me smile. Her small kindnesses were touching. At that time, she was the only person who didn't irritate me just by the nature of her existence. Excluding Kate and Anu. For Kate, I felt a mixture of love, anger, dread and fear. We have to be careful who we love in this life. To give others love is to give them the power to destroy us. It's so easy to love Anu. Unconditional love that she returns out of innocence. I reached into her stroller and she wrapped a tiny hand around my index finger. I wanted to savor her unconditional love now. It wouldn't last forever.

Mike brought the drinks. I grabbed a *kossu* from in front of Sweetness. The shot glass was misted with frost. They kept the *kossu* in the freezer, as it should be. I knocked it back.

"Atta boy," Sweetness said.

It went down with a cold burn that mellowed into a warmth in my stomach and spread all the way to my fingers and toes. The others talked. I ignored them. I wasn't thinking, not anything, just being. When my glasses emptied, both beer and *kossu*, more kept appearing in front of me. Time passed, Milo wandered in, pulled up a chair and sat beside me. We said nothing, just looked at each other. I was certain that, like everyone else, he thought I looked like overwrought shit.

After a couple minutes, he went to the bar and came back with a cola. "What do you want to see happen here?" he asked.

"I want to see Kate here. Whatever it takes."

"What about her brother?"

"What about him?"

"Obviously, Kate isn't going to come back just because I ask nicely, or she wouldn't have gone there in the first place."

I nodded agreement.

"So I'll have to pressure her by threatening to harm John."

He leaned forward with his elbows on the table. He had a

thick black brace on his right wrist and hand to immobilize them. His fingers stuck out of the end. "Fine," I said.

"As long as he's there, she'll always have a place to run to."

"Are you asking me if I want you to kill him?"

He said nothing.

"No. I don't want that."

"I booked our tickets. My plane leaves in two hours. I have an eleven-hour one-way flight. The return flight is in four days, twenty-six hours including one layover. Give me his address."

I memorized it from the return address on the letters John wrote to Kate. All of which asked to borrow money. "Four thirty-seven Grove Acre Drive."

Milo took out an iPad, opened Google Earth, and zoomed in on it at street level. Why the fuck didn't I think of that? My mind wasn't working right. It was on overload and I hadn't realized it. I reminded myself that I had to be careful not to make mistakes.

We saw a small, ramshackle single-family dwelling with a little yard. The street was lined with similar houses on both sides of the street, in various degrees of dilapidation.

Milo pondered this. "Whoever is harassing you is escalating their methods. However, I don't think lives are in imminent danger, as it would be more expedient to have just killed you in the first place."

I nodded agreement, swilled beer.

"Look at me," he said.

I did.

"Do you realize you're in some kind of shock?"

I thought I was just suffering from a combination of pain and anxiety. "I know I'm not thinking straight. My wife, my home, my body all fucked up. I've been coping, but today I feel overwhelmed."

"I have to go," he said. "When I get back, we'll sort this out and put an end to it." He handed me a set of keys. "These are to my apartment and gun safe. If you need to take extraordinary measures, go in there and get the right ordnance for the job."

I finished off another *kossu*. "I owe you."

"Oh, I'm pretty sure you'll have a chance to pay me back."

He got up and left. After a while, the window repairmen called and informed me that my windows were now bullet-proof. I paid our bill, thanked Mike, and dropped him a fifty as a way of both apologizing for the trouble I'd caused and for the good treatment he'd given us.

We went back to my apartment. Only the chair, with the deep cuts from glass shards, gave any indication that some-thing untoward had happened here. It was only early eve-ning, but I was so exhausted that I could barely keep my eyes open, and asked Mirjami if she could look after Anu while I napped. She didn't mind.

I looked around, tried to be a cop for a few minutes. I stood in front of the big window and imagined I was a sniper looking for a firing position to kill someone in here. That couldn't happen now, but we were under surveillance, and our watchers had chosen such a place, as evidenced by the tear gas grenade, which had been propelled by a firearm. I could likely see them too, if I knew where to look.

Sweetness came over and looked out with me. He had no knowledge of such things. He chose civil service over military service, and spent his mandatory time playing with children in a kindergarten instead of with men in the forest playing war games. He asked me what I was doing, and I explained.

"*Pomo*"—boss—"you know the number of people likely responsible for all this can be counted on the fingers of one hand. Actually less. It's just a question of when we get off our dead asses, pay some visits, and put a stop to this bullshit."

"Soon," I said.

My worry for Kate had been so all-consuming, at first it made the harassment, a brick through a window, seem inconsequential. But at least to some degree, I had come to my senses. Someone crossed a line and I was beyond anger. Things were done that could have hurt my little girl.

I went into seclusion with the hope that it would bring catharsis, help rid me of anger. Allow me to reach inside myself and find a pacifist buried somewhere in my soul. Instead, I found a vengeful spirit that demanded a price be paid. The noise of the young people drinking, laughing and listening to music made me want to scream at them all to shut the fuck up. I took a sleeping pill and waited for it to kick in. As I fell asleep, visions of murder danced in my head.

10

July thirteenth. I wake up, plagued by anxiety, frustration and worry. I want to be alone. My apartment is full of people. My mind is bent. My nerves destroyed.

I get out of bed and find the others sitting in the dining room. I go out to the balcony to smoke. Sweetness follows me. "Bad news," he says.

Just the idea of more bad news pisses me off. He points down at the street. The windows have all been beaten out of my Saab. I'm furious but feel no adrenaline. Although my emotions have returned to some extent, they're by no means normal. Part of that abnormality is that adrenaline doesn't accompany rage. I have no fight-or-flight response.

"It was about four this morning," he says. "I heard the smashing and pulled on some jeans so I could go down there, but they worked fast and were gone before I could even get a look at them."

I've been thinking like a victim instead of a predator, working from a defensive mind-set instead of taking the offensive. We must be under constant surveillance in order for our enemies to know the best times to attack us. I do what any cop with half a brain should. I watch for watchers.

I scan the rooftops. It's a clear summer day, blue skies and sunshine. I look for the glint of light on optics. And I find it, but not where I thought it would be. It's in the window of the apartment across the street from mine and one over. It offers a good view of most of my living room. The sun makes a double flare on the optics, so it's binoculars, not a rifle scope. I tell Sweetness to look without looking.

He bends over, lights a cigarette and glances up over his cupped hand. He recently started smoking. He used *nuuska*—a kind of snuff—since he was a kid and so is addicted to nicotine, but women tend not to be turned on by a mouth with tobacco in it, especially since it tends to stick between the teeth, a bit unsightly—women who aren't smokers themselves tend not to be thrilled by cigarettes either, but even less so by *nuuska*—so he traded his lungs for love. Plus Milo and I smoke, and Sweetness looks up to and mimics us, especially me.

"Well, *pomo*," he says, "what's the plan?"

I think it over. Thanks to cortisone shots taking the edge off the pain, my mind as well as my body is working better today. "I'll get dressed, then we'll both go downstairs. I'll go out the front door and check out the damage done to my Saab. You go out back to the inner courtyard, between the buildings, and circle around the block so they don't see you. Just press the buzzers for every apartment, someone will let you in, then you go get them and bring them out so we can talk to them."

"Get them how?"

I shrug. "Knock on the door. That usually works. If they ask who it is, say police and hold up your National Bureau of Investigation ID. If they still don't open, or notice that your ID says you're a translator instead of a cop, use your silenced .45 as a key and shoot the lock to pieces. If you do, call me. I'll come up and talk to other cops if they show, to make it seem like a legit bust. I'll bring some dope to plant on them. If you have to shoot them, try not to kill them. We need to interrogate them."

One of the nice things about being a famous cop is that other police, and everyone actually, tend to believe anything I say.

We get outside. I gimp over to my Saab. There's a note inside, on the driver's seat. "There are ten million ways your family could die, too."

Someone is working very hard to get me to kill them. About ten minutes later, two men come out the front door of the building they were surveilling us from, Sweetness behind them, doubtless with his pistol at their backs. I lean against my Saab. He walks them over to me. They look like bikers: long hair, biker boots, primary drive chains from motorcycles as belts—handy because they can be used as steel whips or turned sideways and swung as flexible bludgeons—and leather vests. They don't have gang colors, though, so they must be independents. One is rail thin, the other on the chunky side. The kind of blubber that comes from sucking down beer day and night for years.

I hold up the note threatening my family. Only someone in the know could have written it, because the official story for the media stated that the ten million euros in ransom money had been recovered. A good ploy. Finders keepers and tax free, too. Assuming they can get it back from me and my colleagues.

"Whatcha gonna do," Chunky says, "gun us both down here in the middle of the street, in broad daylight?"

"I haven't thought that far ahead yet," I say, "but you're doing your best to talk me into it."

They both smirk. Skinny leans against the hood of my car. Chunky stands in front of me with his arms crossed and legs spread. The ignoramus says, "Suck my dick, crip."

Sweetness kicks out in a kind of high stomp that catches the side of Chunky's knee and it buckles. I hear the crunch. Ligaments, tendons, all the shit that holds his knee together, give way. He falls to the street and grabs his destroyed knee with both hands. To his credit, he sucks it up, doesn't make a sound, but the awful pain shows in his eyes.

"Inspector Vaara doesn't likes back talk," Sweetness says.

"No," I say, "he doesn't. No one likes a smarty-pants."

"You're cops?" Skinny asks.

"So they tell me. But you don't have to call me inspector. Sir will suffice."

I carry what is known as a gadget cane. Especially in the Victorian era, canes were made with every conceivable device built into them. Mine is my most prized possession and worth a fortune. Milo gave it to me, a gift purchased with our ill-gotten gains.

It's made of thick ash. The handle is a lion's head made of gold and weighs about half a pound. A cane meant for a big and strong man. Bang down on the floor hard with the tip, it spring-loads the lion's mouth and snaps it open. The teeth are steel razors. Sharp contact, like swinging the mouth against something, forces the fangs backward, they trigger the mechanism, and the mouth clamps shut and bites with about three hundred pounds per square inch of pressure, about the same as a Rottweiler's jaws. Pressing the eyes— one is a ruby, the other is an emerald—disengages the spring and the mouth lets go. Unscrew the shaft and another weapon, a twenty-inch sword, is unveiled.

Chunky has gone silent, sucking up pain. I picture what the tear gas might have done to my six-month-old little girl. I slam my cane's tip into his solar plexus. It knocks the breath out of him and the pressure opens the mouth of the gold lion that comprises the cane's handle. I run my fingers over the lion's razor-sharp teeth, draw a little of my own blood. I shrug my shoulders. The lion's mouth opening means that the fates have intervened and given me a sign. I smack him on his side with the lion's mouth. It snaps shut and gouges a deep wound in his beer-swollen belly. Blood drizzles out of him.

"I think I just invented a poor man's liposuction," I say.

He chokes from pain and vomits.

"Just wait here a few minutes," I say, "while I run an extension cord out here and get the Hoover. We'll have you as trim as Celine Dion in the twinkle of an eye."

He looks up at me and tries to mouth some words, but just pukes again.

"Or you and your buddy seem close. Maybe he'll show his friendship by sucking the fat out of your wound."

I look at Skinny. "And if I tell you to do it, believe me, before I'm done, you'll beg me to let you."

I return my attention to fat fuck biker. "No, wait. That means I have to gouge more pieces out of you, so the fat is removed from various places to create symmetry. It's important to me that you feel svelte and attractive, like an improved person when we're through. It will be good for your self-image. I think a poor self-image is what brought you to this moment of ignominy that you're now suffering. We give you a makeover, put you in a suit, your confidence will skyrocket, and before you know it, you'll have your own office in the World Trade Center, trading stocks and bonds."

I smack the tip on the sidewalk and the lion's mouth springs opens. "Yuck," I say. "On second thought, you really should have a doctor look at that," and shake the bite of beer fat out of the lion's mouth and onto his head. "Well," I say, "now you're going to walk like me." I lift my shirt and show him the handle of the Colt sticking out of the waistband. "Look at my face. Do you want to be handsome like me, too?"

He manages to talk through gritted teeth. "Sir, I apologize for my bad attitude. Would you please stop hurting me now?"

I notice there's a woman standing at the front door of my building, watching. I ignore her.

Back to Skinny. "The story," I say.

"Sir," he says, "we got a get-out-of-jail-free card on a drug bust, plus a hundred euros each a day to watch you."

"So, a cop put you up to this?"

"Yes, sir."

"His name?"

"He didn't give one, didn't even show us ID."

"Then how do you know he's a cop?"

"Because he got us out of the can and got the charges against us dropped. The apartment he put us in is vacant. We didn't know you're police officers."

Like it would have made any difference. "Have you been smashing my windows, writing notes, playing dirty tricks?"

"Yes, sir. But we didn't teargas your house. The cop did it himself."

"You've frightened and endangered my friends and family. How do you intend to make that up to me?"

His voice quakes. "Sir, I apologize for the trouble we've caused you, and we'll do whatever you tell us will satisfy you."

"Tell me about the cop."

"He didn't look too good. Broken nose. Fake front teeth.

Some scars on his face and what looks like a surgery scar beside his left eye."

He's describing Captain Jan Pitkänen of SUPO, the minister of the interior's hatchet man. Milo destroyed Pitkänen's face, reduced it to pulp with the butt of his pistol. Milo beat him half to death, but it was Pitkänen's own fault. When Milo approached him, he failed to identify himself and reached inside his jacket. He might have been reaching for a gun. I told Milo he went too far, though, and Pitkänen wouldn't forget it. However, he wouldn't be harassing me without the knowledge of the minister, Osmo Ahtiainen. Further, he almost certainly ordered Pitkänen to do so.

"You know who it is?" Sweetness asks.

"Yep. You squeezed his partner's shoulder so hard that you dislocated it and broke his collarbone."

"What do you want to do with these fuckwads?" he asks.

I lean against the side of my now windowless Saab. "Be creative," I say.

I look up. Jenna and Mirjami watch through my window.

Skinny's hand is on the hood of my car. Sweetness grinds a cigarette out on the hand, looks thoughtful, pensive. Skinny doesn't move or protest, just grimaces. "You guys ever seen the movie *American History X*?" Sweetness asks.

They both nod.

"You remember near the beginning, when Edward Norton makes the guy open his mouth so his teeth are against the curb, and then he stomps on his head and it mushes like a melon?"

Their eyes go wide with panic.

"Let's do that," Sweetness says.

They don't move. Sweetness twists Skinny's arm behind his back, jerks up and dislocates his shoulder, then throws him onto the asphalt. The two bikers exchange a look that says, *We're helpless, we're better off taking our chances than having this ogre keep wrecking our bodies one piece at a time.* They crawl to the curb, put their arms at their sides, open their mouths and suck concrete.

Sweetness looks at me. I shake my head no. Sweetness stands over them, stomps a combat boot as hard as he can on the pavement between their heads. Skinny recoils, lifts his head and drops it again, knocks his own front teeth out. Sweetness finds this funny, chuckles and says, "Dumbfuck."

"Boys," I say, "you fucked with my family. You come back and we'll hurt you a lot worse than this. I'll kill you both slow. I don't want to see your faces again. My suggestion is that you vacate Helsinki. Do you understand me?"

They're both too fucked up to speak.

"I asked you a question."

They each manage to spit out, "Yes, sir."

"Tell your police buddy I'll be paying him a visit." I gesture to Sweetness to come with me, and we leave them where they lie.

11

The woman still waits on my stoop. "Are you Inspector Kari Vaara?" she asks. Her accent is thick and hard for me to understand.

She's fortyish, has salt-and-pepper hair done up in a bun. She looks older than her years, has the look of hard work and a difficult life that changes people's faces. She has on a plain dress and shoes that speak of a limited income. I expect a complaint for beating people to jelly on the street on this fine summer morning. "Why do you ask?"

"Need help." Her accent is Estonian-Russian, her Finnish broken.

Sweetness tells her in Russian that he can translate for her if she likes. A nasty little piece of history is that during the Soviet occupation of Estonia during the Second World War, Stalin had tens of thousands of Estonians shipped off to Siberia. Russians were brought in to repopulate. Most of the forcibly emigrated Estonians froze and starved to death. Part of the population now speaks Russian as a first language.

I remember that the U.S. had a crisis over busing children as a form of integration. I think Boston had the biggest shakeup over it. I think of Stalin and his form of integration policies with gulags and the deaths of millions. American problems often seem paltry to me. Maybe because they've never been invaded and forced to fight a nation bent on subjugating them, while Europe has been awash in blood and terror since the Pax Romana. I don't count their civil war, a mess of their own making.

She nods and rambles for a minute, nervous.

Sweetness translates. "Her daughter has disappeared from Tallinn. She thinks men brought her here. She says she has friends here, and they told her you're sympathetic to foreigners, that you might help her."

"Tell her to go to the police, explain whatever it is that makes her think her daughter is here, and file a missing person's report."

They exchange a few words. "She's done that," Sweetness says, "and she got the distinct impression that nobody gave a damn."

She says something else.

"The bikers we just stomped the shit out of. She asked if that's what you do to bad people."

"Tell her yes, if I think circumstances warrant it."

Sweetness translates. She answers.

"She says, 'Good. Please do something like that or worse to whoever took my daughter.'"

I give in. She's won me over. "Ask her to come upstairs with us."

Once inside my apartment, I tell her to make herself comfortable and offer her coffee. I ask Mirjami where Jenna is. She went to lie down, wasn't feeling well. I ask Mirjami for a few minutes of privacy and she goes to my bedroom. Milo taught Sweetness how to use the bug sweeper to make sure there are no surveillance devices present. He gives the apartment the once-over. There aren't any.

The woman watches Sweetness with curiosity but doesn't ask about it. I sit next to her on the couch to put her at ease. Sweetness brings coffee for us. He sits in my chair to translate for us. I see the tension melt out of her. Coming here to ask a favor from a stranger caused her anxiety. Kindness relaxes her.

I ask how she found me. The Estonians in Helsinki have their own communities and networks. She says they knew how.

I speak intermediate Russian, studied it in school, but it's rusty and her accent is difficult for me, so I ask her to tell her story to Sweetness and let him repeat it to me. They talk for a few minutes, then he relates it.

"Her name is Salme Tamm. She's widowed. Her daughter's name is Loviise and she has Down syndrome. It's a mild case. Her IQ is over fifty and, within limits, she's functional. She's nineteen years old. She had a job cleaning offices, but through some friends, she met some men who offered her secretarial work in Helsinki. Loviise took a class where they taught her filing and some basic things, and she got excited about it. Salme told her not to trust strangers, but three days ago she didn't come home. Salme thinks these men have bad intentions and Loviise is in trouble. Like most people with Down, she's small, only four foot eleven, but her features are close to normal."

Salme seems to understand Finnish, if not speak it. She takes a picture of Loviise from her purse and hands it to me. She's pretty in her own way. It's not hard to get a handle on what happened. Her diminished intellect makes her easy to manipulate. Her diminutive size makes her excellent fodder for pedophiles, a good earner. Some men involved in the human slave trade duped her, likely brought her to Helsinki, took her passport and whatever money she had, and told her she had to reimburse them for the cost of bringing her here. A scam, as the cost is only about twenty euros. And that she will work off the debt whoring. At the moment, she's locked up somewhere. Not much time has passed yet, it's hard to say what damage has been done to her.

I look up from the picture to Sweetness. "What do you think?"

"You're a physical wreck. People are playing deadly games with us. We have our own to look after at the moment."

An image comes into my mind. Kari Vaara rides a white steed. It runs at full gallop, hooves pounding and thundering. The wind is at Vaara's back. Trumpets sound. Milo bought tickets to bring Kate home three days from now. If all goes well, she arrives to find Loviise here, safe and sound. Vaara has saved a disabled girl from the clutches of villains, from the worst of fates. Loviise can't begin to express her undying gratitude. Everything Vaara has done in the past is vindicated. The horror Kate suffered is given meaning, and her emotional problems stemming from it disappear in the face of goodness. Kate flings her arms around Vaara, the savior of innocents, and declares her undying love.

Kate is constantly on my mind, and I turn ways to earn her love back over and over in my mind. But this isn't just about her. I need this for myself. If I could truly save this one girl, in some tiny way, it would justify all I've done. It wouldn't make things right or restore balance to my inner world, but the symbolism would be there, proof that doing good is possible for me.

"No," I say, "tell her if Loviise is in Helsinki, that you and I will find her and return her to their home."

"You're insane," he says.

"A valid assessment, but I'm going to do this, with or without you."

Sweetness tells her we're going to do our best. I understand well enough to get that he downplayed my phrasing so as not to make her hopeful, and he takes her contact information. She throws her arms around me, careful not to hurt my face, and thanks me over and over. After that, there's no way I can let her down.

12

After Salme Tamm leaves, Sweetness gives me a stern look, as he would a wayward child. "What the fuck is the matter with you?"

"I started this black-ops garbage of ours so I could do things exactly like this. You know, help people, especially young women in trouble. This girl is in deep shit."

He has a pull out of his flask and sits forward with his elbows on his knees. His big frame nearly fills my oversized armchair. "Before you can help anyone else, you have to be able to help yourself. You can barely get around the house.

How are you going to investigate a missing person? Who was most likely conned and abducted by criminals, I might add."

I finish off my coffee. "The cortisone shots are working. My jaw is almost pain free at the moment, and my knee is improved. And I have you to help me."

"*Pomo*, you hardheaded asshole. This is beyond foolish. We have enemies watching us, and we don't know what their limits are, if they have any. We have two women and a baby in this house that we have to take care of. Safeguarding them is our first priority. Call the cops that deal with human trafficking in Helsinki, pass it off to them and let it go."

He made salient points. I weave my way through them. "There are hundreds of prostitutes in Helsinki. There are seven detectives mandated with monitoring the human slave trade. I've spoken with a couple of them. They're pissing in a rainstorm. For every arrest they make, a thousand gangsters are ready to step up and take their place. The profit in buying and selling young women is tremendous. As to the girls, we load them in your Jeep Wrangler and drive around for about an hour to make sure we're not being tailed, then we leave them in a hotel until the job is done. Or pick them up every night after we're done working, if you and Jenna and your love that's bigger than any love that ever loved a love can't stand to be apart for a whole night."

He leans back in the chair and thinks it over. "If Jan Pitkänen is harassing you and it means the minister of the interior is behind him, it's ninety-nine out of a hundred that the national chief of police is in on it, too."

"Those two are like Frick and Frack. Where one turns up, you generally find the other. I warned the chief if he fucked with me anymore, I would kill him."

"You going to?"

I play with my cane, remember I need to wash the beer fat glop out of its mouth. "I don't want to, but can't rule it out. People lose respect for those who don't live up to their threats. On the other hand, Roope Malinen hates our guts, he could have a part in all this."

Roope Malinen, Finland's best hater—he can boast of writing the nation's most popular blog—was elected to parliament and chairs the committee on immigration affairs. He hates us because we humiliated him and exposed him for the dickless coward he is. He most likely hates me the most, since I was the brains behind the operation that helped ensure Real Finns didn't take the election. Plus, Malinen had his eyes on a million euros Veikko Saukko promised as a campaign contribution, and our activities made sure he didn't get it.

Saukko, a billionaire racist, had promised to boot up a million euros to the campaign kitty if a display of serious intent to rid the country of immigrants was exhibited. I'm told that, after neo-Nazis murdered dozens of mostly blacks with strychnine-laced heroin, he was true to his word, but gave it to the National Coalition Party to disseminate.

I haven't spoken to him since the death of his son. Saukko wanted me to investigate the case, the prime minister, who wanted to give Saukko his way ordered me to take it. Saukko, as well as the interior minister, wanted me to find and capture his son, Antti Saukko, a murderer, but not put him in the docks and make him face a court of justice. Saukko wanted to find his boy and give him his freedom, or a semblance of it, since that freedom would keep him under his father's thumb, and the threat of a murder charge hanging over his head forever. Saukko likes manipulating his kids. I can't think of a more effective way.

But Antti wasn't fond of that plan, and when we found him, he drew down, tried to kill us, and he had to be shot in self-defense. Saukko might have been able to live with that, but since Sweetness put sixteen hollow-point slugs in Antti and left him faceless; and since Kate blew the man he hired to find his daughter's killer in half with a sawed-off shotgun; and since the ten million in ransom money Antti stole from him disappeared, as I'm sure Saukko correctly assumes, into our offshore bank accounts, I can understand why he might want revenge.

Upon consideration, it could be that all these people with their various axes to grind are plotting against us together.

Sweetness asks, "We have all these powerful people lined up against us. What have we got to work with?"

I lie back on the couch with a couple pillows under my head and work it through. I was duped into a black op under the belief that its primary mandate would be to save women from being forced into prostitution. The op was self-funded, and we robbed the dope dealers of Helsinki blind to acquire those funds.

The true purpose was fundraising for the National Coalition Party, the party of the rich, and for Real Finns, a populist movement with an often incomprehensible agenda that changed almost daily. They did, however, manage to drain supporters from other, more centrist parties, allowing the NCP to win. The Real Finns garnered enough votes to take part in government, but because of their wilder policy positions, such as withdrawal from the European Union and a return to our old currency, the Finnish markka, were dismissed out of hand. They declared themselves an opposition party, and the NCP victory was complete.

However, in the event that the election didn't work out as planned, I was given the job of collecting dirt on the Real Finns' hierarchy and that of other parties as well, so they could be destroyed by scandal if necessary. Sweetness did the initial surveillance and proved to have a knack for recording people in the most compromising positions, but I needed him for other things. I decided to cover my ass and didn't just collect skank on NCP competition. I hired Finland's premier filth-monger, Jaakko Pahkala, a so-called journalist who freelances for all the skank rags, to surveil the NCP as well. I have something on almost everybody, except those who have nothing to hide, and there are few enough of those about.

And on the interior minister and the national chief of police, I have something special. Sperm samples, currently residing in Milo's freezer, that connect them to the Filippov murder. They thought, pompous fools that they are, that they were so irresistible that Ivan Filippov's mistress just couldn't help herself and had to perform fellatio on them. She was collecting DNA to frame them for murder, though she ended up being the victim herself.

There were four samples, unmarked. Theirs, and those of two other crooked politicians I have yet to identify. Cigarette butts and their attendant DNA, the bane of the criminal. I scooped them up earlier in the summer while we were socializing with the rich and powerful aboard the minister of interior's yacht. They even had the courtesy to smoke different brands and make it easy for me to identify them later. I knew which samples belonged to who. Offenders really shouldn't smoke. I sent them off with the sperm samples to a private genetics testing lab.

The chief, Jyri Ivalo, tried to cover up the Filippov murder because he'd had an affair with the victim. In addition to the sperm, I also have a video of the chief engaging in a fetishistic sex act with her. Making the video public would have humiliated him and ended his career. I saw no need for that and suppressed the evidence involving him. Ivalo made me an offer to run a self-funded black-ops unit mandated to use illegal means to fight crime. Ivalo cited human trafficking as their primary target.

It soon became clear though, that Jyri Ivalo was disingenuous concerning the black op. Although I could fight human trafficking if I wished, Ivalo's main objective was stealing from criminals not only for political fundraising but also personal enrichment. Further, the minister of the interior, who among his many other duties oversees the secret police, SUPO, was in league with him. They insisted that I and my accomplices accept a percentage of the money we stole. They left me no choice. If I wasn't complicit, I wasn't trustworthy. Their ax over my head: my wife isn't a Finnish citizen. They would have her deported. I was stuck between the proverbial rock and hard place.

Flying his sex tape on YouTube would not only make him a laughingstock and destroy his career, but force the reopening of the Filippov case and possibly land him in prison. And now, it appears, he's involved in threatening my family and placing them in danger. His gratitude for suppressing this evidence appears short-lived.

"Skank," I say.

"Skank?" Sweetness repeats.

"The pix you and Jaakko Pahkala took of politicians taking bribes and having extramarital and/or homosexual liaisons. The material I've been paying to collect for months. It's career-destroying material, and it was collected without regard to political party affiliation. It's a powerful weapon in our small arsenal."

"Where is it?"

"In Internet cloud space. Pahkala uploaded it to one account. Milo moved it to another, more secure account and shared the user name and password with me. We memorized it. There's no written record that it exists."

The flask reappears. My two underlings: a drunk and a stoner. Who could ask for anything more. "Killing us would eliminate that threat," Sweetness says.

Yep. I try to think who I could trust to release the skank in the event of our deaths to create a tangible blackmail threat. Only one name comes to mind. Jari, my brother. I'll write him a letter with the user name and password to get to the skank and elucidate.

"I can make that difficult for them," I say. "I just need to have another little chat with Jyri Ivalo and explain the situation. And besides, they could have done that already. They want us alive until we give the ten million back."

"Should we use it to bargain our way out of trouble, then give it back?"

"No. We're in the kind of trouble no bargaining will cure. Not over the long haul."

"Then what's the plan?"

"Kate will be home soon." I say it with confidence but offer a silent prayer that Milo can really make it happen. "I want this over before she arrives. And Loviise Tamm's future is on a tight time frame as well. If it hasn't happened already, odds are good that what they have in mind for her will psychologically and emotionally devastate her, probably for life."

I say another silent prayer that she hasn't been fed to the sharks yet and forced into prostitution. Girls in her position are broken in by being raped and beaten over and over until they just give up and do what they're told. "We start the search for Loviise this evening."

"It's a big city. How?"

I'm suddenly exhausted again. "I'm going to take a nap. I'll let you know when I wake up." I wash the gop off the teeth in the lion's head of my cane, oil them so they don't rust, and lie down in bed.

Sleep doesn't come. Images flicker through my mind like a slide show. A tear gas canister blowing out my window. Kate blowing Adrien Moreau in half with a sawed-off shotgun. The bodies of little children his accomplices left in shallow graves. Sweetness destroying the biker's knee. The sound of it. He'll never walk on it again. Instead, like me, he'll drag his leg around for life. So much violence. I went into self-imposed isolation to avoid it. Or rather, after understanding just how volatile I've become, to avoid hurting others. My emotional state is fragile. I'm unpredictable. I don't want to be. I want to move on from all this ugliness.

The past won't let me be. I have to sleep. I tire easily and may be in for a long night of police work, or some facsimile of it. I dry-swallow a couple pills and wait for them to knock me out, but my mind keeps churning and turns, as it so often does, to Kate.

13

I roll out of bed at six p.m. I slept all day after sleeping fifteen hours last night. I tell myself it's because I tire easily and we have a long night ahead of us, but I know damned well sleeping near round the clock is a sign of depression. Milo said I'm in "shock." I don't know, maybe I am. I don't much care.

The girls are sitting side by side at the dining room table, somber, speaking sotto voce. Sweetness is sitting on the floor in front of the TV, playing the video game Grand Theft Auto. With our watchers incapacitated and the message sent, I think my apartment is safe, at least for now.

Some burgers are in a pan on the stove. We have no bread in the house because Jenna and Sweetness are avoiding the dreaded carbohydrates that would turn them into slobbering fat monsters. I add some salt and eat two with my fingers. I ask Sweetness, "Ready to roll?"

He snaps off the TV and stands up. "Just let me get my stuff."

Said stuff includes a bulletproof vest. It's made of light-weight material, like a mesh T-shirt, with pouches that hold Kevlar inserts. It won't stop a big-bore Magnum round, but is sufficient protection for the greater majority of gunshots, and is unobtrusive, hard to spot under a loose shirt. He puts a windbreaker overtop to provide sufficient pockets and hide his pistols and other necessities: twin .45 Colt 1911s in shoulder holsters that accommodate their silencers, a sap in his waistband, razor-edged knife, Taser and extra magazines for the Colt, and a second backup .45 Colt with a three-inch barrel in an ankle holster. Plus a small flashlight.

I'm carrying all the same gear, except that I only pack one full-sized Colt in a shoulder holster and the smaller backup. Since he's ambidextrous, two benefit him, but not me. It's a warm evening, I'm already sweating from the added clothing and weight. If we're to find Loviise, we have to play to our strengths. I'm a gimp with a modicum of common sense. Sweetness is a physical powerhouse with little of it.

I see now that Milo rounds us out as a team. He possesses little common sense or physical prowess, but his intellect, IQ 172, stoned or not, allows leaps of thought that have moved cases forward in ways I wouldn't have been able to without him. I wish the little bastard were here with us now. Without him, playing to our strengths means strong-arm work and intimidation, methods I hoped to get away from, effective as they may be.

I wish we could carry out this investigation in the proper way and use standard police work. Having experienced both, I prefer it to gangster-style tactics. But police protocol, although effective, is slow and painstaking. Leaving a swath of fear and dread behind us moves cases along at lightning speed.

Sweetness got the girls to pack while I slept and we all go out to the Jeep Wrangler. I install Anu's car seat and belt her in. Sweetness opens the driver's door.

"Nope," I say.

"Nope what?"

"Nope, you can't drive after drinking when Anu is in the car."

His face turns red, embarrassed. "Keep your voice down. I don't want Jenna to know."

Like most juicers, he believes he's boozing on the sly. "She already knows. Everybody knows. Give the car keys to Mirjami."

He goes hangdog but says nothing and hands them to her.

She drives through both the main arteries and back streets of Helsinki for the better part of an hour, until I'm convinced we're not being tailed, and we eventually take the girls to Hotel Cumulus, a ten-minute walk from my apartment, and see them inside.

Then I give the keys to Sweetness—I have no choice, my

knee won't allow me to drive—and actually, I trust him behind the wheel, or almost, but not enough to endanger my child. He's the best drunk driver I've ever seen, better than most people sober. I've only seen him obviously drunk once. In quantities of a bottle a day of vodka or less, usually chased with beer, alcohol has no visible effect on him, and also, he has far and away the fastest reflexes I've ever witnessed on such a big man. He even dances well and with grace.

I tell him to swing by Milo's place around the corner and we take the elevator up. I open the door of the tiny apartment. God, what a shithole. Piles of everything from dirty clothes to unread newspapers to filthy dishes cover every surface, except for his worktable, which is neat, orderly, even polished. His reloading kit and all the accessories—brass, lead, powder, some things I don't recognize—are lined and stacked in rows with obsessive-compulsive precision.

Mounted on the wall behind the table is a long case that displays his war memorabilia, including the Hitler Youth dagger his mother stabbed his father with for philandering. The rest of the apartment is a borderline health hazard, but the display case hasn't so much as a single fingerprint on it. No doubt about it, Milo is three bricks shy.

"Notice something missing?" Sweetness says.

I look around. "Yeah. Where the fuck is the gun cabinet?"

"Stolen," Sweetness says.

I sit down on the edge of the bed. It's cold and hard. The sheet and blanket hang to the floor. I pull them off to reveal a futon mattress on top of the gun cabinet, which lies on its back. I pull the mattress off and fling it aside. "I guess happiness really is a warm gun," I say.

Sweetness yucks and shakes his head. "Fucking Milo," he says.

I open it. Our armory is inside. It's a big one. We're ready for war. I ask Sweetness, "What do you think we need?"

He scratches his head, adjusts his crotch. "We're looking for a girl that's probably locked up. Maybe she's locked up with other girls, and maybe they have a minder with them to keep them in line. Maybe even a few men. We need stuff to B&E them and then take on a few guys if we have to."

I see it the same way. I grab the Remington 870 tactical shotgun and load it with ceramic ballistic breaching rounds, to blow the locks off doors. Then we both take a couple flash-bang stun grenades each, to make a grand entrance if need be. I pocket a .357 snub-nosed that we lifted from a drug dealer a while back, in case we need a throw-down gun to manufacture a frame job. And last, I grab Milo's pride and joy, a 10-gauge Colt shotgun made around 1878. As an antique, it doesn't even require registration. Sweetness is a crack shot with both hands. I can't shoot for shit. Milo has ammo for the sawed-off on his reloading table. Every shell is labeled: rock salt, bird shot, triple-aught buck and flechettes—shot tipped with razors to cut people in half. Kate shot Adrien Moreau with flechettes.

When Milo first bought all this, a mini-armory, I thought it ridiculous. His wisdom stands proven. I load the sawed-off with rock salt and pocket some extra rounds. It will tear the hide off people without killing them.

I hunt around his kitchenette, find an unopened package of big plastic garbage bags—thinking he might actually use them when he bought them was a glaring case of self-denial—and put the shotguns in them so we can carry them around without scaring the citizenry. Good enough. We lock up behind us and go in search of Loviise Tamm.

Back in the Wrangler, Sweetness asks, "Where to first?"

Helsinki is crawling with prostitutes, awash in them. Girls working their way through the university, seasoned pros, sex slaves, and everything in between. Some even advertise, and many are entrepreneurs working out of their apartments. Why not? Pimping is a serious matter, but as long as prostitution isn't organized, there's no law against it. There are several Thai massage parlors on Vaasankatu, near my apartment. I get a kick out of watching middle-aged men glancing around, looking furtive, trying to ensure they enter the parlors unnoticed while inadvertently doing everything possible to attract attention, before they enter and seek a massage with a happy ending.

It makes the most sense to start our search for Loviise with the most popular whore bars. There aren't many, only a couple upscale ones at present, and I'm guessing their owners know far more about prostitution in Helsinki—who does what, who offers what services, who pimps, who the organized-crime figures are behind the slave trade—than the police who monitor such things.

Problems present themselves. There are no good reasons for the staff or prostitutes in the clubs to share such information with us, but many reasons why they shouldn't. And when we announce we're looking for a particular girl, after we leave, the phone lines will crackle red hot as everyone in the trade is informed, then whoever has Loviise will make her and themselves scarce until we give up and go away. I guess I just have to figure it out as we go along.

"Let's go downtown and start with Whitechapel," I say.

It's fashionable among a certain set, expensive and—most relevant to our task—high exposure, so there's not a chance of finding Loviise there. But it's the city's most popular whore bar, and as such, I hope the best source for information. The name Whitechapel comes from the district in London where Jack the Ripper murdered prostitutes. Quaint.

We're silent for a while on the ride over. I know Sweetness, something is on his mind. He works up to it and spits it out. "Jenna knows I still drink?"

"You both drink like pigs in the evening, so she doesn't have much room to criticize, but you're asking me if she knows you drink all day long. The answer is yes."

"What did she say to you?"

"Not a word. We all know, but we don't talk about it. You're an alcoholic and you can't hide it. Why is it you alkies always think your breath doesn't stink like booze if you drink vodka? I promise you, it does. You were a hard drinker and she fell in love with you anyway. In fact, I think she's glad you drink. It gives her an excuse to booze along with you at night and call it 'partying.' But you promised to stop drinking during the day and to quit carrying that flask. You lied to her. My guess is that disappoints and disturbs her."

He doesn't comment, just drives in silence. The truth wounded him.

My phone is on quiet but vibrates. It's Milo. My heart thuds. Anxiety about Kate renews itself. "Where are you?" I ask.

It's a video call. His face looks haggard and grim. He whispers. "I'm on the front porch of the address you gave me, crouched down beneath the window beside the front door. You can look in for yourself." He holds the phone up and angles it so I can see through a gap in sheer tattered curtains. I see a distorted image of Kate and her brother. They're sitting together on a couch that's falling apart. I see a bottle of booze and two half-empty glasses on the coffee table in front of them.

Milo moves the phone and tells me to wait a minute. "I walked away from the house," he says, "so we can talk."

"So talk."

"I got off the plane, rented a car and came straight here. John is a junkie. He's speedballing. In the morning, he buys an eight ball each of cocaine and heroin, sells off most of it and keeps the rest to feed his own habit. Kate isn't using drugs, but is drinking hard. I heard her harangue him about the dope, and of course he swore to stop soon, but we both know that's never going to happen."

"Is he snorting or on the spike?"

"Snorting, but I think he's using more since Kate got here. She's been to the ATM and given him money a couple times. Since now he has her resources at his disposal, he has no reason to show restraint."

"Is there anything else I should know?"

"She cries a lot."

I feel longing and sadness. "Have you figured out how to get her home?"

"I'll give her two choices. She can stay and I can kill John, or she can come with me and I get John into rehab. I get John to help me encourage her by letting him know the rehab is a farce. I get him a large quantity of dope on the condition that he cut off contact with her. He's in bad shape. He'd cut her throat for the free dope."

"It's a solid plan," I say.

"I thought so. And don't call me. I know this is hard on you, but trust me to deal with it, and I'll get in touch when there's something worth telling you."

"OK," I say, and he rings off before I can thank him.

Sweetness looks over at me with concern. "What's the situation?"

"Tenuous at best," I answer, and say no more. I feel like hurting someone.

WHITECHAPEL. A misnomer for this establishment. When the infamous murders were being carried out in 1888, the district was a dangerous and impoverished area of London. This club, though, features a red carpet and two doormen dressed in the best Victorian style: dark tailcoats and trousers, waistcoats, white bow ties, winged-collar shirts and top hats.

One of them queries us before letting us in. "Pardon me, gentlemen, but would you mind opening your jackets for me?"

"Yes," I say, "we would."

"It's unseasonably warm for your jackets, and the bulges under them suggest you're both packing. We don't allow firearms in the club."

I show him my police card. "We're exceptions to the rule."

With a gesture of his arm, he ushers us in.

The décor is garish authentic. Reproductions of period paintings hang against floral wallpaper. The overabundant furniture is a mishmash of Gothic, Tudor, Elizabethan and Rococo. It clashes miserably with a stage that has a dance pole for stripping in the center of it. The bartenders also wear period dress, waistcoats and bow ties. A girl fit for any centerfold undulates on the stage, goes through a series of the classic stripper moves, raises one leg up the pole in a standing split, smacks her own ass and licks her shin.

It's early yet, the crowd thin. A few patrons throw wadded-up bills on the stage. Some girls sit at tables and nurse drinks. All are stunning, won't come cheap. It's clear that Whitechapel caters to an exclusive and upscale clientele.

We go to the bar and I ask to see an owner.

"On what business?"

I show my police card again. "Mind your own fucking business."

The owners aren't in.

"Hey, *pomo*," Sweetness says, "aren't bartenders required to have their alcohol serving certification with them, and if the place serves food—and this place has a small menu— also a restaurant hygiene qualification certification?"

"Yes, they are," I answer. I ask the bartender. "May I see yours?"

He purses his lips, flustered. "Offhand, I don't know where they are. I'm certified, though, and we have them all on file here somewhere."

"'Somewhere' doesn't cut the ice. And I don't see the alcoholic beverage license on display either. I think, in the interest of your patrons, it would be best to stop serving until all these things can be sorted out. It wouldn't do to have someone get salmonella. There are other several issues to address as well, but I haven't decided what they are yet. They'll come to me by and by."

The bartender gives in, exasperated. "Do you want to see the Ripper or the Raper?"

"Excuse me?"

He sighs like I'm stupid. "The owners are the Harper brothers, commonly known as Jack the Ripper and Mack the Raper."

"Gee, they sound so amiable that I'm sure I'd like to be friends with both of them. It's hard to choose. I guess I should speak to both the Ripper and the Raper."

He makes a call and asks us to follow him. We go through the kitchen to the office. The door is open and we walk in. It's seedy, has cheap, battered white office furniture that looks like it came from IKEA. An old gray couch has quite a few stains that look suspiciously like semen.

Two men sit on either side of a messy desk. They stand to greet us, offer us their hands. We shake and introduce ourselves. They look near identical to each other, except that the Ripper is a head taller than the Raper, and they both look like mirror images of Andy Warhol, thin pale ghosts with parchment skin and unkempt white hair, which is strangely disconcerting. Jack, the taller of the two, bids us to sit. No way I'm sitting on that couch. "Thanks, but I'll stand. Hopefully, we won't take up too much of your time."

Sweetness sits on the edge of the desk. I take it he doesn't like the look of the couch either.

They sit. The Raper says, "What can we do fer you two gents? Always obliged to help the police, ain't we, Jack?" He pronounces it "Jeck."

"That we is," says the Ripper.

They have accents like characters in a Guy Ritchie film. I'm certain it's feigned or exaggerated.

"We'd very much appreciate your help," I say. "We're trying to locate a missing person." I show them Loviise's photo.

They both laugh at it.

"And you're amused why?" I ask.

"Listen, mate," the Raper says, "have you 'ad a look at the birds out in the club? This one ain't exactly in their league, now is she." It's not a question.

"I'm not suggesting she's come here to work as a prostitute. I thought, as you two must be quite knowledgeable about the inner workings of prostitution in Helsinki, you might tell us where to look, give us a place to start. She's Estonian. I don't think she's here of her own volition, and if she's engaged in prostitution, it's by force, not by choice."

"We can't help you, mate," the Ripper says. "It would be a betrayal of professional confidence, wouldn't it, Mack?"

"Aye, it would at that, and well said. A betrayal of professional confidence."

"The birds work in here of their own free will," the Ripper says. "We makes our profit on drink for the punters. We're upstanding businessmen, an' the only perk we gets is free pussy now an' again, ain't it so, Mack?"

"So it is. An' what kinda man wouldn't like thet? Thet's what keeps me goin' in this business when I'm feelin' blue. Why don't you toffs accept a little time with a couple birds as a show of respect for your esteemed positions. Get your knobs polished and then go back off in search of your missing girl."

Sweetness stands up, reaches down and snaps a leg off the desk with one hand. He throws it at the Ripper's head. He ducks. The leg has so much velocity that the jagged end penetrates the wall and sticks in it. The desk tips over. Sheafs of paper, bric-a-brac and a laptop slide onto the floor.

Both the Ripper and the Raper sit motionless, mouths hanging open in fear and awe.

"That was your answer," I say.

The Ripper recovers first. "Thet weren't necessary," he says.

I shrug. "Apparently, it was. We expect your cooperation."

"Our Da' were a pimp and a numbers runner, among other things," the Ripper says, "and we been in the cunt business, runnin' his errands, since we was in our nappies. But Da' weren't an honest crook. He skimmed from his masters an' ran his mouth, and Da' ended up fish chum in the Thames. We learnt about this country, a place where a man can make a living and an honest one off the pussy trade, and we came here to start anew. We even donate to the police association, in both official and unofficial ways. We don't want no trouble from ya, we just don't want to be fish chum like Da'. You can understand that, can'tcha?"

I lean against the wall to take the weight off my knee. "Yes, but I don't care." I look over at Sweetness. "Cut off his little finger."

Sweetness takes his Spyderco Delica out of his pocket and snaps it open.

The Ripper holds up his hands in a motion that says *stop*. "You win," he says. "We don't know who has yer girl, but it might surprise yer to know that a big part of our trade comes from spooks."

"You mean spies?"

"I do. They come here because the other punters, just by walkin' in the door, are showin' they got weaknesses. They're lonely, they got problems with the drink, an' they got money, so they got good jobs, like engineers an' such. Many got wives and families."

"And spies make friends with them, then blackmail them for Finnish technology."

"Yeh, the Russians especially try to keep up with the Joneses. And lots of Americans. And Chinese, among others."

"And this is of use to us how?"

"We know the spooks, and some Russian spooks are in the very business yer interested in, includin' the ambassador. If I was you, I'd start with them."

I consider it. If we brace and shake down a Russian spook and he has limited or no information, those phone lines crackle and sizzle, Loviise disappears, and we get nothing. It's a bad bet.

Sweetness and I look at each other. He shakes his head no. He thinks they're holding back.

"More," I say.

The two Andy Warhols look at each other and the room is silent for about sixty seconds. They're trying to decide who they're most afraid of. Sweetness's knife is a lock blade, designed to be opened with one hand. He depresses the lock with his thumb. He closes it, opens it. Closes it, opens it. Seconds tick by.

Mack the Raper stares at me, takes in my cane and gunshot face. "Yer that famous cop I seen on the telly, ain'tcha?"

"Yep."

"Is this method the secret behind yer crime-solvin' success?"

"Yep."

He looks at his brother and nods. The Ripper says, "If I give ya everything you need, I want it forgotten. No rat jacket and coppers showin' up here regular."

"Agreed."

"Yer in luck. Once a month, the real toffs have a poker game, which is tonight. They meet, play, and make deals for women, gambling rights, guns, dope. Even gas and oil. The whole shebang on a global level. Need a tactical nuke to build yer own dirty bomb, that's the place to go. Different men are invited, dependin' on the business at hand, and fly in from around the world to play. I'm told the Russian ambassador was invited tonight. You find him, and he can find yer girl."

"Where?"

"King's Royale. The game starts at midnight."

King's Royale. Helsinki's other major whore bar. Owned unofficially by a Finnish billionaire—actually now a citizen of Monaco—Pasi Palo, who reputedly uses King's Royale to launder money in Finland. Officially, it's owned by a holding company owned by a holding company owned by a holding company registered in Singapore, and there the trail goes cold.

I know this because so many police want to see him jailed for trafficking in arms, women and dope, but especially arms. His business partners are reputed to be Russian mafiosi, including generals in the Russian army and the FSB, the new, democratic Russia's KGB. His best clients are said to include Robert Mugabe of Zimbabwe, Omar al-Bashir of Sudan, and Than Shwe of Burma. Some of the world's most vicious dictators.

"You ever been to a game?" I ask.

"We went once, cuz they wanted to talk to us about girls," the Raper says, "but it costs a hundred thousand euros to get in. Too rich for our blood."

"How tight was security?"

"Not like you might think. It's in Punavuori, and you can't exactly line up fifty men with Uzis in that trendy little part of town, can you, mate? Just a few men. Two at the door that leads from the nightclub upstairs, but they can't hear nor see nothin' downstairs. Two outside the delivery entrance to usher the players in—they come and go that way—one bloke stays at the door and the other escorts the players in when they arrive. A couple are posted outside the door of the room they play in, and more bodyguards are inside the room itself."

It's odd to hear that area, the district of Punavuori, called "trendy." It used to be considered a dangerous place inhabited by lowlifes. Gentrification. "How can they run a high-security game with a nightclub in full swing?"

"For you, mate, that's the beauty of it. Ya got one club upstairs, and another one downstairs, as they spin different kinds of music, so each one's soundproofed. An' behind the downstairs club is a private room, very posh, and also sound-proofed. You could set a bomb off in there and nobody would know. A word to the wise. If ya go there, yer a dead man."

"Do they always use the same security people?"

"Palo's boys."

"And do you know them?"

"Yeh, since he owns thet club we cross paths once in a while, us bein' in the same trade and all."

I snap open the lion's mouth on the handle of my cane, run my fingers along the razor teeth, feel the sting and think. I turn to Sweetness and switch to Finnish. "Do you want to do this? We might get killed."

He puts his knife back in his pocket. "I don't think we have any choice. We probably won't get another chance, and you promised her mom."

At the moment, I'm so depressed about Kate, her problems and our marriage that I don't care if I live or die. "*I* promised her. Not you. Aside from creating an international incident that may land us in prison, it has all the hallmarks of a kamikaze mission that only an addled mental defective would consider."

Sweetness chuckles. "I figured that out on my own. But a promise is a promise, and if you go, I go. I just don't know how you can do it with your knee as fucked up as it is. And if I said no, I have a feeling you'd try to go by yourself."

"Yeah, I would."

"How?"

My pain level has gone down considerably since getting the cortisone shots. "Slowly and carefully. And that's why I brought the sawed-off room sweeper."

"Then let's go."

I check the time on my cell phone, wish I hadn't destroyed my watch. It's a few minutes after midnight.

I switch back to English and say to the whore-mongering brothers, "Put your thinking caps on and figure out how to get in and out alive, because you two are coming with us."

"Why us?" the Raper says. "We gave ya what ya wanted!"

"Because," I say, "the two of you are such harmless, pathetic, brainless morons that no one would suspect you of doing anything that requires balls."

Pissed off and afraid, the Ripper says, "Ya told us you'd leave us be if we told yer what ya wanted."

"No, I promised you no rat jacket. And you may not pimp the girls in your club, but you make deals with their pimps—don't tell me you don't take kickbacks—and in my eyes, that makes you scum."

"They'll fuckin' kill us. We'll have to leave the fuckin' country."

I draw my silenced .45. "It's me now or them later. You boys are good at plying your trade. I'm sure you'll start over somewhere else and prosper."

In fact, I wouldn't kill them or have Sweetness cut off their fingers, but I've done a good job of convincing them otherwise.

"Ya can't just murder us. You've been seen. You'll end up in the nick same as any other murderer, copper or not."

I show him the taped-up .357 Magnum. "You pulled this. It was self-defense. We had no choice."

Fear: the great motivator. He doesn't hesitate, makes a call. The table is full. He says they're happy to sit in when other players want breaks, and really, they want to come to talk business more than play. He gets the invite. My guess is they're bush-league players and the others just think of them as easy money. Two idiots to fleece and send packing.

"You're going to need the cash as a stage prop," I say, "to convince them you're there to play. Find it."

"You expect us to have two hundred thousand euros just layin' around to no purpose?"

"I hope you do," I say, "for your sake."

He turns even paler, scowls, furious at having his life turned upside down, calls me a "filthy fucking rat bastard prick," and says, "I guess we gotta take it with us to flee the fuckin' country anyway, cuz of you."

"It would likely be in your best interest," I say.

He pulls a cheap reproduction of a Pre-Raphaelite painting off the wall to reveal a safe behind it. It's stuffed with cash. He jams it all into a gym bag. "I guess you win, mate," he says, "but goddamn you to hell fer it."

"We're not fucking friends," I say, "so if either of you calls me fucking 'mate' one more time, I'll shoot you on general principles. So fuck you and let's go."

15

We go out to the Wrangler. The Ripper sits in front beside Sweetness. I sit in the back beside the Raper, my silenced Colt pressed against his side. They might try to bolt and run while we're at a traffic light. This gives them incentive to stay in the vehicle and behave. We park down the street from King's Royale. To reach the back of the club and the delivery entrance, a vehicle has to pass through an alley. The buildings on both sides of it make the alley a perfect shooting gallery, while hiding and protecting the guards at the club door around the corner at the back of it. I have no visibility for the first leg of this operation.

How to do this? The Harper brothers could just forewarn the guards that police are coming, walk in, the door locked behind them, and earn some points from Pasi Palo for the tip-off. No doubt they've both already considered this.

"You two remember who you're dealing with," I say. "Two cops from the National Bureau of Investigation." They don't know Sweetness is officially employed as a linguistic specialist. "If you screw us, we'll kill you tonight if we can. If not, we'll ruin your business, charge you with all sorts of shit, have your books examined and nail you for tax fraud. I'll make it my personal business to see you get max prison sentences. The list of our ways to fuck up your lives is long, and if you fuck us over, it'll be your own asses you're peddling, as if anyone would want them, instead of spending your evenings drinking cognac with spies and getting your dicks sucked."

I take the Raper's cell phone, put my number in it, and give it a speed dial with the number one. I call my own phone number, give it back to him and tell him to keep the line open so I can hear everything that's said.

I ask Sweetness for his Taser, take out my own, and show the brothers how they work. "You two are going to talk your way into getting the door unlocked, then zap the men guarding it with these. Keep shocking them until they're unconscious. Look for security cameras and get out of sight of them. Then you tell me and we'll be there in a heartbeat." I pull the sawed-off in its black garbage bag out from under the seat and show it to them. "We'll be right behind you with this, and when we get there, I'll tell you what to do next."

I smell fear sweat and they both tremble. "Pull yourselves together, goddamn it, or you'll end up dead." I hand Sweetness the bag with the lockbuster shotgun and he takes a roll of duct tape from the glove box.

They nod, and we pile out of the Wrangler. They have trouble making themselves walk down the street. Sweetness kicks the Raper in the ass. "Move."

Off they go, and we trail a little less than a minute behind them, shotguns hidden in the bags, but cocked with our fingers on the triggers. It gets dark a little earlier every night as summer progresses. The light is dim. For a moment, I think it makes us unobtrusive, but realize my limp and Sweetness's size make that impossible.

We reach the corner and peer into the alley. The brothers walk into it. We give them a head start and follow. They reach an inner courtyard and turn right. I listen to them blabber inane bullshit to security about why they want to attend the game. But they flash the cash and it gives them an appearance of veracity. I hear electric zaps.

The Raper unpockets his phone and speaks to me. "The blokes are out cold. Me satchel full of cash made 'em believe we're here to play. I got me foot keepin' the door open, an' there's a security camera on top a the door."

Sweetness peers around the corner and blows out the camera lens with his pistol. He motions for me to follow.

I recognize one of the bodyguards. He answered the door once when I visited Veikko Saukko's home. I take it he's on loan this evening. He had an iPad and used it to check

Saukko's appointments, appeared to serve as Saukko's secre-
tary as well as security. We use zip-lock plastic ties to cuff
their hands and feet. Saukko's man is an obvious powerhouse. I double-shackle him to make sure he can't use his
strength to snap the zip-locks. I take his iPad, it might have
some useful information in it. We tape their mouths shut.
They start coming around.

"Can we scarper now?" the Raper asks.

"Soon," I say. "Take us to the game, put on happy faces,
and tase the guards outside the door. Same deal. I'll listen.
Tell me when they're down."

"Yer a God-rotted bastard," he says, and does as he's told.

We follow the brothers through the kitchen storeroom,
they motion for us to stop, and they start down a hallway.
Upstairs in the nightclub, the music must be blaring. Here
in the staff area, I can't hear a goddamned thing. The sound-
proofing is excellent. The Raper gives me the go-ahead. We
start down the hall. I go as fast as I can, which isn't very.
Two more guards are down. We secure them, disarm them,
pull the batteries out of their phones and fling them back
toward the storeroom. I tell the brothers to get the fuck out
of here.

We take the shotguns out of the bags. I cradle the sawed-
off under my arm and take two flash-bangs out of my pocket.
I press myself against the wall to avoid shrapnel. Sweetness
angles himself away from the door to do the same. We do it
fast. He fires and kicks the door open. The roar is deafening
in this confined space. I pull the pins on the grenades and

toss them into the room, turn, plug my ears and close my eyes. Three seconds. Thunders like the cracks of doom and flashes like supernovas.

We charge in. Some made it under the table when the door flew open. Those standing went down. Six players at the table. Two gunmen bodyguards. They're all deaf, blind and disoriented. A couple puke from inner-ear-liquid imbalance. We start screaming. "Everybody facedown on the floor. Lock your fingers behind your heads."

I realize I'm shouting in Finnish. I scream it again in English. Sweetness takes my cue, shouts orders in Russian.

All but two players suck floor. A bodyguard behind the bar must have understood what was happening, closed his eyes and ears. He comes up shooting. He turns his head as I let the right barrel go. Smoke and flame blast out of it. I cut loose with only one hand gripping the gun. It almost flies out of my grasp from the recoil jolt. The guard gets his side and the back of his head scorched with rock salt. He drops his pistol. Not out of fear or pain, but because he sees what he's done. He put a bullet square between Pasi Palo's eyes. That won't be forgiven. As Milo would say, before long he'll be dead as a bag of hammers.

The only man left upright is Veikko Saukko. He's in a chair on the right side of the poker table, resting his right elbow on it and resting his head on his hand. He's drumming on the table with the fingers of his left hand, as if all this bores him. I guess he recognized the flash-bangs, plugged his ears and covered his eyes as well.

I chuck the spent shell and replace it with a fresh one. We keep shouting, keep the fear and confusion maximized. They think this is a heist, that we're taking down their game. I cover the room, Sweetness goes through all their pockets, looks for weapons and electronic devices. Veikko Saukko is an arms dealer. One of the players is Arab. Another is black, so perhaps African. Each has a man of his own race beside him, I assume translators. This really is criminal planning on a global scale. None of them are packing, except for security. Their communications devices—BlackBerrys, Androids, iPads and iPhones and others—go in a pile on the table, so that they neither call for help nor record this event.

It's a nice place for a game. The card table on the left of the room is covered in green felt. Its walnut trim has drink holders built into it. On the right side of the room, leather armchairs are arranged in a semicircle around an entertainment center. A full bar lines the back wall. Another door leads out of the room. I check it out and find a sauna.

I pat down Veikko Saukko myself and pocket his iPhone. Further, I get a pen and paper from beside the game bank, which has hundreds of thousands of dollars in it, and instruct him to write down his e-mail user name and password. I test it to make sure it's correct. There might be messages in it concerning the attacks against us. If he's behind the assaults and threats leveled against my family and me, I intend to find out and put a stop to it. How, I don't know. The über-rich aren't subject to the rule of law as the rest of us are. But

I've learned a valuable lesson over these past months: All men are subservient to the laws of pain.

By the time we've secured the room, tended to our own safety, and made certain our activities aren't on video, its occupants have pulled themselves together for the most part. I tell them all to be seated with their hands placed in front of them on the table, and assure them that we're not here to steal from them and mean them no harm. Sweetness simultaneously translates from my English into Russian.

"Which of you is Russian Ambassador to Finland Sergey Merkulov?" I ask.

"I am." The man is in his late fifties or early sixties, tanned and running to fat, has thinning hair and an Armani suit. He lights a cigar and motions for the flunky who killed Pasi Palo to bring him a drink.

I shove Palo's corpse out of its chair onto the floor, take his seat, lay the sawed-off on the table in front of me, and address the ambassador. "Sir, my business here is primarily with you."

Palo was a billionaire and a man of great power. His death seems not to disturb the other men in the room, his colleagues, one iota. I file this away in the tome in my head titled *What I Know About Human Nature.*

He smiles, reptilian, and answers in English. "I doubt that, unless you're referring to the horrendous diplomatic incident now taking place as 'business.'"

"This is business that, if I went through official channels

to discuss with you, would be dismissed as insulting fiction and result in me being tossed out of your embassy on my ear. Our dramatic entrance was required to get your attention and cooperation."

I take Loviise's photo from my pocket and slide it across the table to him. "I'm looking for this girl. I want you to find her for me. She was lured here from Estonia, was promised work. She's easily identifiable. She has Down syndrome and it makes her stand out."

His smile broadens, then turns to laughter. "Why in the hell would you think I have any idea where this foul little creature is?"

"I don't think you do, but that you know who does."

He exhales a voluminous plume of smoke and knocks his double vodka back in one gulp. "And to what do you attribute this certainty?"

I say nothing.

"And if I refuse?"

I return his smile and still say nothing. The way we made our way in here speaks volumes.

"And if I do locate this child for you, are you going to piss off and let us play cards in peace?"

"Most certainly."

"Then give me my phone."

"In a moment."

I turn to face Saukko. He still wears his façade of boredom. "I've had some problems with harassment. My windows broken out. My family threatened and home teargassed.

Insinuations concerning your ten million euros in ransom money that someone believes I stole and wants returned. Which is impossible for me to do," I lie, "because I don't have the money. And as whoever is threatening me hasn't identified himself, I wouldn't know who to give it to even if I did have it."

He sits upright, drains his glass and folds his arms. "You stupid piece of shit. I know goddamned good and well you and your buddies stole that fucking money. I couldn't give a fuck less. That's candy money to me. I sent you to find my son and bring him home to me, and you killed him. And you killed his pregnant girlfriend and deprived me of a grand-child. You think I would play kids' games like knocking out your windows? If you believe that, you really are one dumb son of a bitch."

I glance over at the security flunky. "Get my friend and me beers and vodkas." He looks at Saukko. Saukko nods assent.

"Your son called you 'a human monster,'" I say, "'the worst sort of pig.' He hated you. He shot at me and tried to kill me. He would have killed my partner if a bullet hadn't stopped him. Adrien Moreau, who you hired, killed his mistress. He shot her through the belly to kill the fetus and watched her bleed out. It may be that I bear guilt for those deaths, but you share it."

The security flunky parks drinks on the table for me and Sweetness, took the liberty of making a fresh gin and tonic for Saukko. Flunky's white shirt is streaked and speckled with blood from the salt that blew through it. His head is seeping blood. I'm guessing that, as the salt dissolves into his system, he's going to be really thirsty for a couple days.

My pain is bad from so much activity. I chase painkillers with beer.

"None of this makes any difference," Saukko says. "You were sent to do a job, you failed, and my boy died. You'll pay dearly, far more than ten million is worth to you. An eye for an eye. Your child belongs to me now. Her name is Anu, isn't it? We'll forget tonight ever happened, because I have dibs on you and want to see you suffer before you die. No one here will have you killed. Finish your business with Sergey and get out."

Sweetness says, "This is a card game. I want to play cards." He points at Palo's dead body. "You've got an empty chair."

The gangsters around the table laugh. The ambassador says, "It takes a hundred thousand to get in the game."

"I'm good for it. An IOU OK for now?" A frank admission that we're crooked cops.

The ambassador waxes indulgent. "Sure."

This is bizarre. I give up my seat for Sweetness. The other bodyguard, not the drink flunky, brings him a hundred thousand in chips. "Whites are a thousand. Blue five thousand, red ten thousand. Max bet is twenty-five thousand, unless upped by mutual agreement."

"Gosh," Sweetness says, "and we're playing for keeps?"

Saukko says, "The money is only a metaphor, now rendered meaningless. We played for blood. Who won and lost the real game is already decided, only the debts remain unpaid."

"It might interest you to know that Inspector Vaara didn't kill your son. I did. I dumped two clips of .45 caliber hollow points in his face and chest. Shit, what a mess. But I guess you saw it at the morgue."

"Good to know," Saukko says, "you son of a bitch. You can join Vaara on The List."

"The List?" I say.

"The Shit List. That's where my worst enemies go. Bad things, horrific things, happen to people on The List. I plan them with care. You, for instance, have some kind of preoccupation with saving women. I'm going to take your child, maybe tomorrow, maybe in ten years, and have her tortured to death. Waiting appeals to me. The older your daughter gets, the more you'll love her. Maybe after I bust her prepubescent cherry, I'll sell her for an Asian snuff film. What do you think, Vaara?"

He wanted to scare the mortal hell out of me, and he succeeded so well that I don't even feel anger, just terror. I unscrew the handle from the shaft of my cane and pull out the thin twenty-inch sword contained within it. I reach across the table and press it against his chest, over his heart. "I think I should just end your miserable, bitter life right now."

On his shirt, a bloodstain flowers around the blade. He pays no attention to it. Instead, he proffers a grin worthy of Satan. "I wouldn't, if I were you. You don't know how The Shit List works. The hits are prepaid, like a debit card for death. It's called the 'button down' method. My death takes the finger off the button, the punishments are carried out, and my enemies join me in hell."

I return the sword to the cane. I'm speechless.

Sweetness, however, isn't. "Are we gonna play or not?"

Saukko laughs out loud. "Boy, you have style. If I wasn't going to kill you, I'd offer you a job. It was Palo's deal. Since you have his seat, I guess it falls to you."

"Give me a new deck," Sweetness says. "I don't trust you criminal fuckers."

The bodyguard who gave him his chips hands him a pack of Bicycle cards. Sweetness breaks the seal, tosses out the jokers and shuffles with speed and thoroughness. Everyone antes. He passes the deck to the right and the Arab cuts the cards.

"Seven-card stud," Sweetness says, and deals with confidence. As dealer, he runs the hand fast, calls out the cards as he flips them faceup. He bets high, but not high enough to drive anyone out of the hand. When he deals the last card facedown, they've already bet seventy thousand per player. No one folded. He tosses in a red chip. Ten thousand more. Everyone sees and calls. Around the table, the players throw their cards down by turn. All have good hands. Saukko has aces and eights, the hand the Wild Bill Hickok legend says he held when he was shot dead. Sweetness flops down three kings, says, "Thanks, guys. I'll cash out now. You know how it is, places to go and people to see."

I give the ambassador his phone. Sweetness takes all the electronica from the table, to make sure we have time to get away. Whether we live through the night is still up in the air. He dumps all the junk into a gym bag one of the players must have brought to carry cash. He takes his half million euros and tosses it in the bag, too.

The ambassador makes a quick call and rings off. He gives me an address and tells me to be there in half an hour. I take his phone from him. Whoever he called knows where the abducted girls are kept. I can track that person through his dialed numbers.

Sweetness says, "Thanks, guys. We'll have to do this again sometime."

The painkillers are kicking in, I push myself to my feet and gimp out the door. Sweetness covers me until I'm out of the room and then follows. "Plug your ears," he says, and tosses in two more flash-bangs behind him as a parting gesture. Even with my ears protected and eyes shut, it's like a nuke went off in the room. We step over the two cuffed guards in the hall and walk away.

We get to the delivery entrance. The guards there remain as we left them. I point at Saukko's personal bodyguard and ask Sweetness, "Would you cut the zip-lock cuffs off his legs and pull the tape off his mouth? I want to take him with us. Men with their mouths taped shut tend to draw attention on the street."

"Why take him with us?"

I want to puke from anxiety. "This Shit List thing. He knows Saukko's business. We have to interrogate him and find out if it's true, and if so, how to nullify it."

Sweetness cuts him loose. This guy is a trained killer. I'm a crip with guns I barely know how to use. I cock the hammers of the shotgun and keep him at arm's length. "Don't say a word. Don't make sudden movements. Or you get both barrels. Walk in front of us out to the street."

He nods.

When we get to the Wrangler, I order him to get in the rear of the vehicle, rebind his ankles, retape his mouth, and throw a tarp over him.

16

We drive away. The dashboard clock reads ten after three. We drive a short distance to the address supplied to us. I ring the buzzer. No answer. I smash the apartment building's front-door window with my sap, an extendable steel baton, reach inside and let us in. We take the elevator to the fourth floor. I ring. Again, no answer. Burning up a clip from my silenced Colt works as a key on the bottom lock. The door swings open a fraction. The Gemtech silencer I'm using, courtesy of Milo, really is a gem. I hear little more than the slide cycling and the used casings pattering on the floor as I'm firing. No waking the neighbors.

Sweetness picks up the spent brass for me. The top, heavy-duty lock is usually meant for extra security when leaving. It's unlocked, which suggests someone is inside.

We enter, and I push the door closed behind us. The reason we weren't buzzed in becomes apparent. A man has his knees on the floor, his head and torso on a couch, as if trying to push himself to his feet. The butcher knife in his back, planted deep between his shoulder blades, prevented it. He's dead.

Sweetness looks at me. "Fuck," he says.

I agree. "Yeah, fuck. We need to take our shoes off, and for God's sake, don't touch anything."

We don't have any latex gloves to keep us from contaminating the crime scene with our own fingerprints. It's a big apartment, with the doors to all the rooms shut. We both pull jacket sleeves down over one hand and use the cloth to turn door handles, hold pistols in the other, not easy with my cane. We split up and go through the place. It has three bedrooms, I suppose necessary for multiple girls turning tricks at the same time.

I hear Sweetness scream, "Jesus Fucking Christ!"

I would have come running if I could, but can only call out and ask if he's hurt.

"No," he answers, his voice calm now. "Come here."

I follow his voice and enter a bedroom. He's staring up into the shelf space over a closet. I look and see a waif of a girl. She's folded herself into the tight space. Her eyes radiate terror. Loviise Tamm.

I doubt if she speaks anything but Russian. "Talk to her," I say. "Tell her we're police, here to help her, and ask her if she can get down from there."

She seems to take our stated good intentions at face value. She pushes her hands against one wall, feet against the other, faceup, and shimmies down, spiderlike. It reminds me of a circus trick. "Can you make her feel comfortable and try to find out what happened here? Ask her to please not sit or touch anything, and tell her we'll take her away from here very soon."

They go back and forth for a few minutes. Some of it I understand, some of it I don't.

When they're done, Sweetness explains. "It's like her mom said, she was promised a job in Helsinki. Then, when she got here, the men who brought her talked about her owing them money for arranging her work and the cost of the trip over, and took her passport. They locked her in this apartment. Other people, including some girls, came and went. They kept her fed, but wouldn't talk to her. Just told her to wait and all would become clear. She was frightened the whole time. Then a man came just a little while ago. He was angry because she was going to leave, and he said he was going to get something from her first. He sat on the couch and told her to take out his 'thingy.' She said it was big and hard, she didn't know what to do, and he told her to get on her knees and put it in her mouth. She froze, it seemed icky and wrong. He started to yell and he slapped her, but the doorbell rang. He answered it and a woman was at the door. She saw

Loviise and looked furious. He told Loviise to get up, go to a bedroom and shut the door. She heard him talk to the woman, but their voices were low and she didn't understand what they said. Then she heard him shout and everything went quiet. She was afraid of him and his anger and his 'thingy,' and crawled up into that space to hide. When I came in, she had a blanket pulled over her and I couldn't see her, but I saw the blanket move from her breathing, I jerked it away and found her. That's when I yelled. She scared the shit out of me."

"Ask her what the woman looked like."

He asks and translates. "She looked like a magazine."

"What does that mean?"

She clarifies. "She was very beautiful, like a woman in a magazine."

Her case of Down syndrome appears to be as mild as her mother claimed. She seems largely functional, but her naïveté likely saved her from a worse fate than she suffered. If she didn't even know how a penis functions, she needed to be broken in, accomplished by raping her on a regular basis until she gave up hope and just succumbed to it. No one had gotten around to that yet. "Thank her and ask her to wait right here."

I go over the rest of the house quickly. There's little to see. Cheap furniture. More IKEA stuff. Some microwavable food in the fridge. A case of Stolichnaya vodka and a crate of beer, I suppose for the clientele. I find some yellow latex cleaning gloves in a closet along with cleaning supplies, and a roll of masking tape in a kitchen drawer. I use it to hide the bullet holes in the front door.

I put on the gloves and rifle through the corpse's pockets. I find two passports, Loviise's and his own. If he had her passport, but no others besides his own, it indicates that he meant to turn her over to me. Something went wrong first, and he was murdered. I also take the corpse's credit card. He was one of those dummies who keeps his bank codes on him with the user number sequence written on it. I take it, too. If he were alive, I couldn't ask him for anything more.

He's a Russian named Sasha Mikoyan and his passport is diplomatic. So he's a spy or an attaché or both, and the Harper brothers didn't lie. People from the Russian embassy are taking part in the slave trade.

The Russian diplomatic mission, given the circumstances of his death, whorehouse, kidnapping et al., will probably exercise their right to keep Finnish law enforcement out of this. I put his passport back in his pocket but take his wallet and iPhone, so I can carry out an investigation of my own. I've developed quite a collection of gadgets tonight.

"Let's go," I say. I check the time, now three fifty-five.

Loviise has a traveling bag. Sweetness carries it for her as we walk to the car. I want to discuss this situation with Sweetness, but don't know if our abductee in the back can understand Finnish. I jam cigarette butts deep in his ears, cover them with duct tape, and put shooting-protection earphones on top of that. He couldn't hear a bomb drop.

We all get in the Wrangler. I sit up front with Sweetness.

Saukko's man hasn't made a sound. Apparently, he's smart enough to know it won't help, and he's just waiting, pondering how to get through this, preparing himself for the worst. This marks him as a cool professional. Sweetness hits his flask.

"This may rank as one of the longest nights of our lives, but we're going to have to make this a murder of opportunity," I say.

He doesn't catch the double entendre. "What do you mean?"

I'm rattled and overwrought, exhausted and in pain. I haven't had this much physical activity since I was shot. I rub my knee. "Saukko said he had nothing to do with knocking out my windows and harassing me. I believe him, do you?"

I start chain-smoking, try to clear my mind with nicotine.

"*Pomo*, that evil fuck is ten times smarter than I am. I don't know."

"Pitkänen isn't doing this alone, that leaves the minister of the interior, the national chief of police, and our new parliamentarian and Finland's best hater, Roope Malinen. I don't think Malinen has the stones for it, but the minister and the chief do."

"What about Adrien Moreau? He was after the ten million and we killed him. Maybe somebody associated with him?"

I shake my head. "He was a self-sufficient loner. I don't believe he would have involved anyone else."

"It could be hate groups as well. We really put the fucks to those neo-Nazis for selling strychnine-laced heroin. And all the groups are interconnected."

Over thirty people died of strychnine poisoning before dealers figured out what they were selling and pulled the bad smack off the streets. "But they don't have a SUPO agent on their side, or if they do, it's because the minister ordered him to work with them. I think we need to interrogate the minister and the chief, and that crime scene is the place to do it."

"Why?"

"Because I told the chief if he didn't fuck off about the money, I'd frame him for a crime and kill him in the process of arresting him. It's late on a weeknight. They're probably in their beds. We should abduct them."

Sweetness chuckles. "Cool. You really gonna kill the chief?"

"No, not cool. Crazy. And I don't want to hurt anybody. But Saukko and his Shit List and his threats, plus the attacks and other threats against my family, have me scared shitless. I'll murder whoever I have to and sit my jolt in prison before I'll let anyone hurt my family. Later, we'll interrogate the guy in the back, and I hope before we go home we'll know where the truth lies and who our enemies are and aren't. We can't protect ourselves and ours until then. That includes Jenna and even your mother."

That possibility seems to have not struck him yet, and when it does, as it did for me, it carries fear with it. He nods his head slow, shakes a cigarette out of a pack and lights it. "You're right," he says. "We deal with this now."

I feel sorry for whoever Sweetness decides is to blame. He'll kill them—after punishing them—and if we can't discover who is guilty, he'll take the position of the crusader leader, a bishop who, when asked by his troops how to tell who was Catholic and who wasn't, answered, "Kill them all, God will recognize his own."

17

Lay out the plan for me," Sweetness says.

I picture the map of Helsinki and think of the most expedient way to do this. "Go to my house so I can grab my crime kit. Then to Milo's. I need something there. I want to at least minimally process that apartment before the Russians claim diplomatic privilege and shut it down. Maybe you could ask your mother if Loviise can stay there until we can make arrangements for her to safely return to Estonia. They have a common language. Loviise could have someone to talk to."

"Mom will probably help, but she'll be furious if I call at

this hour and ask to bring a stranger to her house. It has to wait until a decent hour. And she could be in danger. We'll have to stash them both somewhere."

We have no time to waste. Sweetness pulls out onto the road. "How do you know Loviise isn't lying? She could have killed that Russian."

I just want Kate to see me save the girl. I can't get over the idea that it will redeem me in her eyes, and in some small way, my own. "I don't think Loviise is clever enough for that, but I'll lift prints off the knife and print her just in case. Even if she did, it was justifiable and I don't want her prosecuted. We send her home anyway."

"What do we do with her for tonight?"

I chain one smoke off the other, flick the end of the last one out the window and watch in the passenger-side mirror as the cherry-red end smacks off the street and bursts like a little firework. "Keep her with us. They know we have her. We offended important people. They might try to snatch her back, just to put us in our places."

"They might decide to put us in our places by killing us," Sweetness says.

"True. First, we snatch the minister and the chief and force the truth out of them about the harassment against us. If they pass inspection, we let them go home, if not . . ." I raise my hands, palms up, and shrug, as if to say the situation is beyond my control. "Then we go to Vantaa, to Filippov Construction, and interrogate Saukko's man there."

The construction company specialized in toxic waste

management. It's been closed since its owner, Ivan Filippov, was shot dead while I investigated him for murder. The site has served us well in the past. It has privacy, and we've dissolved the bodies of two gangsters in acid there, to cover up their murders and prevent a gang war.

"And then?"

"And then we make Loviise safe with your mom and go home. It's Mirjami's birthday, and remember, we have to shop for a gift for her when the stores open."

"I could just give her all the money I won. Wrap it up with a card that says it's from both of us."

"That's generous. You cheated, didn't you?"

"Yeah."

"How?"

"I'll buy you a book of card tricks and teach you. But that's why I asked for a fresh deck, so I knew where each card was when I started shuffling."

This gets a laugh out of me. "You're not afraid of anyone or give a shit about anything, do you?"

He looks at me, solemn. "Not much. I'm careful where I place my affections and concerns. I don't have room for many."

Wisdom from the baby-faced behemoth.

WE RUN the errands fast. I have a fishing tackle box with basic crime-scene processing equipment in it. I dump all my newly acquired electronica on the dining room table, grab the box, some other odds and ends, and some photos featuring the minister and chief. I've way overdone it and I'm fading. I scarf some painkillers and tranquilizers to keep me propped up. Then we shoot over to Milo's, and I take the sperm samples connecting the men we're about to abduct to the crime scene of Mrs. Filippov. Both the chief and minister live in apartments in Eira, not far from the scene of tonight's murder.

I check the time. Five ten a.m. I do it the easy way, ring their door buzzers, wake them, and announce that I have business concerning Saukko's money and it can't wait. The greedy fucks both think I'm acquiescing, returning the money, and let us in. I make Jyri Ivalo use his cell phone to call mine—to create the illusion of a phone conversation—and keep the phones open for five minutes, and to fetch his service pistol, which I take. We force them to get dressed and into the vehicle at gunpoint. Back to the crime scene we go.

Loviise is frightened, doesn't want to go back, but Sweetness reassures her that everything is for her own good, that we're trying to stop the people who were bad to her, and we show her our National Bureau of Investigation ID cards, which she can't read, but she seems reassured. Probably more by our demeanors than IDs.

We escort them all up to the apartment. Sweetness and I slip on paper shoe covers and surgical gloves, but don't allow them to do the same. I ask Loviise if she would mind to wait in another room while we men talk. She's nervous to be back in the apartment but complies. The minister and chief view Sasha Mikoyan's corpse with surprise and bemusement. Jyri

Ivalo speaks first. "What the hell are you doing, Vaara? This makes no sense."

First things first. I make them stand on each side of the corpse. *"Sano muikku"*—Say whitefish. They don't smile. I have Sweetness snap pics of them and the corpse together with his cell phone camera.

I keep my .45 leveled at Jyri with one hand, my cane in the other. As with everyone else tonight, I confiscate their electronics to keep from being recorded. I'm aware, though, that some of them will have GPS tracking devices in the event of their auspicious owners' disappearances. Then I think, *So fucking what, they all know I took them and where I live.*

"On the contrary," I say, "it makes perfect sense. I've suffered damage to my property and threats against the lives of my family because of your imaginary ten million euros. I warned you if you didn't let the matter drop, I would frame you for a crime, then kill you when you turned violent resisting arrest. The matter hasn't been dropped. The butcher knife in that man's back—incidentally, he's a Russian diplomat, or more than likely a spy on a diplomatic passport named Sasha Mikoyan—is your sword of Damocles."

I've confused him. "How so?"

I toss a pile of photos on the coffee table. "Have a look, both of you."

They both flip through them. Osmo Ahtiainen, the minister, says, "OK, you got me. I'm not photogenic when I fuck. So what?"

Jyri Ivalo gets the message but pretends otherwise. "So we've fucked some of the same women. Big deal."

"And here we are in a house of prostitution, an administrator of said house is dead, you're both drunk, and your fingerprints are on the murder weapon."

"No we aren't, and they aren't."

"But they soon will be, and you'll be very drunk. Too drunk to recall what happened here."

I pull plastic freezer bags from my fishing tackle crime-kit box. "These are semen samples that you were both stupid enough to deposit in the mouth of Ivan Filippov's mistress." I take out the syringes Jari left at my house. "Your semen samples will be found in Mikoyan's various orifices."

Both of them go pale and reflect shock. The ramifications of what I can do to them hits them like slaps to the face.

I take the samples to the kitchen and put them in the freezer so they don't thaw and deteriorate. I return with beers and bottles of vodka. "Start drinking. Fast."

"Conclude," Osmo says.

"As I'm an officer close to him, even known to socialize with him, Jyri called me and begged me to extricate him from a jam. He was very drunk. You two—given your voracious sexual appetites and lack of choosiness when it comes to your sexual partners, tag-teaming a man won't really surprise anyone—but you had some kind of quarrel. You don't even remember what about, but Mikoyan ended up dead. I came here after Jyri's call, saw the corpse and informed you both that I can't protect you from this. Jyri, in a last-ditch attempt to preserve his freedom, drew down on me and I had no choice but to kill him. Osmo, I haven't decided what to do with you yet. Shooting you as well would be the most expedient. You're not drinking. Chug-a-lug. Mikoyan's DNA, by the way, will be found in your mouths and on your genitals."

They both take deep drinks from the vodka bottles. I think they're glad to have it. "What do you want to put a stop to this?" Jyri asks.

"I already explained the consequences of fucking with me to you. Repeat to me what I told you."

He slurps Stolichnaya, knows his life hangs in the balance of the next few seconds. "We've covered that ground."

I put my Colt to his forehead. "Indulge me, for the sake of clarity."

He doesn't want to say it. I nudge his forehead with the barrel.

"You said you would kill me."

I move the gun fast, shift the muzzle to the right, fire, and shave off the bottom of his left earlobe. Not much, maybe an eighth of an inch. But he doesn't know that. He just feels hot blood drizzling down his neck and thinks his ear is gone. He reaches up, finds it still there and sheds tears of relief.

"By all rights," I say, "I should go ahead and kill you, but I feel generous and forgiving."

He bursts into self-righteous anger. "You wanted to be someone important, to be above the law to further your own agenda. I gave you that and you stole from me."

"How could I steal something from you that didn't belong to you?"

"I didn't send people to harass and threaten you. It's not true."

"But you know who did, don't you? Minders watched my house. Interrogating them proved that they were cutouts run by SUPO Captain Jan Pitkänen, which, Osmo, brings us back to you. He's your axman, isn't he? Keep drinking. If your answer isn't satisfactory, you two begin making your ways around the apartment, leaving touch prints, grab prints, footprints. It will appear that you've been here for hours."

"Here's the truth," Osmo says. "You played a dangerous game and we took you into our confidence. You didn't like the game, you cheated and didn't want to play anymore. But you can't walk away from it. You turned out to be a weak sister and disappointed us, stealing that ten million. You were already well-compensated. We took good care of you, and you betrayed us. The Powers That Be are most disappointed in you. Now everybody wants you and your buddies dead."

He drinks, wipes his mouth on his sleeve. "The truth be told, we never needed you. We didn't care if that left-wing bitch got her head cut off. We needed Milo Nieminen. He's a bloodhound and we knew he'd find the money. It was always about the money. He's shit crazy and needs a handler. That was your purpose. We always thought the kidnapping a sham that would lead back to that racist pig Saukko, via the Söderlund murder, then on to his son, Antti, and the money trail.

"And yes, I put Pitkänen on a detail to watch you with an eye toward recovering the money. He's my liaison to Veikko Saukko, and via Saukko, to the Real Finn hierarchy and every hate group in the country. He has no strict instructions from me. I empowered him to use his own judgment in coordinating the campaign against you. Did Jyri know this? Yes. Did he fuck with you personally? No. And if you frame or kill Jyri and me, it won't help you one jot. You've made too many enemies."

"Pitkänen is your liaison to Saukko regarding what?"

"We were supposed to return his son and money. Instead, he got his son's unrecognizable corpse and no money. Yet he contributed generously to the parliamentary campaign anyway and booted up the million euros he promised. Pitkänen liaises by catering to Saukko's every whim. I don't ask the particulars."

So a captain in the secret police is now an errand boy for an ultra-rich maniac. I look at Sweetness. "What do you think?"

"I don't know. It's probably safer to kill them, but on the other hand, they're important men, the investigation would drag on for months, and who knows how it will turn out in the end. Like the man said, we've made enemies. We might get sold out somewhere down the line, end up in prison ourselves."

"True. And in practical terms, we can always kill them later, but we can't un-kill them if we do it now." I turn to them. "Keep the wolves at bay and I let you live. For now."

Osmo swigs vodka and chases it with beer. Now he feels confident that he'll live through this, and he's deadening his nerves. "Here's what happened," he says. "Pitkänen had a run of shit luck. First your boy trashed his face, then his eighteen-year-old girlfriend got pregnant. She went to his wife, who left him and took their two boys with her. His girlfriend ditched him, too. Since it all started with his face getting fucked, you and your crew symbolize all the bad shit that happened in a short time. He's gone a little bonkers and I sent him to placate Saukko, but mostly to get him away from me and give him something to do while he pulls himself back together. I can pull his reins, get him out of your hair."

I push the silenced muzzle up against Osmo's temple. "If you don't manage to keep your word, the consequences will be dire."

Osmo and Jyri both agree to a truce with me. Since said truce is made under extreme duress, I have no faith in their promises, but the fear factor involved might tame them. I tell them to stand still and suck vodka. A Colt in one hand and a cane in the other leaves me no free hands. Sweetness lifts prints from the most obvious places. Sweetness isn't a cop, but I've taught him this skill. If Osmo and Jyri try something stupid, I'm going to shoot them, and I want to do it myself, not push more killings on Sweetness.

Our backs are to the front door and I don't realize anyone has entered until I hear it squeak when they close it behind them. Three men have guns trained on us. Small-bore handguns. Sweetness and I are about five feet apart. They all three look like nobody, or anybody. Spies, trained to blend in anywhere. I raise my pistol and point it at the head of one spook. In turn, he presses the muzzle of his pistol into my chest. Sweetness's guns are holstered. A spook puts a pistol to his head. The third lowers his weapon and says, in English, "We came for the body and the girl, not to kill you. We'll take what we came for and leave." He looks at me. "Put down your weapon and tell me where the girl is."

His promise doesn't inspire my confidence. I lower my arm but don't relinquish my weapon or answer his question. I look at Sweetness. He's been involved in a lot of violence, but never in an honest- to-God gunfight. I have. I see the look on his face and read his mind. He's going to make a play as soon as he thinks he has a chance of winning. He'll lose.

The speaker of the three seems satisfied that the situation is under control and does a walk-through. He comes out with Loviise slung over his shoulder. She doesn't resist, just looks at me through tears that say I betrayed her. He carries her out of the apartment. Fuck, I can't have found her just to lose her again. What the hell is their motivation? Her future was to be a low-rent hooker. They have no money invested in her.

No way would they go to such extreme lengths out of pride and some ridiculous adherence to gangster code, not when the consequence could involve killing cops. Diplomatic passports or not, it would bring the shit storm of all shit storms down on their heads, and they know it.

I move my arm a fraction and shoot my assailant in the foot. He fires as he goes down and shoots me in the chest. God bless Kevlar. He goes to one knee, I shoot him in the top of his head. It bursts like an egg. Blood, skull fragments and brains splat on the floor behind him.

Sweetness uses the distraction to move his head away from the muzzle pointed at it. He starts to draw. It all goes slow motion for me. I know he'll be dead in under a second. I shoot the other spook in the temple. His brains shower the couch, corpse and wall behind it.

"Go!" I yell. "Get the goddamned girl back."

Sweetness sprints out of the apartment.

Jyri's eyes show wild panic. "We've got to get the fuck out of here."

"Empty the spooks' pockets for me," I say.

He rifles through them fast, tries to give me wallets, keys, phones and passports. I make him dump it all in my fishing tackle box and carry it for me.

"Let's go," I say. "Together. I move slow. Take the elevator with me. Run, and I'll shoot you, too."

We exit the building and find Sweetness alone. "I'm sorry," he says. "He was too fast. A driver was waiting with the car running. I watched it pull away."

The bullet to my chest didn't even hurt much. He'd used a little 9mm pistol. I've learned a few things from Milo's technical lectures and diatribes. The shot wasn't even as loud as a firecracker. He shot me with a subsonic bullet. It didn't break the sound barrier. The bullet packs enough punch to enter a skull but not enough to exit it, just bounces around inside the head ripping up brains. No muss, no fuss. An executioner's rig.

Osmo still has a vodka bottle in his hand. Sweetness grabs it from him and takes a long drink. I tell them they'll be hearing from me and they can walk home. My attempts at pacifism are a failure. Living in solitude in an effort to develop a Gandhi-like inner peace just didn't work out for me.

"What about the corpses upstairs?" Sweetness asks.

"The spooks were already going to dispose of one body," I answer. "I doubt if dealing with two more is much of an additional inconvenience for them."

18

After so much effort, peril and death, the night is an utter failure. Loviise was in dire straits and terrible danger before I set out to save her. Now powerful people who hate me and know that I want to give her life back to her, own her again. Surely, whatever ravages they intended to heap upon her before my interference will be increased tenfold as a way of getting back at me. I'm angry, dispirited and awash in the self-pity of failure.

We arrive at Filippov Construction at a quarter after seven a.m. I'm so tired I can barely hold my head up. We destroyed the locks the first time we broke into this place, months ago. I had new ones installed and have my own key. The bodyguard in the back of the Wrangler has yet to make a sound. Saukko has the best of everything. I'm certain his personal security is no exception, and the man we took prisoner is viper dangerous. Sweetness pulls away the tarp he lies under and blindfolds him. I keep my gun ready. Sweetness cuts the zip-lock shackles from around his ankles so he can walk inside. We have to wait. His legs have gone numb in the cramped position and he can't manage it for a few minutes.

We take him inside a garage where tools are stored and maintenance on vehicles pulled. Sweetness sets a chair in the middle of the room, then zip-lock-shackles him to it. The chair is wooden. His strength is obvious. His forearms are as thick as sturdy oak tree limbs. He could burst the chair to splinters if he wished. I whisper to Sweetness, ask him to add shackles up and down his arms and legs so he can't get leverage for a powerful muscle contraction. We keep silent, work by way of motioning to each other, to build fright. Scary things happen in the dark, in the silence.

I fill the two syringes with Stolichnaya and set out some props. A vehicle battery and cables. A chain saw. Bolt cutters. A burlap bag. Sweetness dumps a bucket of water over his head, refills it and sets it on the floor. The garage has a hydraulic lift for vehicle repairs. We chain his chair to it and lift him off the floor. I would cut his clothes off him— people are so much more vulnerable naked—but I intend to return him later, have nothing against him and don't want to humiliate him by dumping him naked on the street. My knee throbs like hell. I drag a comfortable chair with wheels out of the office and sit down. Sweetness takes off his blindfold.

He looks around, takes everything in. He remembers me from the times I visited Saukko at his home. "Inspector Vaara," he says, "that's an interesting collection of toys you've assembled for my interrogation. Your crime-fighting techniques are unusual."

I lean forward with my hands one atop the other on the handle of my cane. "You're the second person tonight to comment on that. What's your name?"

"Phillip Moore."

"I have no desire to hurt you. I want information. To what lengths I go to get it is up to you. But I'll warn you, I'm in a really fucking bad mood and my temper is short."

"I see two needles there," he says. "What's in them?"

"One is sodium pentothal. The other is LSD."

"So, by the looks of it, you'll start by running me up with jungle juice and begin torturing me with waterboarding . . ."

I cut him off. "Get with the times. It's now called enhanced interrogation."

He ignores me. "And if that doesn't work, you'll use the LSD to drive me out of my mind, then start with electric shocks—tongue and probably genitals—and then finally, if all else fails, start removing parts of my body."

I have no stomach for anything like that. I doubt even Sweetness has that in him. "Something along those lines."

"May I tell you a little bit about myself?" he asks.

Sweetness stands behind and to the left of him, just behind his peripheral vision, to keep him nervous. "Please do," I say.

If he's frightened, he doesn't betray it. His voice is steady, his demeanor businesslike, almost friendly. "I'm retired from the SAS, elite British forces. I know a bit about interrogation, even took a course in how to bear up under it. I could take whatever you have to dish out for a while, but everybody talks in the end. The purpose of enduring torture, usually, is to protect secrets and/or to give your team time to escape. I have no secrets to keep from you and no comrades to protect. As such, you have no need to hurt me, unless you derive pleasure from it. I'll tell you anything you would like to know. Since it saves you time, and my life, it's a bargain that benefits all of us. What do you think?"

I see no reason for him to dissemble. His job is to protect Veikko Saukko, and Saukko is safe. It makes sense. "It does indeed sound like the most expedient route for me," I say, "and the benefits for you are obvious. But if I catch even a whiff of a lie, I'll make you sorry."

"Agreed," he says. "All these zip-locks are chafing, cutting into my skin and cutting off my circulation. Could you let me down and take them off?"

It's stupid to un-cuff such a dangerous man, but I've always been foolish that way. I nod to Sweetness. We take out our Colts. Sweetness lowers the hydraulic lift to the floor and cuts Moore's bonds loose with his Spyderco. Moore thanks us.

"Stay seated and keep your distance," I say.

He rubs his wrists, tries to get his blood flowing. "What do you want to know?" he asks.

I ask a few basic questions to get a feel if he's lying to me or not. "You're Saukko's head bodyguard, correct?"

He switches languages, to Finnish. "Correct."

"What does that entail?"

"I also serve as his personal assistant, in a sense. I keep track of all his appointments, so I know who's coming and going. I run background checks on people I'm unfamiliar with before letting them see Veikko. He has six bodyguards total. I make out the duty rosters, make sure the security cameras are working and monitored, make sure the others are doing their jobs to my satisfaction. In short, I do everything possible to keep a man with as many enemies as Veikko has alive."

I light a cigarette and offer him one. He declines. "He's a grade-A prick," I say. "Why would you want to?"

He chuckles. "That he is. But as I'm entrusted with his life, he doesn't treat me like he does the rest of the world. He pays me a king's ransom, and he treats me with courtesy and respect."

"That's hard to imagine."

"Veikko is motivated by a morbid fear of death. He's a strange man. Afraid to die, but stays drunk from the time he wakes up until he goes to bed—which is saying a lot, since he sleeps very little—and smokes at least three packs a day. He's been doing both for fifty years. He must have the constitution of a rat."

His language skill makes me question the truth of his background. "Your Finnish is excellent. How did you learn it?"

"If I can't speak the language of the country my client lives in, I can't do my job to the best of my ability. Therefore, I learned the language."

Phillip Moore is a formidable man on many levels. "I brought you here because I want to know about his Shit List. Apparently, I and my family are on it, and after tonight," I motion toward Sweetness, "I believe my colleague is, too."

Now he laughs. "Then you, my friend, are in some serious fucking trouble."

"Forgive me if I don't share your sense of humor. Explain."

"Since Veikko has such a terrible fear of death, he assumes everyone else does, too. So some years ago, he started a list of people he wanted dead or otherwise destroyed. He enjoys telling his would-be victims their fates to come. He's had people killed a week after issuing his edict. Some people have been on the list for better than a decade, which he considers worse, since it gives them all that time to contemplate their demises, and just when so much time has passed that they've decided the threat must have been empty, bang! He lowers the boom. As you can imagine, many people try to murder him first. It adds a bit of challenge to my job."

"Who does the killing? You?"

He takes umbrage. "Inspector, I'm a professional soldier and protector of lives, not a murderer."

"Then who does? Just tell me how his fucking Shit List works."

He stretches some kinks out and folds his arms. "Two of the bodyguards that work for him are from the Corsican Mafia. A father and son. The family has been in the assassination business for decades or maybe even centuries, and the son is learning the trade from the father. They have a very formal system. Veikko discusses the punishments he's devised with them. They agree on a price. That money is placed in a safe-deposit box in Nordea Bank, in the branch downtown on Aleksanterinkatu. The father and son have a key. Veikko has a key. He goes with one of them to put money in when a contract is agreed upon, and when a hit is carried out, the money for payment withdrawn. In the event of Veikko's death, they are to complete the list and empty the box. This, of course, is on an honor system, which is why Veikko chose them for the task. He trusts them."

A well-thought-out system designed by an evil fuck. He must have lain awake many nights dreaming it up. I suspect he enjoys pulling the wings off of flies. "How much money do you think is in that box right now?"

"In fact, I heard them discussing the addition of you and yours to The Shit List. Since you're a cop, the price was in six figures. And most of the hits are against high-profile people in other countries, and so expensive to set up. There are at present nine names and nine hundred seventy-five thousand euros in the box."

That's a great deal of money. It makes me wonder about the monetary value of human life. "How much does a murder usually cost?"

"Interestingly enough, most hits are against intimates, jilted lovers and such. A normal hit, the run-of-the-mill murder for hire, killing someone of little or no importance located in the same vicinity as the hit man and so incurring no expenses, runs an average of about twelve thousand U.S. dollars. That's pretty much standard here in the Western countries."

Damn, life really is cheap. "How would you suggest I deal with this problem?"

He shrugs. "Fucked if I know."

I ask Sweetness to bring a pen and paper from the office, tell Phillip to write down the names of the Corsicans and their passport numbers, and his own as well.

"You think I memorized their passport numbers?"

"I'm certain of it."

He laughs aloud. "You're right." He writes them down.

"Would you be interested, Phillip, in helping me fix this? You said you're in the business of saving lives. My infant daughter is on that list. I can't even bring myself to talk about his plans for her."

"You needn't. I already know them. The obvious way is to empty the safe-deposit box at Nordea. The Corsicans won't carry out the murders for free. But Veikko is a billionaire many, many times over. The money in that box is pocket change to him, and even if you could figure out a way to get through the bank's security, Veikko could just put the money back. So he would have to be dead, and thus unable to replenish the fund. That would mean dealing with me, as I keep him alive, and I hope you'll excuse me for saying so, but I don't think you two are up to the task."

I point out the obvious, sarcastic. "A bold statement for somebody who let two shit-for-brains pimps zap him with a Taser."

He smiles and shakes his head at the irony. "True enough. They've been to games before and had cash to play, and I made the mistake of letting them get within arm's reach of me." He chuckles. "Plus, I never would have thought those idiots would have balls that big."

"The choice of being executed with bullets in the backs of their heads or taking their chances with you made their balls grow."

He smirks. "You, a Finnish policeman, intended to execute them? I find that a little hard to believe. When was the last time you killed a man?"

"Since we abducted you earlier, I've shot and killed two."

He senses the truth of it and pauses. "You're thinking, then, that you should kill me now. I'm replaceable and it wouldn't change anything. Veikko would hire another elite soldier with my skill sets to protect him before my corpse is even cold."

I can't think of anything else to say.

"You're not giving my iPad back, I suppose."

I shake my head. "No."

"No matter, I'll get another today."

"What would you want for helping me, if we were to come to an arrangement?" I ask.

He smiles. "Retirement. The contents of that safe-deposit box, of course. However, given the circumstances of my employment, we can't come to an arrangement."

A sudden weariness comes over me. I'm too tired for more of this. I look at Sweetness. "Do you have anything to say about all this?"

He bends over in front of Phillip Moore so their faces are inches apart. "You got one thing wrong. If anything happens to someone I care about—I mean anything—I'll kill you. I'm up to the task."

Moore says nothing, probably because he senses any response at all might result in a bullet in his head, then and there.

"If you play hardball with us," I say, "you'll discover we have skill sets of our own. Skills that you don't possess. I'm not a police inspector for nothing and," I nod toward Sweetness, "I believe his are self-evident."

We cuff his hands behind his back and drive to downtown Helsinki in silence. It gives me time to think. "What are you going to tell Veikko Saukko?" I ask him.

"The absolute truth. I find it really is the best policy, as I never have to lie my way out of it later."

"I've come to a decision," I say. "You work for me now."

He smiles, indulgent. "And how do you figure that?"

"I'm starting a Shit List of my own. Your position allows you access to prior knowledge of actions against me. Knowledge is tantamount to culpability. Should something happen to any of us, I'll consider it a blood debt and I'll collect. I suggest that you ensure the safety of me and mine. And I'm searching for an Estonian girl named Loviise. She was kidnapped for the purpose of forcing her into prostitution. If you gain knowledge of her whereabouts, I expect you to call me." I toss a business card into his lap. "I'll also consider failure to do so as grounds for punishing you. Are we clear on everything?"

"You got a pair on you. I'll give you that."

I cite the SAS motto. "Who dares, wins."

He looks thoughtful, says nothing. I've made another dangerous enemy.

Sweetness cuts him loose, he gets out of the Jeep and ambles away in damp clothing. I hear him whistling a tune, as if none of this had ever happened. Sweetness squirts the vodka from the syringes into his mouth.

19

We drive around the corner. It's a little after ten a.m. Thank God I slept all day yesterday, or I never would have made it through the night. There are no parking spaces, so we use a parking garage and walk a couple blocks. Walking is the last thing I want to do right now. It hurts like hell and I want to go to bed. But our missions aren't yet complete. It's Mirjami's birthday. We go to Fazer, the city's best bakery, and too tired to shop, I just ask the girl behind the counter to give me the biggest, richest chocolate cake they have and to write *Hyvää Syntymäpäivää Mirjami*—Happy Birthday Mirjami—on it in frosting.

We sit and have coffee while she writes it and boxes it up. Sweetness adds a little something to the coffee from his flask. "Jesus, what a night, huh?"

"Yeah," I answer.

I pay. We go to the Alko in Stockmann department store, I buy a bottle of Veuve Clicquot champagne and a gift bag and we head back to the car. Before starting the engine, Sweetness takes a healthy gulp out of a Stolichnaya bottle. I've never said anything in the past because I thought he would stop this on his own, and because since we've been associated, I've been too physically fucked up to drive and, good-natured as he is, he's always offered to take me wherever I've needed to go. More or less been my man Friday. But drunk driving rankles me.

"Has it occurred to you," I ask, "that every time you drink and drive, you're putting innocent lives at risk? You just threatened to kill a man if anything happened to your loved ones. You could kill someone else's loved ones."

He turns to face me, grim. "Am I good driver?"

"Yes."

"You ever seen me sloppy drunk behind the wheel?"

"No."

"You wanna get out and walk?"

He's never taken this tone with me before. "No."

"*Sitten turpa kiinni*"—Then shut your face.

It's my fault. He's exhausted, frightened and frustrated. I picked exactly the wrong time to bring it up. I shut my face, or more literally, my muzzle.

I stop the exchange by calling Mirjami. "Happy birthday," I say.

"Thanks. It's heartening to know I'll never be as old as you."

I giggle. Old cheap jokes always get laughs out of me. "We're on our way to pick you up."

"Did your night work out? Did you find the girl?"

"We found her and lost her. It's a long story and it's been a long night. We haven't slept."

"We'll be in the lobby. Jenna is sick."

"Hungover?"

"No, just sick. She vomited last night and this morning. And I've got Anu, so we didn't even touch the minibar."

We arrive at Hotel Cumulus and escort them to the vehicle. Jenna, even with her normal Snow Queen coloring, looks pale.

We get a parking spot near my apartment building. I get out of the Jeep first, scan the windows and rooftops for watchers but see no one. We tramp inside. I can't remember being this exhausted since before I had brain surgery, when my constant migraine gave me insomnia. Still, there's more to do before I can sleep. I have to download the information from the daunting pile of electronica I've stolen into my computer. The owners will call the service providers, report them as stolen and have them locked. Some already will have. I need to salvage all the info I can before the others get around to it.

I boot up my laptop, stick a USB cable in it and begin.

Mirjami asks what I'm doing and I explain. She calls me a stupid jerk, says she'll do it and tells me to go to bed. I protest, jabber about Blu-ray transfer and the right cables for different devices. She tells me to be quiet, she knows all that.

I double up on everything: tranquilizers, pain medication and muscle relaxants, and wash it all down with a double *kossu*. Mirjami checks my knee and rebandages it. I say, "Wake me up in late afternoon so we can celebrate your birthday."

I force myself onto my feet to make my way to the bedroom. Mirjami kisses my cheek. "Sleep well."

But I don't. Not right away. When it comes, though, I sleep the sleep of the dead.

20

I wake up on my own around five. Jenna is watching Anu. Sweetness and Mirjami sit at the dining room table, have open beers, shot glasses, and a bottle of kossu on it. They've already made a good dent in it. As usual, Sweetness doesn't show it, but Mirjami is a bit giggly and bleary-eyed.

"Give me a birthday hug, then sit down and have a drink," she says.

I'm still a little groggy from my sleeping potion. "I smell like a goat and need a shower," I say. "Give me a few minutes."

I shower and shave, put on new clothes, jeans and a shirt, to look party presentable. Kate bought these clothes for me.

I hide it for Mirjami's sake, but I don't care about her birthday. If all goes well, Milo will bring Kate home day after tomorrow. Worry that all won't go well preoccupies me.

I discover they've finished one kossu bottle, taken another from the freezer and opened it. It's still early. My prognosticative powers tell me this night will end badly. Also, Jenna refusing alcohol is oddly disturbing. Possibly, she's being sweet and staying sober to watch Anu so Mirjami can drink, but I could remain sober and do it. I've never seen Jenna turn down a drink. Forgoing booze on my account is out of character for her. I hug Mirjami and sit beside her. Sweetness pours a shot and pushes it across the table toward me.

I raise my glass. "To you, Mirjami. I hope your twenty-fourth year brings you all you wish for. You've been a godsend to me. I don't know what I would have done without you." This is true.

We drink our shots in one go. I get a beer from the fridge and put on the soundtrack from *Pulp Fiction*. It's one of Mirjami's favorites. We drink, and drink some more. I'm starving and they need some food in them to sop up some of the alcohol in their systems. The head start they got on me has left them coherent but whacked.

"Let's eat," I say.

"I want to go to a nice restaurant," Mirjami says.

Not a good idea. She's already too drunk. I'm not sure a restaurant would even want to let her in. I might have to throw my cop weight around to make it happen. I don't feel like muscling anybody.

"What do you want to eat?" I ask her.

"Sushi." She nods her head with vigorous certainty. "A mountain of sushi."

Sweetness and Jenna both make faces, but it's not their birthdays. Sushi sounds great to me.

"Why don't we eat out in?" I ask.

Mirjami slurs a little. "Whaddaya mean?"

"I'll call Gastronautti."

She pours us all more kossu. "That place where you call and they've got about a dozen different restaurants and you order and they pick it up from the restaurant and bring it to your house?"

"That's the place. And they have three different sushi restaurants to choose from on their list."

She smiles a drunken smile that's both sad and wistful. She forgets the sushi for a minute. "I had the windows in your Saab replaced with bulletproof glass," she says.

Mystifying. "How could you get it done so fast?"

She toys with her glass. "I used my feminine charms."

And her charms are many: She's entrancing, excruciatingly beautiful, intelligent, responsible, has a good sense of humor, is a born nurturer with a great capacity for empathy, and pleasant company as well. She has *vittuväki*, the power of the vagina. I don't know the etymology of the term, perhaps it's lost in the sands of time, but it stems from the era of pagan ritual and the celebration of the feminine, when it was believed the vagina possessed mystical potency. If anyone possesses *vittuväki*, it's Mirjami. Only one downfall prevents me from falling in love with her. I'm already in love with my wife.

Kate is my wife and the mother of my child, and I love her to the exclusion of all others. I lost the ability to feel emotion as a result of having the tumor removed from my brain, but it's drifting back, slow but sure. For some weeks, my primary emotion was irritation. That's fading, too. For Mirjami, although my sexual attraction toward her is magnetic—there are few heterosexual men who wouldn't feel it—my primary emotion is tenderness.

"Thank you," I say. "Let me repay you in sushi."

"Isn't Gastronautti extravagantly expensive?"

I smile. "It ain't cheap."

"What's it like to be rich?" she asks.

I consider it. "Mostly, it relieves some of the pressures of life that plague most people."

"How much did you, Sweetness and Milo steal from drug dealers?"

The questions of a drunk girl, childish in their innocence. My smile broadens and I sip *kossu*. "Oodles."

"This seems like a good time to give Mirjami her present and crack the champagne," Sweetness says.

I had forgotten about the champagne. It's the last thing she needs. But what the fuck, it's her birthday. I hid the liquor store gift bag stuffed with cash in a closet. I get it and set it in front of her, then play the good host and set out champagne glasses.

"Ugh," Jenna says, so out of character that I wonder if she's pregnant and has morning sickness. "None for me."

Strange indeed. I say nothing and pour for the rest of us. We toast Mirjami's birthday again and I tell her to open her gift.

She fumbles with the drawstring, gets it open and stares into the bag. She looks confused, shakes her head as if to clear it. She turns the bag upside down and shakes wads of cash onto the table.

"How?" Struck speechless, she can't say more.

I don't know if she wants to ask how much it is or how we got it. "Half a million, give or take. Proceeds from the evening. It was Sweetness's doing. He should get the thanks."

Drunk, she doesn't hear the part about Sweetness, just throws her arms around me and starts at once laughing and crying. She's got that annoying girl-drunk-weepy thing going on now. She gulps champagne and pushes the cash toward me. "It's too much. I can't."

I laugh and push it back. "You can and you will."

She doesn't argue, just stares at the money with a disbelieving grin on her face.

From a wooden box on the bookcase where I keep miscellaneous odds and ends, I take an unopened pack of playing cards and hand it to Sweetness. "Show me the trick you cheated with."

He says, "I'm pretty drunk, don't know if I can," but opens the pack and discards the jokers. He shuffles, I cut, and he deals. I get a royal straight flush and he gets a pair of deuces.

He puts the cards back in order and does it again, except this time he gets the royal straight flush and I get the deuces. I saw nothing. He's wearing a T-shirt, so has nothing up his sleeves.

"How the fuck do you do it?" I ask.

He zings out the deck in a long string in the air almost too fast for me to see, collapses it back together, hands it to me, and shoots me a sly smile. "Let's just say it's one of those things you learn when you have way too much time on your hands. I could try to teach you. You won't be able to do it, though. You don't have the dexterity."

True. I have the grace of a bear, and a lifetime of weight lifting has left my stubby hands as thick as they are wide. I often break things by accident because I'm too rough with them. My hands have only two settings. Stop and go. It comes to me that, at least in that way, I must be a lousy and clumsy lover.

Impressed, I order a mountain of sushi, and we have champagne, with the ever-present *kossu* on the side, of course, while we wait, and Sweetness and I tell the story of how we found and lost Loviise, *sans* the double killing.

"How do you know she didn't put the knife in his back?" Jenna asks.

"I don't," I say, "and if she did, considering what he had waiting in store for her, I don't care. I tend to believe her, though, and I'm curious about the identity of the magazine-beautiful woman. She's the killer. But given the circumstances surrounding the murder, the Russians won't want Finns investigating the case, they'll invoke diplomatic privilege to shut it down, and it's not my problem. I would give odds on a bet that the apartment is already cleaned out, redecorated and painted, like nothing ever happened there. Out of curiosity, though, I'm going to run the prints we lifted through the computer, just to see if we get a match."

The sushi arrives. Sweetness has never had it before. He gives it a tentative sniff, suspicious. "Is this the equivalent of fucking Chinese girls?" he asks.

I ask what he means.

"It's good, but two hours later you're horny again." He guffaws at the old bad joke. His raucous laughter makes Mirjami and me laugh with him. Jenna scowls, doesn't find jokes about him having sex with other women humorous. Nor will she touch the food. Not feeling well has put a bug up her ass.

Sweetness discovers the pleasures of sushi, and the three of us devour two massive platters of it. The evening has gone well. With so much drink, I expected tears, arguments, the usual drunken party ending. It didn't happen. In the wee hours, we all decide to turn in.

Mirjami follows me to the master bedroom. I'm drunk, but not wasted. She's blasted, weaving as she slips the spaghetti straps from her summer dress over her shoulders. It slides to the floor. Barefoot and braless, she steps out of it, peels off her panties and comes toward me. She puts her hand on my crotch and rubs the hard-on she knew she would find there.

I take her hand away from between my legs and hold it.

"Give me the birthday present I've been waiting for," she says.

Dear God, she's beautiful. When I first met her, I had a hard time not staring at her, and with her naked in front of me, all I can do is let my eyes roam up and down her lissome body. "I can't," I say.

She starts to unbutton my jeans. "Then let me give you the present I know you want from me."

I take both her wrists in one hand. "We talked about this once. I can't cheat on Kate."

The booze and disappointment make her temper flare. Anger flashes in her eyes. "Kate who? I don't see any Kate."

"My wife, Kate. The mother of my child."

Her voice rises to a near shout. "Every goddamned man in Helsinki wants to fuck me, and I don't want any of them except one. You, you fucking bastard. And that one man turns me down. You're an ungrateful asshole."

Drunken braggadocio perhaps, but not far from the truth. "Maybe, but I'm a faithful one. I'm faithful to you too, in a way. I would do anything you asked of me, except this. And if I did do it, would you feel the same way about me afterward? If I dumped Kate for you, how could you ever trust me to not treat you the same way? I'm sorry, but I have a wife."

She slaps the bed, I suppose in lieu of slapping me. "Your wife. Your wife. Where is this fucking wife? Wives take care of their husbands and children. Who takes care of you? Who cares for your child? Who is the woman that has devoted herself to you? I am. I am." She screams the last. "I am!"

She lowers her voice again. "If anybody is your wife, I am. Some stupid vows don't mean shit. Actions have meaning. I show you every day that I love you. In practice, I am your wife. I am your wife." Again, she shouts and smacks the bed. "I am your wife!"

She bursts into tears and sits on the edge of the bed with her head in her hands.

I sit next to her and take her in my arms. "I'm sorry," I say.

She buries her face in my shoulder and sobs. She smells of citrus and flowers. It takes a while for her to cry herself out. Then she looks up at me with heartbroken brown eyes. "Can I at least sleep beside you?" she asks.

I nod. "Yeah." I stand up and take off my jeans. She moves to the head of the bed and pulls back the covers. I can't sleep next to her if she's naked. Something will happen. I take a T-shirt from a drawer and hand it to her. "Would you please put this on?"

She gets it and she's too beaten down with disappointment to argue. It serves as a baggy, miniskirt-length nightgown. It doesn't detract from my desire for her. She would be sexy in a potato sack. I usually sleep naked too, but keep my boxers on.

She doesn't try to snuggle up. I keep turning her words over in my mind, picturing her naked in front of me. Is it possible to pass through this life without causing pain? Not even to the ones we care about the most? I fake sleep.

Mirjami interlaces the fingers of her left hand with those of my right. I feel a slight vibration ripple through the mattress. She's masturbating. She sobs when she comes. I keep my eyes shut and pretend it isn't happening.

21

At nine the next morning, a gentle knocking on the bedroom door wakes me. I ignore it, want to lie here, doze, and enjoy a hangover day. Hangovers get a bad rap. The vicious ones are awful, of course, but the milder ones, if I don't have to do anything, can be rather enjoyable. The lethargy that accompanies them forces me to relax. Pizza and Jaffa—orange soda—the combination of sugar and salt, are the best cure. Most people don't realize that the cause of a hangover is in large part not the consumption of alcohol, but the body's outrage at being deprived of it. Alcohol, in a sense, causes instant addiction. Hence the hair-of-the-dog cure.

Mirjami doesn't wake. The knocking turns to pounding. Jenna shouts, "I need to come in."

"Then come in," I shout back. She enters and sees us in bed together. She already knew Mirjami and I were together in here last night from the shouting. Her expression is neither approving nor disapproving. She couldn't care less, ignores me and begins shaking Mirjami awake. "You have to take me to the doctor," Jenna says.

Mirjami looks dog-sick. "Yeah, OK. Give me a minute."

Jenna returns with coffee for her to expedite the process.

"Why don't you have Sweetness take you?" I ask.

"If you took one look at him this morning, you'd know. Besides, Mirjami promised."

"Take a taxi," I say.

She yells at me. "If I wanted a fucking taxi I would have called one, and if I want your advice I'll squeeze your fucking head!"

I've been yelled at quite a bit in the past few hours, I think unjustly. I cover my head with a pillow and mind my own business. But Anu starts to cry. There will be no late-sleep-in hangover. I get up to tend to my daughter. I'm in her room and hear the door slam as I'm rocking her. Sweetness and Jenna sleep in the spare bed in her room. Sweetness doesn't even stir at the sound of Anu's screams. His hangover must be a killer. I told Mirjami she could use Kate's Audi whenever she liked. They must be taking it.

From outside, I hear a *whoom*. It must have been loud for the noise to have penetrated the thick, bulletproof windows.

I lay Anu down in her crib, grab my cane and hobble to the big window that looks out over Harjukatu. The Audi is in flames, sooty black smoke rolls off it. Jenna is on the sidewalk, not moving. Mirjami is in the road, rolling around. She wore cutoff jean shorts and a light top with straps. They're burning and her hair is scorched off.

At the top of my lungs, I yell for Sweetness and grab my cell phone from the table beside my chair, dial 112, emergency, and explain that a car has exploded, at least two people are hurt, and request ambulances and firefighters.

Sweetness comes out of the bedroom with a hand in his underwear, scratching his balls. "What the fuck?" he asks.

I just point. He looks and tears out the door, runs to the scene in his underwear. He'll take immediate care of them as best he's able. I may be at the hospital with them for many hours. I pull on jeans, a shirt and sneakers, put Anu in her carriage and toss everything she might need for the day into it with her, grab Sweetness's clothes from last night off the floor where he tossed them before passing out, throw them and his shoes in the carriage as well and then go down to the street. A fire truck, police cruiser and ambulances arrived in the ten minutes it took me to make my way down. A good response time, thank God, and the fire is out.

Jenna is in an ambulance. I look in. She's conscious. She had on shorts as well. They're soaked with blood and her legs are smeared with it.

The EMTs have placed Mirjami on a gurney. Her burned-away clothes are stuck to her skin in places. The burns lessen in severity where the flames traveled up her body. She's quaking, in shock. The EMTs inject her with something and insert an IV in her arm.

Sweetness and I talk to the cops. I tell them that Mirjami's parents live in Rovaniemi. Sweetness gives them Jenna's parents' names and address. They'll notify the girls' families.

Sweetness pulls on clothes while I arrange Anu in her car seat, and we follow the ambulances to the emergency room.

After identifying ourselves, we're allowed into the theater where they're being treated. A doctor reports. The brunt of the fire, inside the car, must have been under the floor of the driver's side. Jenna has only minor burns. The doctor discovered, though, that Jenna was pregnant, and the shock of the fire or flinging herself from the vehicle—something about the trauma of the incident—caused her to lose the child. Otherwise, she's fine. Tears bead up in the corners of Sweetness's eyes.

He panics about his mother being in danger, calls and explains, asks her to stay in a hotel. She refuses, says she's not going anywhere. He buries his face in his hands.

Mirjami, however, suffered severe burns. Apparently, in panic, she had difficulty opening the car door so she could get out of it. Her legs are burned so badly that they're charred in places. She'll require skin grafts. Possibly on her midsection as well. Her neck and face are singed and look worse than they are. The scarring in those areas will be minimal. She'll be in severe pain when she wakes. Therefore, the doctor wants to keep her unconscious for a couple days, start her on a morphine drip as soon as she awakens. He advises me to go home. There's nothing I can do here. He takes my number and promises to call me so that I can be with her when they bring her out of the coma.

Sweetness, Jenna—in a hospital gown—Anu and I ride home in silence. We've been at the hospital for eleven hours, with nothing but coffee and tasteless sandwiches. During that time, we mostly sat in the hallway without speaking. To talk would have led to the discussion of who might have done this, and neither Sweetness nor I was prepared for that yet. It would have turned to anger that we couldn't vent in an ER.

We drive through Hesburger and go home. The Audi is gone, towed away by the police to investigate the cause of the fire.

The bags of burgers and fries sit on the dining room table. After the events of the day, no one has an appetite. My everything hurts. I do as my brother, the good doctor Jari, instructed and take some meds. Fast-acting opiated painkillers dissolve in water and bring a near-immediate rush of relief. Jari was right. Tossing out the crutches and relying on a cane puts more pressure on the shot-to-pieces joint in my knee, and I'm paying the price. The cortisone and mild dope keep me mobile, though.

Jenna says she feels disgusting and goes to the shower. Sweetness brings us beers, a *kossu* bottle and glasses. We sit on opposite sides of the table, the junk food between us. We shoot down the shots. He refills our glasses.

"This is one time I'd like to get brainless whacked," I say, "but I can't. I have to look after Anu."

Sweetness says, "Jenna has been off booze, maybe she'll do it."

This is about the most selfish, thoughtless, mindless thing he could have said. She's been through hell and back today, and he suggests asking her to take on responsibility, rather than do everything in his power to see to her comfort. I'm glad she didn't hear it and am about to tell him so when she walks in wearing only a towel, her wet blond hair hanging down to her ass.

Jenna is five foot nothing and max a hundred and ten pounds. Approximately half that weight is in her breasts. She snatches the *kossu* bottle from the table and turns it up. I count at least four mouth-full chugs. She slides it back across the table to us. "Bottoms up, boys."

She just had a miscarriage. To my knowledge, she didn't know she was pregnant and Sweetness didn't know he was going to be a father. Given her illness and being disgusted by alcohol, I should have guessed it. I decide I should get out of the way. "I need to sit somewhere more comfortable for a while," I say, take my beer and shot and go to my armchair. I put my feet up on the footrest, have a sip of *kossu,* and tune them out. Anu is in my lap. Katt climbs to the top of the chair and puts his paws on my shoulders. Within a few minutes, I'm almost asleep and miss what sparks the fight.

"*Haista vittu*"—Sniff cunt—Jenna says.

"Suck my dick."

"Suck it yourself, cuz you're never getting sex from me again!"

So much for my nap.

Jenna is pissed off as hell. "You know why I've been sick and why I was going to the doctor today?"

Trepidation begins to replace anger in his voice. "No, why?"

"Because I was gonna get an abortion, you oversized lump of shit."

Now the anger and trepidation are gone, replaced with sorrow. "I was gonna be a father, and you were gonna do that? Why? It would have been my baby, too. I had a right to know."

He's sitting, she's standing over him, so because of their size difference, they're looking almost directly into each other's eyes.

She laughs in his face. "Your rights. Your fucking rights. You lied to me. You promised to stop drinking twenty-four/seven. Your job is beating the shit out of people." She points at me. "You were a nice guy until you met him. Now you're a drunk and a violent criminal with a police card. You fucking lying bastard."

Now it's my fault? His brother's death made him a violent drunk. I just gave him a job.

"And in case you haven't noticed," she says, "I'm sixteen fucking years old and like to have fun. You think I want to spend my young life changing your baby's diapers? And don't lie to me or yourself and tell me you would fucking help."

He screams. "You were going to kill my goddamned baby!"

He rears back, winds up to hit her. If he does, he might kill her. I scream "Stop!" I take my .45 from its customary place under the cushion of my chair and point it at him.

Anu is in my other arm, upset by the commotion and screaming her lungs out, adding to the chaos.

Sweetness pauses and looks at me. His laugh is so sinister that it's hard to believe it came out of him. "What? You gonna shoot me now, *pomo*?"

"You can't hit her," I say. "You'll break her in half. I won't kill you, but I'll take your legs out from under you."

His mouth moves, but nothing comes as he tries to form some half-assed rebuttal. I watch both of them. Jenna bunches her hand into a little white fist—not much I can do about it, as I'm not going to shoot her—and hits Sweetness with a solid roundhouse to the nose. He saw it coming and let her do it. I hear it snap and his nose folds over onto the side of his face. Blood runs out of it, drizzles like a water tap with a bad gasket.

He doesn't react or complain, just pulls a wad of napkins from a Hesburger bag, spreads them out on the table and leans over them, to keep from making a mess.

Jenna grabs the *kossu* bottle and chugs some more. "Fuck both you guys." She takes the bottle and disappears into the bedroom they share with Anu.

I put Anu in her carriage, walk over to Sweetness and put a hand on his shoulder. "Sorry," I say.

"Naw," he says, "you did right."

"Want to go to the hospital, or do you want me to set your nose for you? The hospital might leave you prettier."

"Fuck it. Just set it. Gimme a stiff drink first." Luckily, he buys *kossu* by the case.

I give him a couple of my painkillers and a half water glass of *kossu*. He drinks both down. He sits and bleeds for a few minutes, waiting for the combination to take effect.

"OK," he says.

We go to the bathroom, where the light is good and the blood can fly and be easily cleaned up. I grab his nose with my thumb and forefinger and jerk. I hear and feel the grinding of cartilage, but it doesn't quite make it. He doesn't make any noise, but it brings tears to his eyes. I have another go at it, and I feel it almost snap back into place, but not quite. This time he winces and yelps.

"Goddamn," he says.

"Sorry. I think I can't pull straight enough with my fingers. I could stick pencils up your nostrils and jerk. That might give me the right angle."

"Fuck that. Give me the bottle."

The break looks clean, since his nose is folded over on the side of his face instead of crushed. "The trick," I say, "is to lift your nose off your face, pull it out and over so it sits back where it belongs."

I go get the bottle and he swigs deep. I have a gulp myself. He looks in the mirror, grabs his nose tight with the meat below his thumbs, and jerks it forward. Cartilage and gristle crackle. His nose settles back in the right place. "Fuck," he says, "that feels better. That dope you gave me, at least with *kossu*, helps a lot, too."

"Yeah," I say, "it does. All of a sudden, I'm hungry as hell."

"Me too," he says.

He jams toilet paper up his nostrils to plug up the bleeding, then we go the dining room and scarf double cheeseburgers and fries.

"It's not my business," I say, "so feel free to tell me to fuck off, but don't you and Jenna use birth control?"

He has half a burger stuffed in his mouth. It takes him a minute to answer. "Sure we do. The rhythm method. Usually the rhythm of the Red Hot Chili Peppers. They're Jenna's favorite fucking music."

22

The sound of the door opening wakes me. I hear the trundle of suitcase wheels. Kate is home. I pull on sweatpants and go out to greet her. Her eyes are flat, lifeless. She looks like she's aged ten years in a week. Milo is behind her, as if to cut off her escape. I hug her. She allows it, but doesn't return it.

"I missed you," I say.

She slurs, "Where is Anu?"

"In her crib, sleeping."

"Would you get her for me?"

"Of course."

I knock on the door, wondering what kind of scene I'll find after Jenna's anger and her TKO of Sweetness last night. "Come in," she says.

I find them in bed, her head on Sweetness's chest. It seems all is forgiven.

"Kate is home," I say. "And Jenna, I think you have an impression otherwise, but I didn't have sex with Mirjami. She just wanted to sleep in the same bed with me. Nothing happened."

"Not my business," she says. "Why tell me?"

"Because I don't want some innuendo about me cheating on Kate slipping out unintended. I've never cheated on her."

And then it comes to me. I intended to change the bedding. It will be redolent of Mirjami. Fuck. Fuck fuck fuck.

I bring Anu to Kate. She takes Anu in her arms, squeezes her so hard I'm afraid she might hurt her, and Kate starts to cry. Not just crying, but wailing from grief. The kind of crying one would expect if her baby was dead, not reunited with her.

Milo whispers in my ear. "She didn't sleep for the whole trip, so she's been up for almost two whole days. Plus, she's been drinking the whole time."

Anu starts to cry, too. "She hates me," Kate says.

"Of course she doesn't hate you," I say. "She loves you. She's just upset because you are."

"I abandoned her and she hates me for it. And she should, I deserve her hatred. And I don't deserve her. A woman like me doesn't deserve a baby."

She sits on the footrest of my chair, holds Anu, rocks back and forth, and just cries and cries. I don't know what to do, so I sit on the couch and wait.

Milo whispers, "Got any tranquilizers?"

I nod, get them and hand him a sleeve of Oxamin.

He goes to the kitchen, and I see him crush some of them to powder with the back of a spoon, make a stiff drink with *kossu* and Jaffa, and stir them into it. He takes it to her. "Here, Kate," he says, "this will help."

She wipes away tears and snot. "My kidnapper and bartender," she says, and sucks down half the drink in one go.

Her crying stops as she finishes the drink, and her eyes start to close. "I have to go to bed," she says, hands Anu back to me, and wobbles to the bedroom.

"Jesus fucking Christ," I say.

Milo sits beside me on the couch. "Yeah," he says. "She's confused and she stays drunk. Not much of what she says makes sense."

"Have you had any sleep?" I ask.

"I didn't have much time to sleep in Miami, so I caught a few Z's on the plane, where she couldn't get in any trouble. I'm in OK shape."

"Thank you for this. I owe you."

"You're welcome, and no you don't. You would have done the same."

"A lot has happened," I say, "and none of it good. We need to trade stories. Who goes first?"

I sit in my chair. He lies back and stretches out on the

couch, legs out straight and feet crossed, hands on his stomach and fingers laced. He closes his eyes while he talks. "I guess I can. Like I told you when I got there, John was speedballing and Kate was drunk. I spent time listening to their conversations through the open window. Kate going on about how killers can't be mothers, talking about a man who fell burning from the sky. Crazy shit."

"She has post-traumatic stress disorder," I say.

"That was apparent, and it was also apparent to me that it was only a matter of time before she picked up his bad habits. She was curious, asked him what speedballing was like. He said, 'Like falling down an elevator shaft.' I saw that the idea appealed to her. He's a 'one more day' junkie. 'Another day and I'll go to rehab.' Which, of course, she believed. So I went to a place called Walmart. Ever heard of it?"

"They talk about it on American TV."

"What a freaky place. As big as a shopping mall and they sell everything imaginable. If a nuke went off, you could survive for years in there without ever leaving the building. They have like a hundred different kinds of potato chips. The place is so big that they have electric carts to ride around in. You would think mostly geriatrics use them, but almost all the people riding around in them are just too fat to walk. It's the fattest fucking place I've ever seen."

Milo and his stories of biblical length. I wish, just this once, he would cut to the chase.

"So anyway, I bought a hunting knife in there. My disguise was a baseball cap and sunglasses I got at a gas station.

The gas stations are weird, too. Huge. They stock like a hundred different kinds of energy drink. Why the fuck would you need a hundred different kinds of energy drink?"

I'm resisting the urge to yell at him.

"John's daily routine consists of going out early, buying eight balls of heroin and cocaine, flogging most of it, and using the rest to support his habit. I followed his dealer, B&Eed his house, and stole an ounce of each. The next morning, I met John on his way out to buy dope. I told him Kate was leaving with me. He got all indignant and threatening until I put the knife to his throat and showed him the dope. I told him I would trade him the dope for Kate. The price: he could never, ever, have contact with her again. And I lectured him, told him he could either put the shit up his nose, or sell it and pay for rehab. He snatched the drugs out of my hands and told me to come pick up Kate later in the day. He sold me his sister."

"No surprise there," I say.

"So I showed up in the afternoon, she was half in the bag, and I told her to start packing, that she was going home now. She got haughty and told me to make her. I showed her the knife and said if she didn't, I would kill John on the spot. He played his role, backed me up, told her she belonged with her husband and child and he was kicking her out."

"How did she take it?"

"Badly. But, as you can see, she did it."

"What do you think will happen to him?" I ask.

"He has a laptop on a table facing his couch. It has a

webcam in it. I infected the computer, so we can watch him with his webcam and find out."

I didn't take Milo's voyeuristic obsessions into account. Of course he has to know what happens to John. His life wouldn't feel complete without it. In giving John the drugs, he played a game. Sell them and detox and live. Put them up his nose and die. Speedball freaks have short life spans. Play for blood. Milo spun the roulette wheel and played for John's life.

"I have hard things to tell you," I say.

I start with Mirjami and work through the murder of the Russian diplomat to the poker game and The Shit List to the harassment and discovering Captain Jan Pitkänen was behind it.

He doesn't say a word while I talk. I watch fury course through him, see veins in his neck and forehead pumping harder and harder as his heart races from adrenaline. When I'm finished, he says, "People will die for this."

"Who? We've made so many enemies that we can't kill them all."

"You realize," Milo says, "that they burned up Kate's car. Your wife was the target and my cousin, Mirjami, was just collateral damage."

I'm pretty sure he's right, but think we should make sure before we let our emotions run high and go on some half-cocked revenge spree. In the end, we could wind up behind bars, and prisons aren't the nicest places for anyone to live, but especially not for cops. "We should find out the cause of the fire before doing anything," I say.

"Fine. Let's go look at it."

"I can't. I want to be here when Kate wakes up."

I also want to find Loviise Tamm again and parade her in front of Kate to prove the sanctity of my mission. I hear the trumpets sounding again.

Milo snickers and talks to me like a child. "Kate hasn't slept in two days, she's got more alcohol than blood coursing through her system, and I just doped her with enough tranquilizers to knock down a horse. She's not waking up today. Maybe tomorrow."

I call her therapist. Torsten asks how I got her home. "It doesn't matter," I say, "but now that I have, I need to know how to best take care of her."

He asks me to bring her to his office tomorrow at eleven a.m. And he would like to talk to both of us, not just Kate. I agree.

Sweetness and Jenna are still in bed. I ask Jenna if she minds looking after Anu for a while. She says she will, and asks if I'm pissed off at her. I say no. I ask Sweetness if he can clean up any blood left over from last night, because it might upset Kate to see it. He promises.

I go to the bedroom to get dressed. Kate snores like a chain saw. Milo is right, she's dead to the world. As he said, "Maybe tomorrow."

23

ilo drives his Crown Victoria, the cliché of all police cars, and we go to the National Bureau of Investigation garage. A forensic mechanic is underneath the Audi when we enter. We announce our presence, he slides out from underneath the chassis, and we introduce ourselves.

"I heard people got hurt," he says, "are they going to make it?"

"Two girls got burned," I say, "one very bad, somebody close to us, but she'll make it."

"I'm sorry for her," he says. "I can picture the fire from the state of the vehicle."

Milo and I nod thanks for his sympathy. "What happened?" I ask.

He wipes grease off his hands with a filthy rag. "To be honest, I'm stumped. You guys know cars?"

We both say yes.

The hood is up, some parts under it disassembled. He points at them as he explains. "You got two of the fuel injectors clogged by carbon, like you were using cheap petrol, but the others are clean. So you had two pistons not working and fuel spraying onto the engine. That could start a fire, but it would take a few minutes until the temperature reached combustion level, and the fire broke out almost as soon as she started the car. Plus, it's a new car, has only seven thousand kilometers on it. Not enough mileage for that dense carbon buildup. And why only those two? And how did the fire make it to the gas tank? The fuel line would have had to lose pressure for the fire to travel backward and ignite there. It's not easy to start a gasoline fire. You can throw a cigarette into a bucket of gas and like as not it will just go out. It's the fumes that ignite, and a little oxygen helps. The gas cap is gone. I guess it blew off when the tank exploded. And last, why the fire inside the car? It came up out of the floor like it had fuel there, like the gas line sprayed it up there. The line is burned up. It's hard to tell what happened with it."

"The car has only been driven a few times in the past few weeks," I say, "and for short distances. I filled it last, and I'm sure the tank was almost full. And no way the injectors were clogged. It's just not possible."

The mechanic raises his hands in frustration, apologetic. "I don't know what to tell you. I can't picture the scenario that led to a fire like that."

Milo says, "Picture this. The car was stolen and taken to a garage where it could be worked on. Two good fuel injectors were replaced with clogged ones. The car was driven back, running on four cylinders. Then petrol was siphoned out of it and replaced with a hot fuel mix, like in race cars, to make the remaining pistons work on overdrive and heat up the engine fast. They probably didn't put a lot of fuel in the car, because a full tank might hamper the combustion with lack of oxygen, just enough to get the car started and travel a short distance, in case it took that long for the car to heat up and the fire to start. The gas cap was left off to provide the oxygen and help the tank blow when the fire hit the fumes. Some holes were punched into the gas line, to spray up under the driver's floorboards. Some volatile accelerant, maybe ether in plastic containers, was placed in the engine compartment and under the driver somewhere. The plastic melted, the ether or whatever accelerant ignited, and then the injector nozzles were spraying fire. The squirting fuel line lost pressure and the fire traveled backward. It shot out of the fuel line and spewed flame into the combustible under the driver, which ignited, and back into the gas tank, which then blew."

The mechanic ponders this. "It's possible, but so complicated that it's not probable. Most murder attempts by tampering with vehicles are conducted in a simple way. Cut brake lines, things like that. But I can look for melted plastic, take residue samples from the engine, fuel line and gas tank and have them analyzed. It's as good as any theory I can come up with."

We thank him and get on our way. I want to run the prints I lifted from the murder scene when we found Loviise Tamm, to find out who visited the apartment and intervened in her intended sexual abuse after the ambassador made his call. We go to NBI headquarters. It's the first time I've been there since I was moved from Helsinki homicide to NBI employ, some months ago. As an inspector, I should have an office. Out of curiosity, I ask where it is. I find it. It's barren, except for a chair and desk with a computer on it.

I log in to the computer and check the database to see what's come of the killing of Sasha Mikoyan and the two Russian spooks. I could have just as easily done this from my apartment. My computer is networked in to the database for a home workstation. There's been nothing in the news, and I think crime scene investigators would have been surprised to find a bullet-riddled door and black fingerprint powder everywhere. The killings are unreported, so the Russians must have spirited the corpses away, replaced the door and covered it all up.

The fingerprints from the butcher knife, though, are on record. They belong to Yelena Merkulova, wife of the Russian ambassador. How could this be? Diplomats and their families aren't subject to arrest and booking. I call the arresting officer. He tells me she's a kleptomaniac who likes to shoplift from the downtown boutiques and Stockmann department store. She was arrested and processed because she had no identification and refused to say who she was for several hours. He also states that she's possibly the most beautiful woman alive.

And she almost certainly murdered Sasha Mikoyan. Interesting.

It strikes me that the Russian ambassador and whatever spooks are in on the prostitution ring might think Sweetness and I murdered Mikoyan. We were on our way there. He must have been told to meet us. Why would they think anything else?

Then it comes to me, the answer that explains the appearance of the spooks at the apartment and their re-kidnapping of Loviise Tamm: because the ambassador's wife Yelena called someone at the embassy—as the ambassador at that point had no phone—and explained what she had done. And the troops were called in to protect her and make it all go away.

24

Milo and I go back to my house. It's time to put the puzzle together and reconstruct the events leading up to Sasha Mikoyan's death. His murder is of little interest to me in and of itself, but Loviise Tamm couldn't have been the only girl pressed into the sex trade by him, and he was almost certainly working with a group of his colleagues.

First, I check Sasha's bank account. It has a hundred and three thousand euros in it. I check his purchases. He lived the high life. Monster restaurant bills, clothing stores, and boutiques that suggest he bought gifts for a woman or women.

And he had a room at Hotel Kämp permanently reserved for nine weeks. At four hundred euros a day, he accrued a massive bill, which he paid once a week. However, Kämp made sense as a place to meet a lover, as it's in easy walking distance from the Russian embassy. Most convenient, especially if that lover was Yelena Merkulova, the ambassador's wife.

True to her word, Mirjami loaded the info from all the electronic gadgets into my computer. Sweetness is in the bedroom with Jenna. I guess this is snuggle and make up day. Some of the info is in Cyrillic, so I need his help to read Russian. I knock and ask if he has a few minutes. "Sure," he calls through the closed door. He doesn't sound aggravated, so they must be all snuggled out at the moment.

He comes out in jeans, shirtless. He looks like a lifelong power lifter, but he's far too lazy for that. He's just blessed with good genetics. He's also barefoot. One of his feet is almost as long as both of mine together. His nose looks swollen near to bursting and both his eyes are black and blue.

"Who broke your nose?" Milo asks.

Sweetness puts his hands in his pockets and stares at the floor, shame-faced. "Jenna."

Milo heehaws. "Good girl."

Sweetness won't meet his eyes. Staring at the computer screen gives him a way around it.

On the night of the poker game, the Russian ambassador's last phone call was to a woman named Natasha Polyanova. The last call Sasha received is identified by the number twenty-three. The number is the same as the last call made by Ambassador Sergey Merkulov, so twenty-three equals Natasha.

An Excel spreadsheet from the iPad has a list of numbers, one to seventeen across, and the time and dates by week for the year down the left-hand column. Another spreadsheet is set up the same way, numbered one to one hundred seventy-nine, gives first names, the capitalized letters of surnames— I'm certain of this because the name Loviise T is on the list—and what appear to be passport numbers, and shows "profit" and "debt."

A debt subcategory is labeled "fines." It seems girls who commit infractions are financially punished. The totals are further split out by percentage, which I interpret as thirty percent for the girls and seventy for Sasha and whoever he worked for.

I think it works like this: Girls are made to work as indentured servants, promised freedom when their debt is paid. But infractions result in fines, and I'm sure that coming close to paying off the debt, manufactured in the first place, results in more imaginary infractions and fines, so that the debts are never paid and freedom never given. An insidious and most efficient system.

I do the math in my head. If I've interpreted the information correctly, Sasha and cohorts have seventeen apartments in Helsinki that each bring in about six thousand euros a month. This comes to about one and a quarter million euros annually. A hundred and seventy-nine girls don't fit in seventeen apartments, so there must be more properties outside

Helsinki, someone else's responsibility, and the real total income is multiples of the amount on his spreadsheets.

Even the finances behind the business revolt me. I don't know what I'll do, how I'll punish people when I get to the bottom of all this, but it must be something severe enough to do justice for the misery and horror they've meted out to these women. I can't turn to the government. Diplomats are above the law, and anyone involved and caught would simply be returned to Russia. I hear myself sigh. Try as I might, I'm just not built for pacifism.

I call Natasha Polyanova. Her phone is disconnected. Sasha's phone contacts include a "YM." I hope this is the number of Yelena Merkulova, the ambassador's wife. I call it. A woman answers. *"Da."*

My Russian is weak. This is too important for me to make a mistake and misinterpret something. I introduce myself in English. Hers is excellent. "How can I help you, Inspector?"

"I'm looking into the death of Sasha Mikoyan. I'd like to ask you a few questions, if I may."

"I know no one by that name."

I take a stab at faking my way through it. "Early yesterday morning, you were with your lover, Sasha Mikoyan, in Hotel Kämp, your normal meeting place for trysts. This is documented by hotel security cameras. Natasha Polyanova called him and relayed a message to him that there was business he must attend to immediately. You followed him to an apartment in Punavuori and found him about to engage in a sex act with a disabled child. Understandably, you were shocked and enraged. Words were exchanged, and the nightmare ended with you stabbing him to death."

Her voice doesn't waver. She offers no more reaction than she would to a waiter describing the evening specials. "What is it you wish from me?"

"A chat. Nothing more. I'm unconcerned with Sasha Mikoyan or your . . . incident. He was involved in human trafficking. I would like to discuss it with you."

"Very well. My husband is in St. Petersburg. Meet me here at the embassy at three p.m."

"Unfortunately, some people in the embassy have negative feelings toward me. If I walk in, I might never come out again. Can we choose a more neutral location? I have no power to arrest you, or rather, to have you prosecuted, as you well know."

"Then meet me on the Esplanade, across the street from the coffee shop, near the fountain. The weather is supposed to be beautiful. Perhaps we'll have a walk." She rings off.

"We need to have a talk," Sweetness says.

"Let's see what happened to Kate's brother first," Milo says, "while Kate is asleep."

"Milo," I say, "can't the voyeur in you wait until you get home? I don't even want to know what happened to him."

"Won't take but a few minutes," he says, and commandeers the computer's mouse. I get up and go to my armchair, to give him the computer driver's seat. Milo the voyeur. A guy who B&Es people's homes, not to steal from them, but just to see how they live. If I don't let him look, I won't have his attention while we talk, because all he'll think about is this. Our computers are networked, so he's run John's to his to mine.

"I used a motion sensor to activate his webcam," Milo says, "so the only things recorded are when he sits on his couch, where he likes to sit when he snorts drugs."

I pet Katt and ignore Milo while he plays.

Sweetness watches with him. After a few minutes, I hear them start making noises and swearing under their breaths.

"Ouch."

"Fuuuccckkk."

"Jesus fucking Christ."

"God fucking damn."

"Fuuuuucccckkkkk."

Milo turns to me. "Jesus, that was enough to puke a dog off a gut wagon. Well, that's one problem you won't have to deal with again."

I suppose I have to see. I sent Milo there. Whatever happened is in part my responsibility. I push myself out of my chair and lean on the table to keep the pressure off my knee.

Milo starts at the beginning. John lays two big bags of dope on the table, side by side. He pours some powder from each and cuts it into rails with a razor blade. He rolls up a twenty-dollar bill, snorts them and cuts two more. And then two more. And then two more. He sits straight up, eyes wild, like he's plugged into an electrical outlet. I expect his hair to stand on end.

Milo fast-forwards. John slumps forward. Blood shoots

out of his nose and mouth. He jerks and twitches. The blood keeps gushing. He pulls a pillow up to his mouth and bites it, as if it will stanch his internal bleeding. He topples over, out of sight.

I'm not sure if I should be angry or not. "Did you give him bad dope?" I ask.

"Of course not. I stole it from his dealer. It's the same shit he's been using."

"So," I say, "he did the coke, and then heroin. The coke ran through his system too quickly, and without it to hold him together, he ODed on heroin and his heart pretty much exploded."

"You are correct, sir."

"Erase it," I say, "and forget it ever happened. My marriage would be over if Kate found out."

"He did it to himself," Milo says. "He could have gone to rehab."

"I know," I say, "but I never want to speak of it again."

Milo knew that John, given that amount of drugs, would OD. Milo killed him as surely as if he put a gun to his head. He set up the webcam so he could view his handiwork, but he did it for Kate and for me. Kate can never go to her brother to self-destruct again. I feel only gratitude.

I sit back down with Katt for a few minutes until the mind movie of John dying fades. Suddenly, the pain is excruciating. My knee screams a shrill throb. I've done everything Jari told me not to when he shot it up with cortisone, and I'm paying the price. A half glass of water sits on the table beside me. I drop a couple codeine and Tylenol tabs in it and wait until they stop bubbling, then chase a couple tranquilizers with it.

I take back the chair in front of the computer. I still have all the files from the kidnapping of Veikko Saukko's son and daughter in it. Included in them is information concerning his employees. I look at Phillip Moore's file. At the time of the kidnapping, going on two years ago, he had a boy, now age eleven, and a wife, although they were estranged.

His son attended the International School of Helsinki. His wife taught English in a high school. Pictures of both of them are in the file. I bump the pics over to my cell phone, and find Moore's number in the download from Saukko's iPhone. I send him a message with the photos attached. The message is short. "Burned car. Girl dead. Blood debt."

Moore calls me straightaway. "What is the meaning of your message?" he asks.

"We had that discussion before you got out of our Jeep. Knowledge equals collusion."

"I told you I'm a soldier and a bodyguard, not a murderer, and I disapprove of hurting women and children."

"I'm uninterested in what you approve or disapprove of."

"I had no prior knowledge that your car would be fire-bombed."

"You're a bad liar. Tell me the truth."

"I only know that his girlfriend had a miscarriage, and that the girl who was burned so badly is your subordinate's cousin and your mistress."

I don't bother to clarify the mistress comment. "Lie to me again," I say, "and I'll hang up and proceed to make good on my word."

"So you're ready to take me on. It could prove fatal."

Sweetness sets a *kossu* on the table beside me. "I agree that people will die. Who they are remains an open question."

He hesitates, thinking. "In the interest of saving blood from being spilled, I'll tell you what happened. In return, you give me a chance to get my family out of the country."

I sip the *kossu*. The pain in my knee is calming down. "I'll agree to make that part of the arrangement. Tell me the story, and I'll decide if I feel it fair to place other demands upon you."

"We have to come to an arrangement," he says, "or I have to hunt all of you down to save my family and my own skin."

I say nothing.

"I had nothing to do with firebombing that car, and I didn't know about it until after the fact. It was Veikko's idea, I believe after consulting with some Russians. NBI Captain Jan Pitkänen and the two Corsicans carried it out."

"Even if you didn't learn about it until after it happened," I say, "you failed to inform me. I told you that you work for me now. Kill the Corsicans."

"Are you shitting me?"

"You're lucky I'm not demanding that you kill Veikko Saukko, but especially after the kidnap-murder of his daughter and shooting death of his son, it would spark the biggest manhunt in Finnish history and you would be caught. Kill the Corsicans, and they'll just have their bodies dumped and be forgotten."

"That's a fucking lot to ask," he says. "I'll have to leave the country as well."

"Not my concern. No Corsicans, no Shit List until they can be replaced. It buys me time. Call me when it's done."

"I'll get you for this one day."

"Fine. I'll see you then."

He rings off.

"Damn," Sweetness says. "You're not fucking around, are you?"

I close my eyes and think. It goes against my nature to threaten a man's family, but my own comes first.

Pitkänen. The minister of the interior's axman. I spared Osmo Ahtiainen's life and this is the thanks I get. Maybe he doesn't know his man is waging war on me. I start to call him but think better of it. It would tip him that I have someone inside, and as head of the secret police, he could run phone records checks and know who it is in about two and a half minutes.

Impressed and a little shocked, Milo asks, "Were you really going to go after Moore's family?"

"Of course not," I say, "but my track record left him uncertain about it. I didn't think he would take the risk, and I was right."

"We need to have a meeting," Milo says.

Milo has changed. Before, he had a needy side to him. A need to impress. A need for recognition. A need for approval. All that seems gone now, replaced by self-possession and confidence. Being shot and cut, maimed and disabled, has tempered his steel. Suffering made him grow up.

25

We check the bedrooms. All the girls, including Anu, are asleep. I put the sauna on to ensure our privacy. We sit in silence in the living room and think our private thoughts while it warms. Sweetness, of course, breaks out more alcohol. I unwrap my knee and inspect it. It's more swollen than it should be, but not oozing pus, and considering the abuse I've put it through, I suppose it's OK.

We crack beers, hose ourselves down with the shower, and sit down in the sauna. Milo throws three dippers of water on the stones without asking. I've been to sauna with him before and he has the young-man, sauna-is-a-contest mentality. I was the same in my twenties. Now, in early middle age—and I've noticed most men get like me—I want to work up a good sweat without scalding myself. When it gets so hot that it burns the inside of my nose, I get out, shower in cold water, and cool down before going back in.

"Take it easy on me," I say. "And sauna etiquette dictates that I should sit in the corner and toss the water."

Milo is too thin. If he turned sideways and stuck his tongue out, he would look like a zipper. I once asked him if those were his legs or if he was riding a chicken, and it got under his skin. He's by no means weak, though, just skinny and covered in ropy muscle.

He ignores the rebuke and gets down to the meat of the situation. "Who lives and who dies?"

The Gandhi pacifist life may not be working out for me, because of necessity, but I just don't want to hurt anyone else. "We could begin by looking for a way out of this where nobody dies."

Sweetness turns his beer upside down with his thumb covering the top, to cool down the neck so he can drink out of it without burning himself. "Sorry, *pomo*, not possible. My baby died."

I don't point out that it would have been aborted anyway. I suppose he doesn't want to face it.

"And besides," he says, "we have so many enemies, how can we ever make peace with them all?"

Milo ticks them off. "Veikko Saukko, and if Moore doesn't

kill them, the two Corsicans, the minister of the interior, the national chief of police, the Russian diplomats you're trying to nail for human trafficking. Every fucking one of them is above the law and has people that do their dirty work for them."

I let out a hopeless sigh. "And don't forget Roope Malinen."

He got his seat in parliament, but we hurt the extreme right and fucked up his hate agenda by exposing their drug pushing.

"I have another goal as well," I say. "Those spreadsheets are all about human trafficking. I want those girls helped, especially Loviise Tamm."

Milo and Sweetness nod agreement. "The men that brought her feel they own her now," I say. "She needs protection."

"Her mother called me," Sweetness says. "She made arrangements for them to live in the countryside where they can hide and Loviise will be forgotten." He swills beer. "I know you want Kate to see Loviise to prove something to her. But, *pomo*, I don't want you to be disappointed if it doesn't make everything right between you and your wife. It won't."

I built it up in my mind as if it would, but he's right and I'm aware of it. "I think maybe we should all go stay at my house in Porvoo for a while. The windows are bulletproofed and the river runs in front of it, which is one less angle we can be easily attacked from. Plus, it's bigger. This place is too small for five adults, a baby and a cat to live in."

I inherited the house from Arvid Lahtinen. His wife of fifty years was in agony from bone cancer. He helped her die. I helped him cover it up. We became close friends. He was like a grandfather to me and made me his heir. Then, I suppose, feeling he had nothing left to live for, alone at age ninety, he blew his own brains out.

"I'm living here?" Milo asks.

I throw water on the stones. Steam rises and hisses. "I think we all have to stay together. The easiest way to get us is to cut us out of the herd and take us down one at a time."

"Killing cops is a huge deal," Milo says. "We take care of our own. If you and I or our families were killed, Helsinki Homicide would pursue it to the ends of the earth, never let the case die."

I finally understand what has happened. It comes as a revelation, and with it, I see the inevitable outcome. There are certain men in this world who refuse to succumb to pressure, who will see things to the end of the line no matter the cost. Such men are shunned by society as dangers, and feared by the powerful. Such men are begging to be killed.

Milo, Sweetness and I are three such men. Brothers in arms. Brothers in blood. Each of us bound to the others by the knowledge that only we can count on ourselves not to kill one another. We did our jobs too well, observed no limits, not even legal boundaries, and served justice instead of our masters. This, not theft or crime or deaths, was the infraction for which we must be punished.

I know where Milo's thought train is headed. It's insanity. Still, I need to let him articulate the plan he's cooked up so I can punch holes in it. "You have an idea," I say. "Let's hear it."

"Give me a minute to think. Let's cool off."

We step out of the sauna into the bathroom, take turns running cold water over ourselves, slurp long hits from the *kossu* bottle, and go back into the heat.

"OK," I say, "tell us."

"We massacre them all in one day."

This idea is so typical of Milo that I almost laugh. "Spell out who all is included in 'them.'"

"Veikko Saukko, the national chief of police, the minister of the interior, and Jan Pitkänen."

"I like it," Sweetness says.

Now the laughter bursts out of me. "You just talked about how the murder of a couple cops would spark an investigation that would never end without a prosecution," I say. "You're discussing a mass murder of historic proportion. We would never, ever, get away with it. Not to mention that it's hard to justify murder at all, let alone such a bloodbath."

I toss more water on the stones, fill the room with a satisfying blast of steam.

"Of course we wouldn't," Milo says. "Unless we had a fall guy."

"A fall guy?"

"A lone gunman. With good luck, we could even end up investigating the murders ourselves."

"A patsy, who more than likely would spend most or all of the remaining years of his life in a mental institution. Who would you condemn to that?"

"The man who deserves it: Roope Malinen."

Malinen does deserve it. He got away with, among other crimes, accessory to murder. Because of him, Lisbet Söderlund was murdered and decapitated, her head mailed to a Somali political organization.

Söderlund was a Swedish-speaking Finn, and so white, politician belonging to the Swedish People's Party. She dedicated her life to public service. After the 2007 elections she was chosen to be the new minister of immigration and European affairs. She became a tireless champion of immigrants' rights. She was their foremost advocate in government, and so came to be the object of contempt and hatred of the extreme right and racists. For a time, until it was removed because of its criminality, a Facebook page existed named "I Would Give Two Years of My Life to Kill Lisbet Söderlund." The page attracted some hundreds of members.

Prior to the parliamentary election, the Real Finns, a supposed party of the people, was and is officially headed by Topi Ruutio, a member of the European Parliament. Its unofficial second in command is Roope Malinen. He held no office at the time, but his blog is the most popular in Finland, sometimes generates fifty thousand hits per day. The Real Finns agenda was unclear, except that they were anti-immigration, anti–European Union and wanted Finland to leave it. They denied charges of racism and euphemistically called themselves *"maahanmuuttokriitikot,"* critics of immigrants. Malinen blamed immigrants for the majority of Finland's social ills.

Malinen hated Söderlund. He made that perfectly clear

in his blog. A rumor spread that whoever killed Lisbet Söder-lund would get her job, but it was only that, a rumor, started by Roope Malinen. Although he had no authority to decide such matters, it was taken seriously. Malinen also associated with right-wing activists, including neo-Nazis who sold heroin. They distributed, on the street level, to blacks, in an effort, as Saukko put it, "to sedate the nigger population," and to some extent, Malinen helped orchestrate it.

None of his followers would roll over on Malinen. None of this could be proven. Veikko Saukko's daughter had been assassinated by a sniper a year earlier in the aftermath of a bogus kidnapping. Her brother, Antti, absconded with the ten million euros. His partners in crime killed the girl as payback. Antti tried to kill us. Sweetness shot him into dog food and we kept the ten million, recompense for pain and suffering, because Saukko is such an asshole, and because if we didn't keep it, corrupt politicians would.

We recovered the rifle used to murder Saukko's daughter, used transfer tape to put Malinen's prints on it, and turned Malinen in to the detective handling the case. Malinen hadn't taken part in that murder, but given his other crimes, for which we believed with reasonable certainly he wouldn't be prosecuted, felt a frame-up was justified. We hid the rifle in Malinen's summer cottage and told the detective where to find it. The Powers That Be found Malinen more useful as a nutcase parliamentarian than behind bars, had the rifle wiped clean and suppressed it. It disappeared from the investigation, never made it into evidence, and showed up in no report. And so Malinen got away with conspiring to murder Lisbet Söderlund.

Now my curiosity is piqued. I'm not prepared to condone Milo's plan, but I want to hear it out. "Continue," I say.

"I'm going to create a lone gunman out of Malinen that will make the JFK cover-up look like something concocted by schoolkids."

He takes his characteristic moment for melodrama, flips his beer upside down to cool the neck, flips it upright again and drinks. Working with Milo has significantly improved my ability to exhibit patience. I note that the irritability that nagged at me for weeks has now passed. My brain chemistry and the effects of brain surgery are stabilizing. I say nothing, wait on him.

"I write a two-thousand-five-hundred-page manifesto detailing the reasons behind his heinous crime. It will be simple, as he's written thousands of pages in his blog, much of which can be construed as the hate-mongering of a deranged madman. I combine it with the manifestos of Ted Kaczynski, the Unabomber, Seung-Hui Cho from Virginia Tech, some others. With so much material to work from, and since it's supposed to be the rambling, semi-coherent tract of a psychopath, it won't take too long or be very hard."

"Won't you find it hard to type thousands of pages with only one working hand?" I ask.

"Nope. I'll use dictation software. I'll get it done faster than if I typed it."

"Suppose you make Malinen the lone gunman. What if he has an alibi for the time of the killings?"

Milo's look says I'm stupid. "Duh. His killing rampage has to end in suicide."

"Of course, how silly of me. And we have enough firearms for an army, but we need guns that can be traced back to him."

"We check the database, find someone who has what we need, and B&E them. To do it right, we'll have to make some videos of me posing as Malinen firing the weapons and fly them on YouTube, and also the most humiliating sexual ones starring the minister of the interior and the national chief of police. Their depravity will draw some attention away from the killings themselves. Malinen is about my size. We steal some personal items to make videos of him firing the weapons—I'll wear a balaclava—return the items, and they'll turn up during the investigation, along with the guns, which he'll fingerprint for us before his unfortunate demise. I think I'll even force him to make a voice-over for the video."

"And his 'unfortunate demise' will take place how?"

"In his summer cottage, which is a short trip from my summer cottage by boat. We either lure him there, make him believe he's meeting someone, or take him there by force. It doesn't matter much, just so long as we get him there alone, without his family."

Milo has all the bases covered except one. "How do you plan to get all those people in one place?"

His smile is knowing. "I don't. You stole all of their phones,

BlackBerrys, iPhones and iPads. They contain their calendars. We know where they'll be and when. If they're too spread out for us to shoot them all in one day, we plant bombs."

"Bombs. So you're not concerned about collateral damage?"

"If I wire them up so that a cell phone completes the circuit—Iraq jihad style—we can do it in line of sight and ensure no innocents are injured. There are three of us, after all. We choose which of us kills who, with time intervals to support the lone-gunman theory, and it should work out."

"And where will you get the explosives?"

"Helsinki is expanding at a tremendous rate. Because of geography, we can't grow outward, and nobody wants skyscrapers here, and so we're building downward instead of up. Underneath the city, there's an ever-expanding warren of tunnels. And those tunnels are created with explosives. It won't be hard to liberate a small amount for our purposes. There must be tons down there."

"And what if Moore doesn't kill the Corsican father and son who intend to wipe out everyone on Saukko's Shit List?"

"We either murder them too, or the money disappears from the safe-deposit box—I'm not sure how to pull that off yet, but I'll work it out—and their deal is off. According to Moore, there's nearly a million in it. I wouldn't mind to heist it. Let's see what comes of it."

"Let me think about this," I say, and step out for some cold water and *kossu*. It doesn't take me long to make up my mind.

I sit back down in the sauna. I'm cold from the shower, splash some water on the stones to warm me up. "No," I say.

Milo's eyebrows furrow. "What do you mean, 'no'?"

"I mean no. I don't want to murder all those people."

"Jesus fucking Christ. They want to murder you and your family, and I'm sure mine and Sweetness's along with them. You think they knew Mirjami and Jenna were going to be in the Audi when it blew? They assumed it would be Kate."

"Sorry," I say, "I just can't see us doing it."

"*Pomo,*" Sweetness says, "I'm with Milo on this one."

These two have never put me on the defensive before. "When did this become a democracy? Sweetness, you call me *pomo*—boss—doesn't that imply I make all final decisions?"

Milo gulps beer, now hot and ruined, says "Yuck," and goes out to get a cold one. He sits down beside me. "We don't want to usurp your authority or make you angry, but you're the boss in work-related matters. When it comes to protecting ourselves and the people we love, we get a say in what happens. I won't ask you to participate if you're dead set against it, but this is going to happen."

I think of Kate. My extra-legal activities were the spark behind her emotional trauma. If she found out I murdered someone, or was even an accessory to murder—which, having heard the plan, I de facto am—it could end our marriage and make her even sicker. I have to balance this against stopping further attempts on her life. I explain this to the others.

Milo replies, "The manifesto, the guns and possibly explosives will take us a couple weeks to get together. You have time to think about it. And as far as Kate goes, if you decide to take part, just hide it from her. You would anyway."

"Let's let it go for now," I say. "We'll move to Arvid's place, and in the meantime, keep me posted on the progress you make. Deal?"

"Deal," he says.

"Anybody have any ideas about how to find Loviise Tamm?" I ask.

"The way I understand it," Milo says, "she was snatched by Russian diplomats. Right?"

"Yeah."

"So they probably either took her to the embassy or to another whorehouse. Another whorehouse seems way more likely to me."

"Me too," I say.

"And Russian diplomats are overseeing the operation?"

"Well, I think most aren't really diplomats, but spies here with diplomatic passports for cover. With some hired help from a few Finns, according to the files we pulled out of their electronics."

"Then we need to tail the people working at the embassy until they lead us to the right whorehouse. The problem, of course, is that there are twenty or thirty of them, and only three of us. It would be fucking helpful if we had the manpower of the police department for this."

I lean up against the wall and pull one knee up, let the bad one lie flat on the bench. The heat is easing the pain in both my knee and my jaw.

"Let me think about this," Sweetness says, and fetches fresh beers for all of us.

He sits down and says, "I'm hesitant to suggest this, but I could call my cousin, Ai."

"Ai," Milo says, "as in what people yell when they're in pain?"

"Yeah."

"Why is he called Ai?" I ask.

"He's my cousin, my dad's sister's kid, sixteen now. My aunt was a bad drunk and drug user, turned really mean when she was high. When Ai was about three, he tried to take a cookie or something, and she smashed his hand when he reached for it. She hit him hard with an iron skillet and broke bones in his hand and wrist. He screamed 'Ai' and started to cry, which made her madder. She said she'd give him something to really cry about, and she stuck his hand in a pot of boiling water and held it there. Dad went over there about three days later and Ai hadn't been given any medical treatment. The skin peeled off like a glove almost to his elbow. Dad didn't want his sister to go to jail, so he just took Ai home, put burn ointment on it and wrapped it up till it healed. Sort of."

"Sort of?"

"His hand is withered and all the nerves in it are dead. Plus, it always looks worse than it is because he puts cigarettes out on it to impress people and make them think he's tough. Which he is."

"That still doesn't explain why he's called Ai," Milo says.

"I told you his mom was fucking mean. She started

calling him that to make fun of him. She would actually tell the story when she was drunk and stoned, like it was funny, and the nickname stuck. Now he doesn't like to be called anything else. Like it's some kind of badge of honor."

"You said 'was' mean. Where is she now?"

"Disappeared three years ago. Ai says she went out to score and never came back. I think the truth is he killed her. He's meaner than she was. He's like the fucking devil, that's why I hesitate to call him. She was on permanent disability because of her substance abuse, and Ai lives alone, has since she disappeared. I think nobody ever reported her as a missing person and he lives off her social security pension."

"What about his father?" I ask.

"He doesn't know who his father is."

"And he can help us how?"

"He runs a gang in East Helsinki. They would follow the Russians for us, if the price was right."

Jesus, what a story. "What the fuck," I say. "Give the kid a call. It might be interesting to do business with a teenage devil incarnate."

26

Sweetness secures an invitation to visit Ai for us. Despite Sweetness's assurances that he's in fit condition to drive, we're all drunk, and I insist that we take a taxi. It pulls up in front of a building that screams government subsidized. A place to warehouse refugees, dopers, drunks, the mentally ill, and some people who just suffer the misfortune of being poor.

Garbage is strewn around the door. Said door has the glass knocked out of it. Little kids are playing out front, despite it being past midnight. I notice they're all white. Most often, quite a few of the tenants in these places are black immigrants. The government likes to dump them in shitholes like this. Usually, the government will control a portion of the apartments in a building like this, and the rest will be privately owned.

We take an elevator to the third floor and ring the buzzer. A teenage boy opens the door. "I'm not fond of cops," he says. "Your ID cards."

He holds out a hand, gnarled, withered and scabbed. His small and ring fingers are bent and twisted. He puts a cigarette out on his palm, flicks the butt into the hallway and keeps his hand out, faceup. The stench of burnt flesh sickens me. No doubt his intention. It's apparent that the hand has little or no mobility. Seeing our police cards was a command, not a request. We lay them down on his dead hand. He inspects them with the other hand and gives them back. "Come in."

We enter, and other than being polluted with blue cigarette smoke so thick it makes my eyes water, the place is immaculately clean. And well-decorated. About a dozen young men, aged about fourteen to early twenties, are hanging around, most of them sitting on the floor, almost all smoking and sucking on beers or ciders. They wear the white-trash uniform: black boots or sneakers, black jeans, hoodies, some of them with the hoods over their heads, some with baseball caps cocked at forty-five-degree angles. These are the kinds of kids I loathe.

Ai, however, doesn't fit in this picture. He's dressed in

neat, preppy clothes. His Lacoste shirt is blue and pressed. He appears to be aged a hundred years old, the oldest teenager I've ever seen. His face isn't scarred, it's ravaged by life. He sits in a leather wingback chair, which obviously serves as his throne, and lays his forearms and hands on the armrests. For lack of anywhere to sit, the three of us stand in front of him, like petitioners to a king.

"No hello for your cousin?" Sweetness asks.

Dismissive, Ai says, "Hello, Cousin."

He turns his attention to me. "State your business." So he noticed that I'm ranking officer here from my police card. That escapes a lot of people.

"Let's start with your business," I say.

"Very well. If we must."

The other hoodlums listen in rapt attention, hang on his every word.

"You're a teenage boy. I'm given to understand you've lived alone since age thirteen. How did you manage to get that by social services?"

He lights a cigarette. He has an ashtray in a stand by his throne. "I gave them no cause for inquiry. I haven't missed a day of school in that time. My grades are the highest in my class. I dress well."

I feel like I've entered a fictional world. That this is a Sherlock Holmes tale and I'm surrounded by the Baker Street Irregulars, but they answer to a pint-sized and disfigured Professor Moriarty.

"My business is this," I say. "I'm looking for a girl named Loviise Tamm. She's been kidnapped by a member of the Russian diplomatic delegation. Their embassy is Russian soil. I can't enter it and search for her any more than I could the Kremlin. She is to be forced into prostitution. The delegation has, to the best of my knowledge, seventeen houses of prostitution, but I don't know their locations. Sooner or later, she'll likely wind up working in one of them. I want you to use your people to surveil the diplomats, many of whom are actually spies, identify the people involved with prostitution, find out where the houses of prostitution are, and locate the girl if possible. She's easy to spot. She's tiny and has Down syndrome." I take out her photo and pass it around the room. "It seems to me that the easiest way to do that would be to enter the houses as customers. Your crew looks like it would have few qualms about using the services of prostitutes."

He looks thoughtful for a moment. "Why don't you just use police for this?"

"For personal reasons, it falls outside their purview."

He glances at a kid on the floor. Said kid hops up and brings him a beer. "I know a little about surveillance," Ai says. "Why don't you just GPS and monitor their vehicles? Chalk-mark their tires for certainty. Use security camera footage to get the license plate numbers and images of the people involved."

Milo breaks in. "The cars are swept every day for bugs and bombs. The vehicles all have tinted windows. They've arranged their transportation so that no one can see who enters or exits the vehicles coming and going from the embassy."

Ai turns sarcastic. "So you're an expert on Russian embassy surveillance countermeasures."

"No," Milo says. "It's standard diplomatic security protocol."

Ai sips beer. "But yet, you believe we can accomplish all this and defeat their security measures, when you, trained detectives, are unable to do so."

"Sulo thinks you can," I say. I use his real name, as I doubt Ai knows his nickname. "Can you or can't you?"

"That would depend on my motivation."

I take Sasha Mikoyan's credit card and account access codes from my wallet. "This is the account of a dead man. I checked it today, it's still active and contains a hundred and three thousand euros. More than likely, you can withdraw three thousand euros a day in cash from an automatic teller machine, or if you prefer the safety of emptying it into another account, in the event that it gets locked, my colleague"—I gesture toward Milo—"will help you set up something offshore."

He holds out his hand, I put the card and codes in it, and he looks them over. I'm certain he's never had a chance to make so much money.

"Agreed," he says.

"Do you have the means and will to accomplish this task? For that much money, I expect a successful outcome."

"We do, and you'll have it. Our means might be," he pauses, searching for the correct word, "zealous."

I turn to face his friends. They've listened and are dumb-founded at the prospect of so much money. I have their respect now. I could ask them if they had fucked their sisters and they would tell me the truth. "How many of you have felony arrests?" All but two raise their hands. "How many of you are armed?" Four hold up pistols. A few display knives.

I ask Ai, "Would you like me to open rat jackets on all of you? Odds are good some of you will be arrested, and if I say you work for me as informants, I can almost certainly get the charges dropped."

He considers it. "A gracious offer, but we decline. It strikes me as something that will come back to haunt us later. If we need to do something drastic, we'll use juveniles."

I hand him a business card. "I want regular reports."

"You'll have them."

My earlier curiosity is renewed. "Don't any blacks live here?"

"No."

"Why?"

He gets up, goes to another room, and comes back with a Crossman air rifle. He loads a pellet into it and pumps it a dozen times to get a lot of pressure behind the projectile. He goes to an open window. A girl of about five plays downstairs in the yard. He shoots with it. She shrieks in surprise and pain.

"We prefer the company of good, God-fearing white folks," he says. "After being stabbed, shot, beaten and so on, the blacks all decided to seek their fortunes elsewhere. Besides, it made room for my friends to move into their apartments. Most of us live here now."

Yep, the kid is like the devil. I've never seen a child in such mental anguish. "Regular reports," I say, and we take a taxi home.

27

My phone rings at nine a.m. It's the National Bureau of Investigation forensic mechanic.

"I got fascinated by the explosion in your Audi and pulled an all-nighter," he says.

"Thanks. I appreciate that."

"You may not thank me when you hear the findings. First, there was a hot fuel mix in the gas tank. Enough to start the car, but not enough to keep it running long. There was ether both in front of the fuel injectors' carbonized nozzles and under the driver's seat. I'm pretty sure a hole had been drilled so that it aimed up under the driver's seat and squirted fuel.

When the line lost pressure, fire shot backward up the line, ignited the ether under the seat and also set off the gas tank."

"So it was a pro job."

I hear him suck hard on a cigarette and gulp what I assume, from the blowing then slurping sound, is hot coffee. "And very slick. Here's how pro it was. Ether eats through plastic, so the ether was poured into plastic bags, probably freezer bags or something, and those bags were placed in thin, watertight balsa wood boxes, so that a portion of the ether leaked into them. The flame coming out of the carbonized nozzles set the balsa wood, which is absorbent, on fire, which in turn ignited the ether and started the process. It was hard to spot the remains of the burned-up boxes, because balsa doesn't leave much and there was already carbon all over the place. I picked up traces of acetone from the balsa leftovers, so I'm pretty sure that was the scenario. Somebody wants you dead, or at least burned to a crisp."

"What do you preferably drink?" I ask.

"Good single-malt scotch. Why?"

"I'll bring a bottle by for you by way of thanks."

I can almost hear his smile. His job doesn't garner much appreciation. "Stay safe," he says.

KATE AND I take a taxi to see Torsten Holmqvist. I met Torsten not long after moving to Helsinki. I had broken the Sufia Elmi case, one might say by attrition, because so many people under suspicion died. I was shot in the face. I had been promised a slot in Helsinki Homicide, but the department decided I needed my psyche delved into before starting in my new position.

I never liked Torsten. He's a Swedish-speaking Finn, wealthy, and I got the impression that like many rich Swedish-speaking Finns, he believes he's *bättre folk*, as I've heard them call themselves, a cut above the rest of us commoners. I find everything from his expensive preppy clothing to the apple-scented tobacco he smokes in his briarwood pipe pretentious, and he thought I couldn't see through him when he tried to manipulate me. I interrogate people for a living. He never seemed to understand that he and I are, in a sense, in the same business, and it annoyed me. It wasn't that he's bad at his job, quite the opposite. He was just the wrong therapist for me.

I think, though, that he truly cares about his patients. Seeing Kate today, on short notice, because she's in crisis, serves as proof of that. His office is in a beautiful home in the district of Eira, near embassy row, and worth millions. A bay window looks out on the sea. It's a perfect day, warm enough for T-shirts and shorts, the sea dotted with pleasure craft under a cobalt-blue sky.

When I woke Kate and told her we were coming here, she didn't resist. She must know she needs this. She looks bad, haggard and worn. It took more than booze and jet lag to do this to her, more like something that gnaws at her soul.

"Do you mind if Kari joins us in our session today?" he asks Kate.

She shakes her head no.

"I thought," Torsten says, "as an outside observer and as a witness to the trials you've been through, he might be able to shed some light on how I might best help you. If at any time you feel uncomfortable with his presence, if you feel it inhibits you or prevents you from sharing a confidence with me, I'll ask him to take a seat in the waiting room until we're done here. Is this acceptable to you?"

His English is excellent. She nods her head yes.

Torsten offers us coffee or tea. I take the coffee. Kate takes some herbal tea blend. I sit on the couch, a little away from them, and Kate takes a chair, separated from him by a small table. He provides me with an ashtray, fills his pipe and lights it.

"Would you like to begin, or shall I?" he asks.

She starts trembling. "You."

"Very well. I thought we were making progress here. What prompted you to run away?"

Tears appear in the corners of her eyes. "I couldn't remember things. I was afraid that I was unable to care for Anu. I wasn't getting better, I was getting worse. I killed someone. Killers aren't supposed to be mothers. Mothers aren't supposed to be killers. I don't deserve her."

"So you left her to punish yourself?"

She pauses, wipes her eyes. "At least in part."

He crosses his legs, sits back, puffs. "I smell alcohol on you, on your breath, and so much that you're sweating it out. Why?"

She nods. "I was drinking more and more, and that's another reason I thought Anu was better off without me." She sobs, starts to cry.

"May I ask why you've been drinking so heavily?"

"I'm self-medicating. It's the family way. My father was a drunk. My brother is a drug addict. We can't cope with life."

"Your brother. Is that why you went to him?"

She nods. "I knew he would understand."

"Do you crave alcohol and feel you're an alcoholic?"

She shakes her head no.

"I don't think so either. Before you leave, I'll give you a prescription for something that should make you feel better than alcohol."

Silence.

"Even before you left for the U.S.," Torsten says, "you were reluctant to see Kari. Why?"

"Look at him. He's a wreck, and it's my fault. He did wrong things, but he asked me first. I told him to do them. Even Adrien, the man I killed. I told Kari to take him into his confidence, to work with him. And then he shot Kari and Milo and a woman close to giving birth. She and the baby both died."

She stops and looks at me, shame-faced. "And I'm not always sure who he is. I get confused about where I am and who people are. Not all the time, but sometimes. And then all that goes through my head is that day on the island when I killed Adrien Moreau."

She bites her nails. I've never seen her do that.

Torsten leans forward, elbows on his knees, hands clasped. "Kate, would you like some time to rest? There is a facility called Aurora, and occasionally, when life becomes too hard to bear, people go there for a little while. You don't have to do anything. Your every need will be cared for. Would you like that?"

Her face blanches from terror. "You mean a mental institution?"

He puts on his consoling face. "Yes, it is. But of a benign nature. It's nothing you should be afraid of. The workers there are very kind."

She shakes her head so hard I think it will turn a circle, twist off, and fall to the floor. "No no no no no no . . ."

I'm tempted to ask him if, since she doesn't want to go, I can go there and have people be nice to me, I can rest and have *my* every need cared for. I hold my tongue.

He pats her knee to reassure her. "It was just a question. You don't have to go there. Your other option is to go home. You can go there and be with your husband and daughter."

She looks at me, expression flat. "He doesn't need me. I've been replaced by a twenty-three-year-old beauty queen."

Torsten raises one eyebrow. It calls to mind bad soap opera acting. "Replaced?"

Kate says, "By a girl I thought was my friend. The bed reeks of her soap and perfume."

Torsten's glance asks me to explain.

"Kate, I haven't cheated on you. Ever." Which is true, but the exact circumstances will still distress her, so I tell a white lie. "When you left, I was in bad condition, unable to take care of Anu. Mirjami, Jenna and Sweetness came to stay with me and help out. I gave Mirjami our bed and I slept in my chair. I suppose I should tell you now. Mirjami borrowed your car and there was an accident. She was very badly burned and will be in the hospital for some time."

This leaves her speechless.

"I've done things you found questionable," I say. "Those things weren't your fault. They were my choices. And you blame yourself for approving my actions. You believed you were granting the wishes of a man dying of brain cancer. It was unfair of me to place you in that position. You blame yourself for killing Adrien Moreau. He gave you no choice. He would have killed the rest of us, and you saved our lives. He brought his death on himself. Your action wasn't criminal, it was heroic."

"I hated the way you lived, the way you changed. Committing criminal acts. Stealing. Dissolving people in acid."

Torsten gawks at me.

"I didn't kill them," I say. "I made two bodies disappear to avoid a mafia gang war."

I light a cigarette to buy a few seconds and consider my words, then return my attention to Kate. "Brain surgery impacted me more than I knew. My recovery isn't over yet, but I'm much improved. However, some of the things I've done upset important people, mostly because I no longer want to do questionable things on their behalf. If you come home, we're going to stay in Arvid's house for a while. You'll like it. It's pretty and spacious. On the river. A good place to rest. Jenna, Sweetness and Milo will come, too. Jenna was in the accident with Mirjami. She was pregnant and lost the baby. She needs a change of scenery. It's sort of a vacation for all of us."

"You still do questionable things," Kate says. "You more or less had me abducted and forced me back here."

Torsten helps me out. "I told Kari he had to get you back here in order for me to treat you. Your illness had become a life-threatening situation. I didn't say it to Kari, but I was afraid you might harm yourself." His smile is gentle. "You were abducted on doctor's orders."

She doesn't find it humorous and scowls at me. "You think you're the fucking Godfather. I'm married to Michael Corleone."

A penetrating observation. Especially since Milo and Sweetness want the next step in our illustrious careers to be much like the end of *The Godfather*.

"If Kate goes with you," Torsten asks, "will she be safe?"

A half-truth. "Of course she'll be safe. She'll be surrounded by law enforcement officers around the clock." Followed by a truth, as without me, Milo and Sweetness to protect her, she's in dire peril. "There's no safer place she could be."

"Tell us, Kate," Torsten asks, "what do you feel would be best for you?"

"I want to sleep for ten thousand years with my baby in my arms."

"Are you comfortable living with Kari?"

"I don't know who he is or wants to be. I don't know if we should be married anymore. I avoided him for weeks and kept his baby from him. That wasn't fair. And it wasn't right for me to leave him alone when he was so weak and sick and then to dump Anu on him out of the blue. I will try to be comfortable with Kari, one day at a time."

"You aren't well enough to live on your own. Do you see that now?"

She hesitates, doesn't want to admit it. "Yes."

"If you run away again or if your condition deteriorates, Kari is to call me, and you'll have to take that rest we talked about. Do you both understand this?"

We nod.

"And Kari," Torsten says, "you must understand that Kate isn't well, and that living with her will sometimes be uncomfortable. You're obviously in poor condition yourself. Are you prepared for that?"

"Of course."

He writes a prescription for Kate. "This is for Valdoxan, an antidepressant. It's a relatively new drug, but results with it have been very good. The side effects are minimal, it will help you sleep, and stopping it when the time comes is much easier than with other antidepressants."

He hands it to her. "Kari, this is a safe place for Kate. If you have something you want to say or anything you would like to ask her, now would be a good time."

I look at my wife and barely recognize her. The changes wrought by her suffering fill me with sadness. "Why did you leave?" I ask. "When you came out of your dissociative stupor, you left within hours. I don't understand. You were in a safe place, loved and cared for."

"Except for Anu, I wished we had all died on that island. I wish we had never come to Helsinki. I wish you could have been content to be a good and honest policeman, even if you didn't make a difference. I just couldn't stand the sight of you. It made me think of all that ugliness."

"And now?"

"I still wish we were all dead, and I can look at you, but it's hard."

Question asked and answered. I should have known better. Never ask a question if the answer may destroy you. I say nothing else.

"Let's call it a day," Torsten says.

28

We go to a pharmacy, Yliopiston Apteekki, to get Kate's prescription filled. It's downtown in a large shopping district, a mall across from it. The main train station is on the other side of the street. Kate and I go there by taxi. It's packed. Kate and I don't speak. She takes a number to get in line and we browse in different aisles so she can avoid looking at me.

My cell phone rings. A nurse from the hospital tells me Mirjami is awake and would like to see me. I say I'll be there as soon as I can. We go home. Milo is sitting on the couch with my laptop, jotting notes, going through the vast amount of information accrued from the numerous communications devices I confiscated. Jenna and Sweetness are sitting at the dining room table, dressed in raggedy house clothes and sipping their early-afternoon beers. The swelling in his nose has gone down, but the bruises around his eyes have deepened, and the spectrum of their colors is a rainbow of light blue to near black.

I ask Kate, "Does their drinking bother you?"

"I don't care what any of you do. I just want to sleep."

I ask her to please wait, ask Jenna to help me, and make up the bed with fresh linens. I don't want her to sleep in a bed that smells like Mirjami. I've always found changing the blanket covers—which are like very wide and long pillowcases—near impossible to do by myself and wonder at how women are able to reach inside the little armholes in the corners of the covers, reach through the bottom, grasp the blanket and shake the cover in a whipping motion so that the blanket doesn't hang out the end.

Kate tells me that Americans seldom use blanket covers and sleep under bare blankets. It seems a dirty habit and vile to me. During the short time I spent in the States, there were no blanket covers, but I thought it was because I lived in student housing and people made do with whatever was at hand. And when I watch foreign television or movies and people hang around on the bed with their shoes on, it makes me cringe.

Kate waits with impatience in the kitchen. I give her a dose of Valdoxan, and take my own array of painkillers, tranquilizers and muscle relaxants. The tranquilizers seem useless to me, as I have no problems with nervousness, but the neurologists tell me the relaxing effects will help my injured muscles from tightening. My knee hurts like mortal hell at the moment. I'll eat whatever to make it stop. Kate asks for Anu and I put my girls in bed together.

"Mirjami is awake and wants to see me," I say to Milo. "Could you drive me to the hospital?"

"Sure." He shuts down my computer. "Let's go."

WE DRIVE to Meilahti Hospital, a huge facility surrounded by a warren of smaller buildings. We get directions to the burn ward from the front desk. We know we're on the right track because patients in later stages of recovery wander the halls, going to the canteen, outside to smoke. Some miss eyes, ears, noses, fingers. In comparison, Mirjami got off easy, but these people *could* be her, and it makes me furious.

I ask Milo to wait in the hall. He's her cousin and her friend. I promise to ask her to talk to him. A nurse escorts me in.

There's not much to see of Mirjami. Burns of various degrees of severity cover almost sixty percent of her body. She's wrapped in gauze and some kind of plastic wrap that I suppose keep the ointments on her from rubbing off. I don't know, maybe it also reduces the risk of infection. I pull up a chair next to her bed and she offers me a gauze-covered hand. I take it gently.

"Is it hard to talk?" I ask.

"Not if I don't open my mouth too wide."

"It's a stupid question, but how are you?"

"Do you want the gory details?"

"Yes."

"I'm burned to a crisp from the midsection down. I'll need several surgeries, skin grafts, I can't remember what all they said, but it's bad, and it will be a couple years until it's over."

The only thing I can think of to say is *I'm sorry*, but those are paltry and tepid words, inadequate to her suffering, so I say nothing.

She can't smile because of the burns, gauze and plastic, but she tries. "You should have made love to me when you had the chance. Those parts won't be in working order again for a long time."

I lie. "Yes, I should have. I wish I had." I change the subject. "Where are your parents?"

"They flew in from Rovaniemi and have been here most of the time. I told them to go to a hotel and get some sleep."

"If they need anything, have them call me."

"Do you know anything about my condition?" she asks.

"The doctor told me what he could after he finished with you in the ER."

She has a self-administered morphine pump. She doses herself. "I'm afraid they lie to me, to keep my spirits up. Please tell me what happened to my face. Tell me the truth."

"Your face was farthest from the fire and so the least damage was done to it. You suffered third-degree burns to much of your lower body. From your lower torso and upward, you suffered first- and second-degree burns. If you looked at yourself in a mirror now, it would startle and frighten you, but it will pass, and most of those more minor burns will heal to a great degree within a few weeks. Your hair burned off. But hair grows."

She sniffles, tries to keep from breaking down, keeps trying to smile. "I was beautiful just a couple days ago. This seems impossible."

Her eyes are uncovered. She closes them and I kiss her on their lids. "You're still beautiful, inside and out. It's hard, but try to be patient. When they unwrap it and you see your face, you'll realize that for yourself."

She tries to squeeze my hand. It makes her wince. "Kari, I love you. Whatever and whoever else you have in your life, I want you to know that."

I take a moment, try to decide what to say to make her feel the best. "And I want you to know this. If circumstances allowed it, I would have returned all the love you've shown me. I would have been proud for you to be my life partner. I would have been proud if you were the mother of my children. Since you walked into my life, I've thought of you as a godsend, and I love you, too." There is a modicum of truth in most of this, but the last is a blatant lie. I just don't love her.

She weeps quietly, and we share a few moments of silence.

"What will happen to me?" she asks. "I won't be able to walk for a long time. Who knows when I'll be able to work. I don't want to live in this hospital for months."

"You'll stay with us. I'll get you in-home care."

Mirjami gives herself another jolt of morphine. "I don't think your wife will appreciate that."

No, she won't. "You two were becoming friends. You took care of her and Anu when they needed it. You took care of me when I needed it. I can't imagine her objecting to us taking care of you."

Yes, I can. I picture strenuous objections. But that will be a few weeks away. I'll deal with it then. It's the right thing to do.

I wait for Mirjami to speak, but she's passed out. The combination of morphine, burn trauma and exertion from talking put her lights out. Before I leave, I inform her doctor that I'm treating the fire that put her here as a criminal investigation, and ask him to call me immediately if there are any changes in her condition.

29

I have an appointment at three p.m. with the Russian ambassador's wife. I ask Milo to drop me near the fountain where we're to meet. She's already there. Loviise said she "looks like a magazine," and indeed she does. Many fashion models would envy her looks. She wears pumps with one-inch heels and, with them, is about as tall as I am. But unlike me, most of her height is composed of thin, coltish and spectacular legs. She's model skinny, dressed in a not quite mini-skirt and sleeveless top. Her honey-blond hair is cut above shoulder length and curls over her ears, toward eyes the color of glacier-blue ice set in a face that speaks of childlike innocence. Hardly the face of a killer.

She, of course, recognizes me because of my wounds. We greet, shake hands. The esplanade is one of my favorite spots in the city, a long and well-manicured park that runs through the city center. The harbor and a market square are at one end of it, the trendy restaurant Teatteri—Theater—occupies the other. A Dixieland jazz band is playing on a pavilion not far from Kappeli, one of Helsinki's oldest and most classic restaurants, close to the fountain. Both restaurants have large outdoor patios, places to people-watch, to see and be seen. The sun, warm weather, sea breeze and blue sky make a day spent with beers here on a patio inviting.

"Where would you like to go?" I ask.

Her smile would melt the heart of any man. "It doesn't matter. You can choose."

An ice cream stand is near to us. I nod toward it. "How about a double-scoop cone and we sit here on the edge of the fountain."

I didn't think it possible, but her smile broadens even more. "It's been ages since a man bought me ice cream. You're quite charming for a policeman."

I laugh. "You just don't know me yet."

Yelena turns flirtatious. Her eyes dance. "You seem to presume I will get to know you."

"Trust me," I say. "I presume nothing."

We get our cones and sit on the edge of the granite ring

surrounding the fountain. "I've never known quite what to make of this statue," Yelena says.

"You're not alone. Opinions have been divided since it was erected in 1908. It's called the Havis Amanda. A mermaid standing on seaweed surrounded by four fish and four sea lions."

"So you're a charming detective and a historian as well." Her smile disappears, replaced by the expression of a shrewd and calculating woman analyzing me. "What is it you wish to discuss with me?"

Pistachio is my favorite flavor of ice cream. It's starting to melt. I lick a ring around it to keep it from dripping. "Several things. Why did you murder your lover?"

She screws up her mouth with distaste. Or disgust. "Where to begin? I am chattel. My husband, the ambassador, is a wealthy and powerful man. My father is an even more rich and powerful man. They reached a bargain for me. My husband paid for the privilege of my hand in marriage, primarily with oil and gas stocks. Our marriage was a kind of merger."

I joke. "No pigs or sheep involved?"

It gets a grin out of her.

"And why the shoplifting?" I ask, more out of curiosity than anything else.

This gets a belly laugh. "Because it drives my husband crazy! I may be his wife, but I'm still Daddy's little girl. My husband must take everything I do in stride and fix the problems I create for him. I get bored and create problems."

"Does 'everything in stride' include your affair with Sasha?"

"In a sense, but he punished me by telling me the truth about Sasha, that he was deeply involved in human trafficking and forced other women to have sex with him. I was in love with Sasha, my husband ruined it, so he got his revenge."

"And you got yours and killed Sasha."

"He went from my bed to that apartment, where, by the looks of things when I entered, he intended to defile a filthy little urchin. Every person has limits, and I confess, I do tend to let my temper get away from me."

"And you possess a keen gift for understatement."

She licks her ice cream. "It's not so terrible being married to my husband. He insists that we have sex twice a week, which amounts to about half an hour of my time. But still, I hate him for ruining what I had with Sasha. It lent meaning to my otherwise futile existence. You do realize that you're powerless to do anything about the murder, don't you?"

"Yes, I'm aware of that. I'm not interested in the murder. Your lover got what he deserved. Less, in my opinion. By the way, are you aware that your husband's colleagues came to collect Sasha's body to cover up the murder, and they kidnapped the so-called urchin? I assume because she was a witness."

She smiles her charming smile. "Of course I know. I tried to call him but couldn't reach him. So I called one of his minions at the embassy, who knew where he was. When he finally returned my call, I told him what I had done and to have the mess cleaned up. He was most displeased."

"Do you know where the girl is?"

She takes a bite of the cone. "How would I know that? And why would I care?"

"I'm here because Russian diplomats are involved in forced prostitution. I believe that this is orchestrated by a woman named Natasha Polyanova. I want to find her and what appears to be about a hundred and eighty women in the region, many housed in at least seventeen apartments in the Helsinki area. I hoped you might help me find her, and the women, so I can put a stop to this."

"This, I can help you with," she says. "The Russian trade delegation owns close to a dozen apartments. They've rented several more. Natasha Polyanova manages the properties for the trade delegation."

"Can you get me a list of the properties?"

She broaches no foolishness. Her tone turns put out. "As you can see, I'm a busy woman with weighty matters to attend to. Surely a detective as astute as yourself can secure the list without my assistance."

"I can indeed. However, her phone number is no longer in service. Do you know where I can find her?"

She's getting a little pissed off. "If she manages so many properties, don't you think it likely that she lives in one of them? Do I have to do all your thinking for you?"

"No, you've done quite enough." I reconsider. "One more question: Why leave fingerprints on the door handle and the butcher knife?"

Her eyes glitter again. "To make more problems for my husband, of course."

I thank her for her time.

"Actually," she says, "I'm going to do one more favor for you. I've considered it for some months, and now the timing is perfect. It will both ruin my husband and help you accomplish your mission of mercy. Or, at the very least, render him unable to do anything to stop you. He'll return to Helsinki in a couple hours and get his surprise in the morning."

My curiosity is piqued. "Would you care to share your plan with me?"

Her face returns to its former reflection of innocence and her laugh is delighted and genuine. "Inspector Vaara, hasn't anyone ever told you that you should be careful what you wish for? Come visit me in my room at Kämp tomorrow morning. All will be clear then."

She takes out a wallet from her purse and offers me a key card. "Let yourself in."

"I already have a card," I say. "I took Sasha's wallet."

"Efficiency," she says, "something I admire."

And with that, she gets up and walks away.

30

I find the situation at home much as usual. Sweetness and Jenna slurp beer. Milo lying on my couch, his head propped up by pillows, my laptop balanced on his knees. His eyes are blood red. I take it he's stoned.

"Where is Kate?" I ask him.

"In the bedroom with Anu."

I feel foolish, but we haven't established the rules of engagement, and I knock on my own bedroom door.

"Come," Kate says, and I feel like I should be in livery, awaiting her instructions.

She's lying on top of the covers, wearing sweatpants and

shirt, old workout clothes. No books or magazines are in evidence. She's staring at the wall, a vague expression of terror on her face, and doesn't look at me when I enter. "Am I in the hospital?" she asks.

"No, you're in your home. Do you know who I am?"

Her eyes don't waver. "No."

I sit on the edge of the bed. "I'm Kari, your husband."

"I'm tired," she says. "Would you leave so I can rest?"

"OK. Can I take Anu with me, so I can feed and change her?"

She nods. I pick up Anu and close the door behind me as I leave.

I sit in my chair, Anu in my lap. Katt hops on top of the chair, now mended by Jenna, and mercifully only wraps his paws around my neck as if trying to strangle me rather than using me for a scratching post.

"How's Kate?" Milo asks.

We keep our voices low. Kate sometimes understands Finnish. It depends mostly on the subject matter. "Bad. How's your diabolical plan to overthrow the government coming?"

"Pretty well. Every Saturday, Osmo Ahtiainen and Jyri Ivalo play golf together at the Vuosaari Golf Club. They're members, tee off at eleven, play the first nine, have lunch in the restaurant, then play the second nine. So I've placed them together in an open area. In Phillip Moore's iPad, it says that Veikko Saukko 'drives' every day at noon, including Saturdays. He, incidentally and unfortunately, plays golf on a course every Sunday, and not at the Vuosaari club. I need to know what 'drive' refers to. It sounds promising, some kind of activity that takes him out of his house. As far as the two Corsicans go, I only have their work schedules."

"Are you still going to murder them all?"

He looks up at me. "Oh, yes, there's no doubt about that. Of course, if Moore follows through and murders the Corsicans, it's one less thing we have to do."

"And after all these people are dead, what becomes of us? Do we wait a reasonable length of time, leave the country and live on our accrued ill-gotten wealth? Just cite our injuries and retire from the force? What?"

He chuckles. "Well, speaking for myself, I'll just go back to being a cop, solve crimes, that sort of thing. I like my job. Why would I leave it?"

I mull it over. "I guess that goes for me, too. Like they say: do what you know. But why kill Osmo and Jyri? They've done nothing overt to harm us."

"And they haven't because they're too smart for that. They put Jan Pitkänen together with Veikko Saukko and knew the consequences would be disastrous for us. And with them gone, I don't think that leaves anyone alive who knows enough to get us indicted for any crimes. And without Osmo to cover his ass, Pitkänen has to be prepared to do a prison jolt as a cop killer, and it would be a long one. I doubt he's prepared for that."

"And if I forbade it?"

"I would ignore you. I'm going to leave the Crown Vic here tomorrow and take a bus to my summer cottage to get my sailboat tonight. I'm going to Roope Malinen's cottage. I'll take some small belongings to implicate him in the video. His boat is docked there and I want to check it out. I either have to steal his on Go Day, or make mine look like his, swap the GPSs on our crafts, put his serial number on my boat, and make it appear that he used it for transportation while committing his string of barbarous murders. Stealing Malinen's boat seems the more elegant solution. Then I'm coming to Porvoo. I'm going to dock my boat near your house and start working from there. Soon, I'll sail down and surveil Saukko's place from the sea and find out what 'driving' refers to."

"Yeah, I guess we should move tomorrow," I say. "How do you sail with one hand?"

"I don't. I can't negotiate the ropes or tie a proper knot, so I put a big engine in the back and keep the sails furled."

My phone rings. It's a doctor from Meilahti Hospital. He's sorry to inform me that Mirjami is dead.

"How can that be?" I ask. "I just saw her today. She was talking, her prognosis was good."

"Such severe burns cause trauma that sometimes the body can't cope with and it just shuts down. The burns on the lower portion of her body were very bad indeed. Nothing went wrong, her treatment was excellent. She just died anyway. Again, I'm very sorry for your loss."

"This is now a murder investigation. I want an autopsy performed." I'm angry with the doctor, want to shoot the messenger, and ring off.

"Milo, it's bad news. Mirjami died."

Jenna and Sweetness hear me. We all just sit and stare at one another for a while. There are no words. After a while, Sweetness motions to me with a tilt of his head to come to the dining room table. He pours us all Koskenkorva, and we drink to Mirjami. I'm glad that the last time I saw her, I lied about my feelings for her. At least in that small way, she could die believing what she wanted to be the truth.

None of us speak for the better part of half an hour, then Milo says, "You still think my plan is too harsh?"

"Do what you want," I say. "Jan Pitkänen belongs to me." He and I don't have a vendetta, we have a reckoning. His blowing up the car, burning Mirjami to a crisp and hurting Jenna in a murder attempt created a situation in which one of us must die. I wonder if he recognizes this as well. I wonder if he created this situation out of jealousy, because he was the golden boy of illegal activity, Osmo Ahtiainen's chief axman, and then all the dope money and power that goes with it, illegal surveillance, strong-arm work, as well as the nation's most prestigious crime cases, all fell to me. I would have been happy to hand it all over to him. Spilt milk. Now he has to play for blood.

Even as I plot revenge, I realize that my thoughts about them are false and I want to push them all out of my mind. I'm sickened by corruption, death and murder. I want to live in harmony with my family. Nothing more.

Kate comes out of the bedroom in her bathrobe, a smile on her face. She says hello to everyone and disappears into the bathroom. She comes out, goes back to the bedroom and returns in a summer frock and her hair done up in a chignon. The ten years that fell upon her when she came unglued have disappeared. She looks like my Kate again.

"Anybody have a beer for me?" she asks.

Torsten didn't mention anything about her staying away from alcohol altogether, and I don't want to deny her and ruin this good moment.

"There's plenty in the fridge," I say.

She cracks one and sits down with us. We're all a bit mystified by the mood swing, but what the hell, it's great to see her happy.

"What's with all the glum faces?" she asks.

I answer. "Do you remember Mirjami? You and her and Jenna spent a lot of time together this spring."

"Don't be silly. Of course I remember her."

"She died today."

Kate's brows furrow as she ponders this. She doesn't think to ask how Mirjami died. "Mirjami would want us to celebrate her, even if we're mourning her at the same time."

Words of wisdom. She would indeed.

"I'll put on some music," Kate says. "What should we listen to?"

Sweetness doesn't hesitate. "Some tango, please."

Kate can't picture Sweetness being a tango fan. I suppose I've never told her about the tango palaces all over Finland. Our tango is usually sad music in minor keys, appropriate for this moment. I choose a CD by Unto Mononen. The song "Satumaa" comes on.

Sweetness asks Kate if she would like to dance. She giggles. "My feet are bare. Are you going to stomp on me and break them?"

With pride, Jenna says, "Sweetness is one of the best dancers I've ever met."

"I've won tango contests," he says. "My mom made me take lessons, and I studied gymnastics, too. I know Kari thinks my dad is a piece of shit, and he's probably right, but about once a month he made up for making Mom miserable by taking her out to tango. I've been doing it since I was a little kid. Watch this," he says.

He has another *kossu* to fortify himself, moves to the middle of the living room floor for space, and does a standing backflip. A six-foot-three-inch, two-hundred-sixty-five-pound man. I never would have believed it possible of him. "Will you dance with me now?" he asks.

Kate giggles with delight. "I don't know how to tango."

He takes her hand and urges her from her chair. "I'll teach you."

Kate limps from a broken-hip injury, but has learned to move so it's hard to notice. Sweetness guides her, moves her about, and before long she does a basic tango. She's in heaven. They dance for near an hour while Jenna and I look on, and then I see Kate start to fade. She takes a break and sits down, breathless. She still smiles, but soon announces she should go to bed.

I make sure she takes her medicine, tuck her in and tell her I'm going to stay up for a while. In truth, I'm afraid she'll wake up next to me and panic for one reason or another, perhaps not recognize me. I have one more beer with the others, medicate, and go to sleep in my chair.

31

I wake early, about eight a.m. The first thing that comes into my mind is that when I was in the sixth grade, a boy in my class and his mother were abducted and driven into the forest. He was kicked in the head multiple times and left for dead. Her throat was slashed. Was this a dream, or did it happen? It seems real to me, but after brain surgery, I sometimes doubt my own perceptions. I send my brother Jari a text message and ask him if he remembers the Ruoho murder case from when we were kids, and if so, what was the outcome?

The way I remember it is that Tapani Ruoho came back to

school after a couple weeks. He sat in front of me in home-room. One morning not long after, he asked me to feel his head. I ran my fingers through his hair and felt a big scab from the kicking. He told me he played dead, the man tied his mother to a tree and cut her throat while he watched. He said nothing about rape, just pure murder.

I remember the newspapers following the murder. The prosecution had a solid case against a man, based on foren-sic evidence and Tapani's testimony. But Tapani stuttered. The defense used this to discredit Tapani, portrayed him as a confused mental defective. Not true. He was a bright kid, he just stuttered. His family moved away not long after the trial.

Jari texts back. Yes, he remembers. The defendant was acquitted. I've blocked this from my memory for all these years, never once thought of it. Does this mean my brain is returning to working order, or that the emotional events of recent days have triggered something in me? It leaves me in a quandary, disturbs me.

And then I remember something else. When I was eleven, I wore hand-me-downs and wasn't well-nourished. At the time, the tax returns of every citizen of working age were published in a book, allowing, through extrapolation, a deter-mination of income. At school, a child from a well-to-do fam-ily stood on his desk and read from said book, pointing out certain children, saying, "Your family is poor." "Your family is poor." "Your family is poor." I was among those singled out.

In the seventies, many people then considered middle

class would be considered almost destitute by today's standards. However, it was the first time that I realized I was entrenched as a second-class citizen. I haven't thought of that day in thirty years.

Although the tax book is no longer printed, tax returns remain a matter of public record, and each year, due to my phobia about poverty, I check the record and compare myself to others, to reassure myself that I'm no longer poor. Until this moment, I had no idea why I feel this compulsion. Further, I realize that most likely it was these suddenly recalled memories that led me into police work, as it's the second-most-respected occupation in Finland, after the medical profession. Why am I remembering these things now?

I think about Kate. When she ran away, Torsten said he could help her in a short time, if given the opportunity to treat her. I know enough about psychology to comprehend that his statement was simplistic and overly optimistic. I ask myself: What if she never recovers? Will I sleep in this chair and tend to her for the rest of my life? At present, a frequent topic of conversation and much written about in magazines is the importance of personal happiness. The trendy belief is that without personal happiness, we can't make others happy. A euphemistic way of saying that selfishness is paramount, and a twisted argument that disavowal of responsibility is desirable, not only for oneself but for the good of others.

Whatever happened to the concept of duty, that sacrifice for the good of others is not only laudable, but expected, especially when it comes to family? I'm scared for Kate because of the psychological dangers that lie within her, and the physical dangers that loom from without. I will sleep in this chair. I will retire and devote myself to her care for the next forty years if need be. And I will protect her from the dangers of the world as best I'm able.

Milo went halfway around the world and saved her for me. He's crazy as a shithouse rat, but I owe him a lifetime debt. He's asleep on the couch, stirs and wakes. We have coffee and cigarettes and decide this should be moving day, to the home I inherited from Arvid in Porvoo. I consider the ramifications of taking Kate away from familiar surroundings to go on our "vacation." It could be considered as such. A lovely home with the Porvoo River directly in front of it, close enough so that I could step off the porch, onto the wooden walkway and jump into the river if so inclined. In practical terms, it's a safe move. The water, like a moat, adds a measure of protection.

Milo's complicated plan to perpetrate the mass-murder frame-up of Roope Malinen requires a .50 caliber Barrett, as it's a sniper rifle he's familiar with, but he doesn't want to use his own because of a possible ballistics match. He has cheap automatic pistols we stole from drug dealers and kept to use for frame-ups or as throw-down guns, but he needs a military automatic or semi-automatic rifle for a frame-up video he wants to make. Something that can at least be fired as fast as the trigger can be pulled.

This presents a problem for him because of the severely

limited use of the fingers of his right hand. Physical therapy is improving it, but we don't have six months or a year to wait while he regains sufficient mobility to rapid-fire a weapon. It is, however, he says, sufficient to pull a hair trigger on a sniper rifle. Via his home network connection with the police database, he's found a person with the firearms he needs to do the job. A retired army major in Helsinki has a Barrett, a pair of Sako military-issue RK-62 assault rifles, and an Israeli Uzi submachine gun. He intends to B&E the major and steal his arsenal.

I ask him what kind of plan might require that many weapons. He doesn't know, but all the bases will be covered. He also intends to visit an underground construction site and use his police card to weasel his way into an explosives cache, claiming a need to inspect them. He'll take Sweetness, create a diversion, and they'll steal a small quantity of high-grade explosives. A little, he says, goes a long way. But that's a project for another day. Today, he'll get his boat and dock it in Porvoo.

"And how do you intend to kill the minister of the interior and national chief of police?" I ask.

"Don't know for sure yet, but probably while they're golfing, which means we have to pick a Saturday for this."

"We?"

"Aren't you going to kill Jan Pitkänen?"

I don't want to think about it. He tried to murder my wife and child and killed an innocent girl instead. I have no way of stopping him from attempting the same again. I have no legal recourse. I can't see that I have much choice. Still, I'm so conflicted about it that part of me wants to let him live, just put all this behind us, and internally, I keep waffling about it. Not killing him, however, is a threat to us all, and this isn't all about my wants or feelings. I sigh. "I guess so."

He senses my reluctance. "Do you want us to do it for you?" Milo asks.

I can't ask someone to commit a murder on my behalf because I don't have the will. "No."

"Then you have to time it with us. He'll just be another dead guy in a crowd."

I nod. This is at once all logical, pragmatic and insane. What's more, I have no doubt that we'll get away with it, for the simple reason that no one would ever believe it. I picture the headline: HERO COPS ON CRAZED SHOOTING SPREE. That's never going to happen. As Arvid Lahtinen once told me, "It would be like trying to convince people that Jesus was a pedophile."

Milo gets in the shower. Anu sleeps in her stroller beside my chair. I warm her formula, put cups of coffee on a tray and, precarious, carry it with one hand and rap on my bedroom door with my cane.

A sleepy voice says, "Come."

I walk in, sit on the edge of the bed and lay the tray on it. "I thought you might like to have a little family time this morning," I say.

Kate looks at me, her face blank. "What family?"

I don't know if she's being sardonic or genuinely doesn't know. "Your husband and daughter."

I see confusion in her eyes. She doesn't know who I am. Then, maybe because daughter equals Anu, and our baby is a touchstone for her, even when she was in a dissociative stupor, she snaps back into reality and the present. She tries to cover her lapse with cynicism. "Oh, *that* family. Applied to us, doesn't that make a mockery of the word?"

She radiates anger, but truly because of frustration caused by her lapse, not by me. "Anu doesn't need a bottle. I can breast-feed her."

"I'm sorry, Kate, but you can't. You're using medication that prevents it."

This makes her choke back a sob, but she says nothing.

I don't know if she remembers this has been discussed. "We're leaving today," I say, "to take a little vacation in Porvoo. It's a charming town, mostly Swedish-speaking. The old town has the kinds of arts-and-crafts stores you enjoy. We'll stay in the house Arvid left me. It's a lovely home on the river. I think you'll be happy there."

Kate has always been so demonstrative. Now I find her inscrutable. "Who knows," she says, "maybe I will."

If I could jump up and down for joy, I would. Kate has uttered something positive to me for the first time in weeks.

I ask Milo if he minds to drive me to Kämp for my meeting with Yelena. He says, "Sure," and gets dressed.

We take his Crown Victoria. My phone rings as we pull out. Phillip Moore.

"Vaara," I answer.

"Hello, lad. I've called to give you a heads-up. Is your phone secure?"

"The securest."

"My situation went slightly awry. I decided to decline your generous offer to let me and my family live unless I committed double murder. I intended to take my family and leave the country instead, and so I resigned my position, effective immediately. Saukko took exception to my resignation, never mind that I've worked for him for five years and said nothing against him, just said I'd like a change and to move on. He said, 'Congratulations, you just made my Shit List,' and had me escorted off the property without even letting me get my kit. I took great umbrage at such treatment."

"And you'd like me to help you how?"

"It's me trying to help you, despite the fact that I may kill you one day. I wanted my things and had no intention of being on a death sentence list, neither yours nor his, so I went back and cut the throats of those two Corsican bastards— they were sleeping like babes—took their passports, and appropriated the keys to the safe-deposit box, both Saukko's and theirs. I did a little passport doctoring and replaced the elder Corsican assassin's photo with my own, went to the bank, emptied the safe-deposit box and took my retirement fund."

"A mocked-up passport altered by hand in a hurry got you into that box?"

"It's July, I took a gamble that the regular admin was on

vacation, and it was more than sufficient to get by the zit-faced zombie summer intern from the university."

"You've been a busy man," I say. "Why are you calling me?"

"To let you know the Corsicans are dead and end our relationship. For now. You know, I never truly feared you. Your torture-session stage props were a bit over-the-top, like a movie cliché, and it wasn't sodium pentothal and LSD in those syringes, was it?"

"No, it was vodka."

"The poor man's truth serum. Injected alcohol works to a certain extent. Good thinking. The reason I'm calling is that I'm no longer in the country, and both keys to the box are at the bottom of the Baltic. Saukko has to find himself more killers, and there aren't so many proficient ones around. Then he has to have the box drilled, which he will find empty. So he has to fill it back up. Even billionaires don't generally have a million in cash just lying around the house. It will take him at least a couple weeks to sort it all out, which gives you a window of opportunity."

"To do what?"

He laughs. "Anything you like, lad. Anything you like."

"A couple questions," I say, "just so I can believe you."

"Fire away."

"In your iPad calendar, you list 'driving' almost daily. What does it mean?"

"Working on his golf drive. He has some buoys out in the sea at different distances. He aims at them and drives a bucket or two of balls. He has his own green and sand trap as well, to practice putting and chipping."

"What about the dead Corsicans and body disposal?"

"Saukko has had too many bodies about. Daughter. Son. Now this. A background check on the dead men would turn up suspicious things. Too much trouble, too much publicity. They'll also be at the bottom of the Baltic by now. Maybe they'll find their key down there."

"How did you defeat security and get in the house?"

"I designed that system, left myself default security codes. And the easiest way in is by sea. It was a fine night for a swim."

"Thank you, Moore," I say. "Just one last thing. You said Saukko has a morbid fear of death. I put a sword to his heart and pushed it hard enough against his chest to draw blood. He never flinched."

"A sword?"

"Long story."

"Saukko is a master of façade. He has terrible psychological problems but is very good at masking them."

"Enjoy retirement," I say.

"I promise you I will. Take my advice, lad. Help yourself while you can. There are other men with the same set of skills as myself, and when Saukko gets himself a roguish one, it'll be time to say good-bye to your family."

I start to say that the last time a man with his skill sets tangled with us, he was so careless that my wife killed him, but too late. He rang off.

"What did Moore want?" Milo asks.

I consider the subtext of his call. He didn't call me for his stated reasons. He called to get a job done. "Because he wants us to kill Saukko."

Saying it out loud sparks other truths. Saukko talked about waiting years to take his vengeance on me, yet tried to kill my family within days. He fears death. He reads people. He knows I'll stop at nothing to protect my family. He fears me. He called the tune. Play for blood.

Moore killed the Corsicans but let Saukko live. Especially after the kidnap and following murder of his daughter, then the drama of the death of his son, the murder of Saukko will generate the biggest manhunt in Finnish history. Moore foresaw this. If Saukko were murdered and Moore disappeared, the investigation would focus on him from day one and he would be apprehended. So he spared Saukko and left us to clean up the mess.

But we have more than just Saukko to deal with. Through some twisted logic, Jan Pitkänen hates both Milo and me for the cards life has dealt him. Jan Pitkänen arranged the car bomb, ultimately murdering Mirjami, proof of said hatred. Jan Pitkänen works for the minister of the interior. Thus, Pitkänen had Ahtiainen's implicit or explicit blessing before acting. Ahtiainen almost certainly discussed it with his best friend, Jyri Ivalo, before giving the green light. Thus, they are all complicit in the murder of a sweet and innocent young woman. I have too much dirt on both of them. Ivalo fears me. Ivalo will find a way to either kill me or put me behind bars. I have no doubt the pair of them have put as much time and energy into collecting dirt on me as I have on them.

The value of all these lives is reduced to a kind of balance sheet. Either me, my family, Milo, Sweetness or maybe even Jenna must die. Or Saukko, the minister, the chief, the murderer and the patsy hate-monger must die. There are no smaller, neater options. There's no room for negotiation. There's no way everyone can live. It's a terrible decision to have to make, but only one choice is possible.

I pat Milo on the knee. He looks at me, quizzical.

"When we get back to my house," I say, "I have a present for you."

32

We arrive at Kämp. I ask Milo to wait in the car. It makes him unhappy, so I explain that I would bring him but the invitation was extended only to me. He accepts it.

The doorman recognizes and greets me. I limp down the long carpet into the lobby, pass by the marble pillars, under the chandelier and rotunda, then take a left to the elevators. Sasha was no more careful with his hotel security than he was with his finances. The key card is in the hotel's paper holder with the room number on it. I take the elevator to the fourth floor.

Kämp has gone through various renovations. About half of the hotel has security cameras mounted in the hallways. The other half doesn't. It also has a security staff of one. He mostly attends to preparations for visiting political dignitaries, rock stars, people of that ilk.

I let myself into Yelena's suite. To the left of the door, Yelena used her blood to write on the wall in big letters. Blood dribbled down the wall as she wrote, I suppose finger painting. "My husband killed me." I use my cell phone to take pictures. I follow the blood trail to the bathroom, Yelena stills wears the clothes she had on when we met, minus shoes.

What happened seems obvious. She slashed her wrists, wrote her message, then came in here to avoid making a mess, and I think to maintain dignity in death. She knelt over the tub. Eastern Orthodox prayer beads are laced around her fingers and her hands are folded. She prayed as she bled out. A green rubber duck sits on the edge of the tub, as does one in every room. It seems to make light of the scene, a kind of accidental mockery, and I'm tempted to move it, but don't.

I take my shoes off and walk around her suite, looking for anything that might indicate that her husband truly did play a part in her death. I find a letter addressed to me on the nightstand beside the bed, written in impeccable English.

Dear Inspector Vaara,

As you see, I've provided you with ammunition against my husband. You seek that urchin. He knows her whereabouts. My husband is a lapdog to his masters. He will not

part with that information easily. I have no doubt you will
have to torture it out of him. Then, as a favor to me, to
reciprocate the favor I have done for you, please photo-
graph both my writings on the wall and myself. Send them
to my father (note his e-mail address at the bottom of this
note). I promise you that any and all problems concerning
my husband will come to an abrupt end, as will he.

> *With Warm Regards,*
> *Yelena Merkulova*

The logic of her note is faulty. It expresses the frantic and des-
perate state of mind of a woman about to end her own life.
There's no need to torture him if I have photos that guarantee
his death. I can offer to give him his life back, use them for
barter, trade them for Loviise Tamm. Her less than lucid rea-
soning probably caused her to think she was covering all the
bases, and perhaps the idea of her husband being tortured
pleased her so much that she thought, *What the hell, can't hurt*
to try. Such pure hatred is seldom seen.

Yelena said she was still "Daddy's little girl," that her father
was a rich and powerful man, and her husband was charged
with her care. When her husband discovers what's happened
here, he'll try to cover it up, to save his own life. I take copious
photos to ensure that doesn't happen. She'll have her dying
revenge for being reduced to "chattel," in a way no different
from the poor girls bought, sold and traded by men like her
lover and, I feel certain, under the direction of her husband. I

also feel certain that within a day or two, her father will have her husband recalled to Russia and murdered. This, I believe, was the purpose of Yelena's suicide.

I have the ambassador's number in my phone. I send him a couple of poignant images. He calls me immediately. As much as I would like to honor Yelena's final wishes, I won't torture her husband. I do, however, offer to suppress the images in trade for the return to me of Loviise Tamm. He says he would if he could, but he doesn't know where she is. He offers me a quarter of a million dollars to suppress the pictures. His voice trembles with fear. I tell him money won't cut it and hang up on him.

I call Milo, tell him to come up, and to bring protective gear to prevent us from contaminating the crime scene. I then call Helsinki Homicide to report the death. Milo arrives and we suit up. He sees nothing I've overlooked. The ambassador text messages me, asks me again to please not release the images. He writes that the last time Loviise was seen, she was in the company of Yelena as they left the embassy on foot.

Inka and Ilari from Helsinki Homicide come in. I assume they're competent detectives, but they're annoying. They've had an affair going on behind the backs of their families for years, I'm told, but bicker and treat each other like dogs when they're around other people. I suppose they think it maintains their charade. They sometimes forget themselves and talk to their colleagues in a similar way, and it makes them unlikable.

"Vaara," Ilari says. "What the fuck are you doing here?"

"Milo and I were out in our patrol car and caught the squeal. We were nearby and first on the scene." It was a joke intended as a little display of my disrespect for his attitude. We use cell phones, not police radios, and we never use a patrol car.

"Well, get the hell out. This is a potential international incident. It isn't—and it's not going to be—your goddamned case."

"Fuckin' A right," Inka says. "You're on leave and have no right to be here. Out."

I have what I came for, and it's only going to be their case for about two and a half seconds. "No problem, and good luck."

Milo and I walk out of the room and find the Russian ambassador, surrounded by an entourage of five men. The forensics team has also just arrived. The ambassador is raising hell, demanding to see his wife, demanding Finnish police leave the scene, invoking various articles about diplomatic privilege. No one is interested. Until Moscow intervenes, it's a potential crime scene that belongs to the Finnish police.

Milo and I strip out of our protective suits. The ambassador realizes it's me. "Hi, Sergey," I say. "Sorry for your loss."

He points a trembling finger at me. Surging adrenaline turns him to raging jelly. "You."

"Me," I say, and we take the elevator to the lobby.

Aino is Kate's assistant restaurant manager and replacement while Kate is on maternity leave. She's a pleasant young woman. I want to reassure her. We find her in her office. She's been crying. "Everything is fine," I say. "Finnish authorities are in control. There's nothing for you to do. If something is needed from you, you'll be asked. So don't worry. Call me if you need anything."

"Thank you," she says. "I've never been through anything like this, and I lost my nerves."

If I cited statistics about deaths in hotels, she would likely leave right now, never return, and find a job in another line of work. "Hopefully, this is your first and last time," I say.

33

Back in my apartment, I hand Milo my phone. Like so many things right now, I don't want to do this, because it's disrespectful of the dead. It's a necessity. "Can you plaster the photos of Yelena Merkulova all over the Internet without them being traced back here?" I ask him.

He doesn't bother to speak, boots up my computer, connects the cable from my phone into it and logs in to his own computer through our network. He bumps the photos from the phone over to my computer and says, "Going viral in thirty seconds."

The Russian embassy, out of fear, will delay informing

Yelena's father of her death until the ambassador can find a way to weasel out of the culpability she ingeniously hung on him by writing on the wall in blood. In the interest of survival, the ambassador will try to have it scrubbed off the walls and have the fact that it existed suppressed. He'll then claim it was an attempt to frame him. I'll preempt that. Her father will learn of her death through these photos rather than through an e-mail. It's mean. It's ugly. It serves a purpose that justifies it. Her father will kill Merkulov because it will make him appear weak in front of the world if he doesn't. The ambassador is neutralized, one less enemy to deal with.

I sentenced him to death. I feel remorse. Guilt is the overarching emotion that has defined my life. After having the tumor removed from my brain, I felt no remorse about anything. I knew it was a symptom of post-surgery illness, but I was glad of it. Of the many negative changes the surgery wrought in me, freedom from guilt was one I was glad of. I'm not sure if I should feel relieved that I'm healing, that the hole the tumor removal left in my brain is filling in with tissue and returning me to who I was before, or anger that unwanted emotions are rearing their ugly heads. I suppose I feel both.

"Going, going, gone," Milo says. "Where's my present?"

I look around. I hear Sweetness and Jenna in the kitchen and smell frying bacon. Part of their carb-free health diet. Kate must be in the bedroom.

In the foyer, over the coatrack, is a shelf for scarves, gloves and hats. Over the rack is a small storage compartment filled with junk. I point at it. "In there, on the left, in the very back corner, in a Stockmann gift bag."

He takes a dining room chair, stands on it, finds the bag and gets down. He looks inside and pulls out something square, wrapped in brown paper. He starts to tear the wrapping off.

"Don't," I say. "I don't want anyone else to see it."

He grins, giddy with anticipation. "Then it must be extra-special good. What did you get me?"

"I didn't get you anything. I hid it from you. I found it when we B&Eed a dope dealer and stashed it in the bag of cash that was in the same closet. It's two bricks of Semtex."

He cradles it like a baby and mimics Gollum from *The Lord of the Rings*. "Oh my precious. My sweet sweet precious. You've come home to me."

His impression is so good that it's eerie, and since his "precious" is plastic explosives, sounds psycho and a little scary.

"Semtex plastic explosive," he says. "A Russian classic. And enough to take down a building. You really do love me, don't you?"

I snap open the lion's mouth on the handle of my cane and wonder what in the name of God I've just done. "With all my heart."

"Can I kiss you?" He steps toward me. "Give me some tongue."

I raise a hand to keep him at bay. "Down, boy. Down," I say, as I would to a dog.

He grins and calms himself. The permanent pools of black

around his eyes from self-imposed sleep deprivation glisten like oil. "Why did you keep it and hide it?"

"I couldn't think of a way to dispose of it, stuck it there and forgot about it. I hid it because I was afraid you'd blow up a building with it."

"So now you're supporting my plan?"

I gesture toward the balcony. We go outside, close the door so no one can hear us and light cigarettes.

"So now you like my plan," Milo says. "That makes me happy."

I stare at the parking space where the Audi blew up. "No, I don't approve. Not in the least. I just can't find another solution and don't want you to get caught. That's why I gave you the Semtex. Not having to steal plastique is one less risk you have to take. What's your timetable? Phillip Moore said we have a couple weeks."

"Then we have a lot to do in a short amount of time. I have to burn the midnight oil and finish writing a crazed mass-murder manifesto, surveil the targets and figure out the most economical way to take them all out in one day. And most importantly, we have to learn to shoot. You can't shoot for shit, and I have to learn to shoot left-handed. You're still taking out Jan Pitkänen, right?"

I sigh and nod.

"I'll GPS tag his car so you can find him when you're ready, but he'll kill you in a heartbeat if you don't improve your shooting skills."

So he will. We both light another cigarette and stand side by side in silence. My eyes keep drifting to the blackened spot where the Audi burned. "I forgot to tell you," I say, "Moore said that 'driving' means that Saukko goes out in his yard and knocks golf balls into the sea."

Milo flips his cigarette end down to the street. "I'm leaving now. The day is getting on. I'll see you at Arvid's—I mean your house in Porvoo—tomorrow."

I make the sign of the cross in the air. "*In nomine Patris et Filii et Spiritus Sancti.* Go with God, my son."

"Forgive me, Father, for I am about to sin oh so grievously." He laughs. "See ya."

I let him show himself out and stay on the balcony. I turn what we're doing over and over in my head, searching for a way out. It occurs to me that I haven't called ace pseudo-journalist and collector of filth, dreck and skank Jaakko Pah-kala, Helsinki's king of reputation destruction via its scandal sheets. He's on my payroll, supposedly collecting skank on politicians of all stripes for a planned hate rag. The plan for the hate rag went to the wayside, but I told him to keep working, collecting blackmail material for my own use should the need arise. The need has arisen. I sit in my armchair, rest my throbbing knee and call him.

"Hello, Inspector," he says. "I'm surprised to hear from you."

"Why?"

"Haven't you heard? I'm in Copenhagen."

"Your line isn't secure. Call me back from a pay phone or bar phone or something." I hang up and wait.

Ten minutes later, he calls back. "I just spent money I don't have on a disposable phone," he says. "It doesn't have much time on it."

"What happened?" I ask.

"SUPO agents came to my house. I told them I work for you, thinking they would go away. Instead, they beat me up, confiscated just about everything I own and told me to get out of the country. Do you know how much time and expense I put into my literature collection?"

Meaning he collected hate. Prewar anti-Jewish propaganda and what he considered the best Finnish skank, his specialties.

"What about the stuff you collected for me? Have you acquired anything new and valuable over the past weeks that I haven't seen?"

"Quite a bit."

"Where is it?"

"It's the digital age. All the photos were in my computer, which they confiscated."

"You have no backup?"

"Of course I do, in cloudspace, at a different address than the one I gave you before. But you can't have it unless you pay me real money for it. You've cost me enough as it is. Do you have any idea how hard a time I'm having finding work here? My Danish-language skills are somewhat lacking."

His whiny, pathetic voice has always grated on me and he's a duplicitous prick. And I paid him a generous salary to collect the skank, so technically it already belongs to me.

But he has a valid complaint, so I don't point this out or make any demands of him. "How much?" I ask.

"Fifty thousand."

"Do you really have anything I can use?"

"I did a good job, as promised. People across the political spectrum in the most compromising positions. Most of them sexual in nature. A few involving money."

"Get on something secure. Buy another throwaway phone or something. Send the cloudspace web address and passwords, along with your bank account number. I'll give you thirty K, not for the skank, because I already paid you for it, but for the loss of your stuff, job, and the beating you took. Fair enough?"

His phone runs out of time and the line goes dead.

I make one more call. Mirjami's autopsy should have been performed by now. I couldn't bring myself to attend and so didn't ask about its scheduling. One of the coroners gets furious when detectives don't attend and then call him for results. He believes cops should be present in every step of an investigation. Getting transcriptions takes forever. I call the stenographer, ask him if he'll do me a favor, just listen to the end of the recording and tell me the cause of death. He's nice about it, says he'll call me back.

It doesn't take long. "She died of morphine overdose," he says.

I start to ask how such a thing might be possible, then remember he's a stenographer, not a doctor, thank him and figure it out for myself. She had a morphine pump. She could barely negotiate it with her bandaged hand, and I don't think it's even possible to OD with one. Someone went to her room and finished the job of murdering her.

I remember Moore's reference to her being my mistress. The two bikers spying on us for Jan Pitkänen must have come to that conclusion because they saw her entering my bedroom at night. I check my received calls and count them down to one identified only by number, not by name. That's the doctor's number. I call. He doesn't answer. I send him a text message and ask if he can check with the staff on duty and ask if a man with a scarred face visited Mirjami. A few minutes later, he answers. He doesn't have to ask, he saw a man fitting that description himself. I thank him and ring off. So Pitkänen killed my friend.

Pitkänen. I said I would kill him, and a big part of me wants to. Mirjami's murder deserves to be avenged. But I'm hedging again. Blood, as often as not, brings more blood, and another part of me wants to hurt no one. So much blood has already been spilled. I ask myself what Mirjami would want. She was a gentle spirit, a healer, would likely want nothing done. I could try to make a deal. After Milo kills his boss, Pitkänen will have lost his sponsor, will be acting alone. I could offer him a cash settlement, compensation for his face and a truce. But revenge, like a funeral, is for the living, not the dead. Will I really kill him? I don't think I'll know until the moment I'm forced to make the decision.

Sweetness comes out of the kitchen and belches. "We moving today?"

"Yeah. Get your stuff together and we'll leave in an hour or two."

I check on Kate. She's showered, dressed, and has her makeup and hair done. She's also breast-feeding Anu.

"Hello, husband," she says. "How are things?"

I've come to suspect from our interactions since she left me that, when she ran away from home, first to the hotel and then to Florida, her hateful attitude wasn't really directed at me, but a façade designed to mask that she knew I played some part in her life, but wasn't sure what it was or who I was, whether I was friend or foe.

On rare occasions, she would snap to reality enough to comprehend that I'm Anu's father and would bring her here for visits, but remained confused about the state of our relationship when she saw me. She probably thought she left me for a reason, but couldn't fathom what it was, so her natural assumption was that she had a reason or she wouldn't have left. So she treated me as an enemy. I was really just an unknown quantity, and as such, frightening. She's getting past that now.

I get a text from Jaakko. Cloudspace user name and password and banking info.

"Things are fine," I say. "Can I hold Anu?"

"As soon as she's done here."

How to do this without causing upset and trauma? I'm not a psychologist, I have to feel my way through these situations. Kate must have felt the same dealing with me after my brain surgery. "I'm sorry, but you shouldn't be breast-feeding her while you're taking antidepressants."

She takes Anu away from her breast and shakes her head. "I don't know where my mind is. I knew that and I just forgot."

A reasonable response. Her medication must be kicking in. This makes me so happy I could burst. I sit down on the bed.

"You said we're leaving for Porvoo today," she says. "What should I bring?"

"Mostly summer clothes. It can get chilly in the evening on the river, so some jeans and a sweater or two as well."

She screws up her mouth, thinking hard. "I have to get back to Helsinki for therapy twice a week."

This conversation is pleasing me more than anything that's happened since Anu was born. "It's not that far. I promise we'll get you back here for therapy. And if you need more clothes, we can always pick them up while we're here."

"Thank you, Kari," she says.

I was hoping for an *I love you*. But one step at a time.

34

We get to Porvoo around eight p.m. We travel light, it doesn't take long to get our things out of the Wrangler and inside.

It's called a shore house—a few stand in a row along the river—built after the great fire of 1760, and by tradition painted ocher red. They were built to house goods traded with German ships from the Hanseatic League. Given its size, picturesque location and place in history, as well as being situated in the tourist mecca of the old town, it's worth a small fortune.

When I told Kate it would be a kind of summer vacation,

I lied. I believed she and Anu would have to be constantly guarded, unable to venture out without Milo, Sweetness or me for protection. Changes in circumstances have made a real vacation possible. The Russians have other fish to fry— trying not to die—Veikko Saukko's killers are dead, thanks to Phillip Moore. The only immediate threat known to me is Jan Pitkänen. He's not stupid enough to kill a cop's family by himself. We have those most valuable of things: time and freedom. I believe this place will help Kate heal.

I show her around. For decades, Arvid and his wife Ritva made this their home, and it's been untouched since their passing. Their ghosts and shadows seem to be everywhere. It's an odd feeling, but not a bad one, as they're the ghosts of friends. It even makes the place seem more friendly, in a strange way is a source of comfort.

I turn Katt loose out of his travel carryall. He leaps out to investigate. Arvid and Ritva had four cats. He has much to occupy him, rooting them out, until his tiny mind reaches the conclusion that they're no longer here. They mourned for Ritva after her death. Their constant meowing was a reminder to Arvid of the death of his wife of half a century. He couldn't bear for anyone else to have them, so he drowned them. He built a square box for a coffin and left it in the backyard. It was winter, the ground too hard to dig. It's nailed shut. Kate can't look in it. Still, I need to bury it or throw it in the sea or something.

The downstairs is one large, almost open space. In the front of it, a davenport and three well-worn, comfortable armchairs surround a coffee table. Against the wall to the left of it, an antique bookcase with glass doors serves as a liquor cabinet. To the right, a fireplace. A big, dark oak dining room table is farther into the room. Behind it, a massive soapstone stove stands floor-to-ceiling and is the room's only divider. Behind and to the left of it is a well-equipped kitchen with both gas and wood-burning stoves. Pots and pans hang from hooks on the ceiling. A half bath is next to the back door, which leads out to a sizable backyard surrounded by a brick wall, with an untended flower garden. It feels like a home.

Upstairs are two bedrooms and a full bath. Kate and I put our things in the master bedroom, Arvid and Ritva's room. Everything is antique. The bed. The wardrobe. The chest of drawers. A writing desk. They were together for fifty years. They might have bought them all new. The closets and drawers are full of their things. I make room for ours and wonder if I'll be sleeping in here tonight.

Everyone is hungry. For the first time in a long time I feel that I can take Kate and Anu out and they'll be safe. I suggest Wilhem Å, a restaurant just a few minutes' walk from our house. It's atmospheric. Its large patio extends out over the river. Moored boats are lined up in front of the patio. It's a lovely evening, still daylight, a breeze coming off the river. We order beers, except for Kate. She orders orange juice. What Torsten said appears to be true. Valdoxan appears to have replaced alcohol as her nepenthe.

She's healing. I offer a silent prayer of thanks and hope

that she continues. I have an inkling that her situation is like falling down a well. She can see light at the top, and it's narrow enough for her to climb out, but the walls are slick and precarious. It would be all too easy for her to slip and hurtle back to the bottom and land with a splash, once again in the freezing water.

Sweetness, of course, lines up three *kossu* shots and knocks them back one after the other, "to build his appetite," which is already enormous and needs no enhancement. In keeping with their diet, he and Jenna order steaks. He orders two.

I would like to join them, have a good piece of red meat— I miss it—but my gun-shot mouth isn't up to chewing it yet. Instead, I have roasted salmon in mushroom sauce. Kate has a perch fillet in dill and remoulade sauce.

We take a stroll down the boardwalk after dinner. Pushing Anu's stroller spares me the decision of whether to hold Kate's hand or not, as I have to guide the pram with one hand and limp along with my cane in the other.

We get home. Kate announces she's tired, needs sleep. I'm exhausted as well. Carrying Anu, I tag along up the stairs behind her and into the bedroom. She cocks her head and looks at me, quizzical.

This is a kind of litmus test. I'm nervous. "Can I share the bed with you?" I ask.

She sits down on the bed, mulls it over and nods. "You have to sleep somewhere."

I feel a great sense of relief. That's good enough for now.

We perform our pre-bed ablutions, take our medications, stand side by side as we brush our teeth. Without speaking, we climb into opposite sides of the bed. I kiss her shoulder and wish her good night. She doesn't respond.

35

In the morning, there's no food in the house, so we go out for breakfast. Kate is polite, if not warm, toward me. On occasion, I see her face go blank for a moment, as if she's having little lapses, either unable to recall something or remembering something she would rather not.

Afterward, she asks if we can explore the old town. It's a little maze of arts-and-crafts stores, antique shops and junk for tourists. She loves this shit. I play the good husband, trail around behind her with my wallet ready as she chooses little things that catch her eye.

Handmade place mats for the table, some candles, a bottle

opener with a handle made from a reindeer antler. This is tourist season. A small army of husbands and wives follows exactly the same routine. Porvoo is primarily Swedish-speaking, so I can at least be of some use, translating questions to clerks for her on occasion. Mostly just for fun. The clerks cater to a lot of foreigners, and most speak English well.

Kate tires easily. We go to a grocery and do a little food shopping. By the time we get home, she's ready for a nap. She has therapy at four. Sweetness promised to drive, and I promised to come along. The bus ride is only about an hour, but I worry that being surrounded by strangers—or even just the social pressure of having to spend so much time alone with Sweetness—would be unnerving for her. I picked up two newspapers at the grocery. One shows a couple of my photos from Yelena's suicide scene. The other, showing more taste, chose not to run them.

The Russian ambassador was recalled. Soon he'll be, as the Ripper and the Raper put it, fish chum. I killed him with my photos as surely as Milo killed Kate's brother by giving him so much dope. I can't bring myself to care. I hope his gangster partner, Yelena's father, hangs him from a cross and crucifies him. Finland requested permission to remand him pending further investigation. Moscow refused, and made a formal complaint because Finnish police processed the crime scene without diplomatic consultation. Exactly what I expected.

But it reminds me that I have another task to carry out, and soon: finding the nearly two hundred girls pressed into sexual slavery on the list Sasha had in his iPad. And Loviise. They suffer as I procrastinate. For a man hanging around doing nothing, I have much to do. Try to bring my wife back to good health and keep my family together. Play whatever part I must to end our feud with the greater powers of the establishment and make us all safe again. As the homicidal Adrien Moreau would have put it, restore harmony to all our lives. No small order.

But when I think of those women, again I hear the trumpets sounding and the pounding of my white charger's hooves as I engage in battle to save the day. I see the look of love and adoration on Kate's face, the ugliness of the past erased, my reward for all the good I've done. And if I manage to free all those women, it would no longer just be the act of symbolism of saving a single girl, but an act that helps a great many people. Some true vindication of the vicious things we've done.

In our time as a black-ops unit, we may have crossed the line, but the people we hurt were bad. The world would be better off without most of them. In those cases, justice was served. I served it through criminal actions. That was wrong, but I believe in the adage "Who must do the hard things? He who can." Though I don't regret my actions, I don't want to repeat them. I don't like hurting people. I don't want to jeopardize my marriage. I need only to look in the mirror to see that I've done my duty. Now I wish only to live in peace.

Milo shows up around two, comes to the house and asks Sweetness to help him bring his things in from the boat. Sweetness is the only one of us undamaged, and as a result, finds himself constantly playing errand boy for all of us, but he never complains. Alcoholism and sociopathic tendencies aside, he's a good kid.

I go out with them to have a look at Milo's boat, moored near the house. It's a twenty-five-foot Coronado with two cabins, about forty years old but well cared for. Milo, convinced as he is that everyone is fascinated by technical details, fills us in on everything from its masthead sloop to its draft to how many watts the solar panels generate to details about its engines and props and even its Danforth-style anchors. For Sweetness and me, much of his lecture might as well be in Greek, but we've learned it's easier to indulge him than shut him up.

Even by his standards of haggard appearance, he looks exhausted. Eyes like bloody holes in his head may be the result of his smoking dope along the ride, but still. "Hard night?" I ask.

"I was up all night writing the manifesto," he says. "It's not hard, and I'm having fun with it, but it's pretty time-consuming."

Most of what he's brought along is guns and bullets. He's hesitant to leave the sniper rifle in the boat, but I don't want Kate to see it or the massive amount of ammo. Enough to fight a short war, there's no way to explain it. His pistol is fine, standard police fare, but I especially don't want her to see his beloved 10-gauge Colt sawed-off shotgun, as she used it to blow Adrien Moreau in half.

The three of us sit down on the dock, let our feet dangle

over the water and light cigarettes. "I cruised by Veikko Saukko's mansion," Milo says. "Sure as shit, just like his calendar says, he was out behind the house, knocking golf balls into the sea. Kind of weird, isn't it? I'm going to kill one man practicing golf and two men playing it on the same day. Generally, people don't consider it a dangerous sport."

"Do you have a plan and a schedule yet?" I ask.

"One time, I went to a junkyard looking for a carburetor for a car I used to have," Milo says. "A piece-of-shit Volkswagen from the seventies. This big fat fuck was in a shack—the so-called office—lying on a couch with the springs popping out of it, watching a soap opera on a TV so old it was black-and-white and had rabbit-ear antennas, eating a bag of candy. I asked him if they had one. He said, 'I dunno.' I asked him if they had that make of Volkswagen. He said, 'I dunno. Maybe. You gotta go out and look around.' I said, 'Well, goddamn it, what the fuck *do* you know?' He said, 'Not much. The less you know, the less you have to do.' I thought that was true and pretty wise, especially coming from that dumb shit. And it applies here. How much do you really want to know?"

I shrug and flick my cigarette butt into the river. It goes out with a hiss and starts its journey toward the sea. "What I need to know, I guess." As I said to Moore, pre-knowledge of a crime is tantamount to collusion. I'm as guilty as Milo and Sweetness.

"What you need to know is that every morning, you and I are going to get up before dawn and claim we're going fishing. What we're really going to do is go to a little unin-habited island I know and learn to shoot with our disabili-ties. That OK with you?"

"Sure."

"But to pique your curiosity, a little B&E last night reveals that Jyri Ivalo keeps his golf clubs in the trunk of his Mercedes."

He gets up and grabs the bag with his computer in it, Sweetness shoulders his duffel bag and we go inside. Milo looks around. "Nice place. Where should I sleep?"

I point at the davenport. "I guess there. The beds are already taken."

"I'll just sleep in the boat," he says. "The bed is comfort-able, and I can keep an eye on my Barrett."

I go upstairs and find Kate awake, getting ready to go to therapy. "I heard Milo's voice," she says. "Why is he here?"

"He's going to stay with us for a little while."

"I don't understand. We're supposed to be having a vaca-tion, but you brought everyone that works for you with us."

Think fast, Kari. "I can't get around very well, and you have some . . . problems. While you were away, Sweetness came to help me out, especially because I had Anu. I was in so much pain, it was all I could do to make it to the grocery store and back. Jenna goes wherever Sweetness goes. Milo has been away. I haven't seen him for a while, and he's not in very good shape either: He's partially disabled and depressed about it, and I thought our company might do him some good. Besides, he's going to sleep in his boat. He mainly wants to fish. You won't see much of him."

She looks at me askance. "And you had Mirjami with you as well, a small army of helpers. Good for you."

"Mirjami came one day because she and Jenna had become good friends, and I guess they just wanted to party together. Mirjami was a registered nurse, saw what bad shape I was in, and threatened to call an ambulance if I didn't do something about it, so I called Jari. He agreed to shoot up my knee and jaw with cortisone to relieve my pain, but thought I needed to have my knee professionally bandaged and braced daily so I wouldn't damage it further. Mirjami volunteered for the job. And so it ended up that I found myself living with an apartment full of kids."

"Did you really not fuck her?"

"I swear to you that I didn't."

She turns toward me and brushes the back of her hand against my cheek. "After what I've done, I wouldn't blame you if you had, but I'm glad that you didn't."

We make the forty-five-minute drive to Helsinki, mostly in silence, and drop Kate off at Torsten's door. Sweetness and I go to a little grocery store down the street and buy a six-pack. We take it to Kaivopuisto, a big and beautiful park, sit on the grass, enjoy the beautiful day and sunshine and drink a couple. Sweetness pulls out his flask.

"Please," I say. "Not with Kate in the vehicle."

He takes a second to decide whether to argue with me, then screws the lid down and puts it away.

We're waiting in the Jeep when Kate exits. She asks if I'll ride in the back with her on the return trip. Her eyes are red and puffy from weeping. I get in the back with her and she takes my hand. When we get out on the highway, she lays her head on my shoulder. Sweetness leaves the stereo off, I'm sure to give us time for Finnish silence. It often relates more meaning than spoken words ever could. We spend the trip home in the quiet.

36

We arrive home to an empty house. Jenna is out. A note on the table says she got bored and went exploring. There's little to do except housework. The place has stood empty for a while and needs a good dusting. I'm not in the mood, and while my knee hurts less than it did before the cortisone, it's still a pain in the ass to perform simple tasks with only one free hand, my cane always in the other.

I browse Arvid's book collection instead. He—or maybe Ritva or both of them—was an ardent crime and thriller novel fan. Complete works by Dashiell Hammett, Raymond

Chandler, John le Carré, Graham Greene, Jim Thompson, Maj Sjöwall and Per Wahlöö, and Mika Waltari. I decide to work my way through the whole 87th Precinct series by Ed McBain. That should keep me busy for a while. I settle down in what was Arvid's armchair and start reading *Cop Hater*. The others wander in. Sweetness has been to Alko, bought a dozen bottles of *kossu* and a case of beer. Milo has been on his boat, working on his computer, I imagine writing his manifesto.

Jenna and Sweetness do what they do best, sit at the table and drink. They whisper the private jokes of young lovers and giggle. In a little while, everyone gets hungry, and by general consensus, we decide to go to a good restaurant. This trip feels more and more like a vacation than I thought it would.

We go to Wanha Laamanni. It's only been a restaurant for a few years, but the building was constructed near the medieval cathedral around 1790. The menu is gourmet. Sweetness complains about the lack of steaks. As far as he and this place are concerned, it's like lipstick on a pig. He turns up his nose at the snails in gorgonzola. Roast lamb, after a few aperitifs, pacifies him. For me, wild boar rillettes as an appetizer and a main course of charcoal-grilled Arctic char with choron sauce, saffron and fennel. Kate chooses salmon infused with the flavor of tar. She pronounces it inedible, so we trade. This should be the test for Finnish citizenship. If you enjoy the taste of tar, you pass. If you don't, you should spend a few more years here until you do. I find it delicious.

Milo has to eat left-handed. He has a hard time keeping

food on his fork. He has to learn to do almost everything in his life over again. I hope surgery repaired his carpal tunnel and radial nerve sufficiently so that he regains some function in his hand. Being disabled makes for a hard life.

After dinner, when the coffee and cognac arrive, Sweetness announces he's talked to his mother and she checked his mail for him. He's been accepted at the police college in Tampere and as a Russian-language student at the University of Helsinki.

Slots in universities and polytechnics are competitions. Often, six hundred people will sit down together and test for a position in a department, and only fifty will be accepted. The smart thing to do is to treat studying for the examinations like a job and apply to more than one department to increase your odds. Sweetness has actually done this. He now has a possibility to build a career that doesn't involve beating the hell out of people.

I'm impressed and order champagne to celebrate: a bottle of Dom. I wonder if Kate considers where the money for these extravagances came from. They're reminders of our various and sundry crimes that left Milo, Sweetness and me millionaires. Maybe she's pushed it out of her mind and tells herself I'm wealthy from my inheritance from Arvid. It's partly true.

Sweetness's success is a bright note in a stressful, even frightening time in my life. I'm afraid my wife's mental illness will cause me to lose her. I'm afraid that, in the end, I'll lose my leg. I'm afraid for all our lives, least of all my own.

And my friends are planning to change the course of Finnish history to save all our lives. I'm afraid of what will happen to all of us if they fail. Good news in this time of confusion and mayhem was much needed.

We walk off our meal and go home. This appears to be the pattern we'll follow. Quiet days, good meals, long walks and early nights. For Kate and me and our relationship, my devout hope is that this pattern will be therapeutic and bring catharsis.

Milo invites Sweetness to go drinking with him. Jenna assumes she's included. She's not, and miffed about it. Sweetness cites a need for "guy time."

Kate and I get ready for bed. I set an alarm on my cell phone.

"What are you doing that for?" she asks.

"Milo and I are going fishing early tomorrow morning."

Fearful of upsetting her, I stick to my side of the bed and avoid anything that might be construed as physical contact.

We lie in silence for a while. "Don't you want to touch me anymore? Are you so angry?" she asks.

I'm flummoxed. "Angry for what? I'm not angry about anything. I'm afraid you're angry, and I don't want to do anything to upset you."

She lies on her back, arms at her sides, stares at the ceiling. "I left you when you were too weak to care for yourself. I was cruel to you on the rare occasions I saw you, refused to let you see your child very often, and then I dumped her on you so I could run to the other side of the world to turn into a drunk."

I'm taken aback, wasn't expecting this. "You were sick.

You're suffering from post-traumatic stress disorder, so says Torsten. How can I be mad at you for being traumatized? And I was behind the trauma. I did many questionable things, some ugly things, some wrong things."

"Your brain surgery made a mess out of you," she says.

"Yes, it did."

I don't say that if I was put in the same situations now, I don't know what I would do differently. I began with the best of intentions and slowly sank into the sewer of corruption. I always meant well. My biggest mistake was not understanding that I was being used, that my greatest flaw is naïveté. I'm naïve no longer. I know what I *would* change. I wouldn't have let myself be manipulated and put in such positions in the first place.

"I told you to do those things," Kate says, "I advised you to do the very things I came to loathe, the things that made me wonder who you are and where the man I married went."

"You had little choice. You were scared, afraid I would die of cancer. It's hard to say no to someone under those circumstances. And like me, you kept believing I could extricate myself from the corruption. We didn't understand that would never happen. As it was put to me, 'This isn't a game you can just decide you don't want to play anymore.'"

"Are you going to do things differently now?"

"Yes."

"No more robbing drug dealers. No more taking money you didn't earn. No more bodies dissolved in acid. You'll become an honest cop again?"

I wish I could preface my answer with the absolute truth. *After I make the people in my world safe again, I will return to honesty and abide by the law.* "If I decide to be a cop again. I'm tired. I'm shot to pieces. I'm mentally and emotionally worn down. I may retire."

"I'm done advising you. Do what you think best for yourself. Have I done such terrible things?"

"No."

"Do you still love me?"

"Heart and soul."

"Can we be a family again?"

"That's my greatest wish."

She scoots over and lays her head on my shoulder. "Good." Within minutes, she's asleep there, in an old and familiar position. It seems like centuries have passed since she slept there, and having her there again, I feel those years fall away from me in a kind of spiritual rebirth.

37

I step off the dock into Milo's boat at five thirty a.m. He's already up, slurping coffee and dictating into a microphone. Judging by his eyes, he's had a wake and bake. I pick up the hashish pipe next to his computer. It's pungent, freshly used. Its warmth and smell confirm it.

"So where are we off to?" I ask.

"Let me show you something first. Sweetness and I didn't really go out drinking last night."

He leads me to the other cabin and pulls a tarp away to reveal a gun safe lying on its back. The lock is gone, drilled out. I comment on it. Milo sighs. "Like everything, lock picking is hard for me just using my left hand. This belonged to the good major. Sweetness and I B&Eed him and boosted it. It's made of cheap metal and not that heavy, so we just hoisted it up and carried it out to the Jeep on our shoulders."

He flips open the door. "A .50 cal Barrett, two assault rifles, and a small assortment of handguns. Another step in the plan accomplished."

We go to the kitchenette and he pours me a cup of coffee. He takes some gun parts out from the cabinet he keeps cups in.

"Have you learned how to fieldstrip your Colt?" he asks.

I had so little to do when I was sitting home alone, and had promised myself that I would learn to shoot, so I practiced until I could do it with my eyes closed. "Yeah, I learned."

He hands me a barrel and firing pin. "After you kill Pit-känen, the first thing you do is replace the ones in your Colt with these and fire it a couple times. That way, the rifling and pin mark on the brass will clear you if you're caught. Just tell the truth and explain that you've been practicing marks-manship, and it will explain the powder residue on the gun and your hands."

He seems to have thought of everything. "How are you going to get Roope Malinen out to his summer cottage where you can kill him after his frame-up rampage?"

"What happened to the less you know, the less you have to do theory? The more you know, the more culpable you are."

"I'm already culpable."

"We're not sure yet. Either entice him out there with a

phony meeting he believes has to be held in private, or just abduct his sorry ass and force him there. That doesn't concern me as much as making certain his family isn't there. He has to go there alone in order to commit suicide after his atrocities. Sweetness will attend to that part of things."

"Have you got a Go Day yet?"

"Not yet. Soon."

"I've got another aspect to it that might deflect some media attention. All those girls in the apartments owned or rented by Russian diplomats. Raiding them and freeing them on or around the same day seems like a good idea. Every day that goes by, those girls suffer, so if you're bent on doing this, do it soon. We release the info on the girls forced into the slave trade, it has to be dealt with immediately. It will create havoc in the police department, among the media, everywhere, just overload them all with more than they're able to deal with efficiently."

"A good idea," Milo says. "I'll get this together as fast as I can."

I ask nothing more for now. Lying to myself about not taking part in an event that will change history is the ultimate in self-deception.

Milo pilots, I fish. By the time we've reached his uninhabited island destination, I've got a pretty good catch: some nice salmon, perch and pike.

There are actually two islands, a little less than a kilometer apart. Milo chose this spot so he can practice with his sniper rig, shooting from one to the next. Vegetation is sparse on both of them, but there are a few trees he can shoot at long distance.

He says we're going to learn to shoot pistols the way Adrien Moreau taught us. No using the back sight. Just using the front sight, as if pointing with our index fingers. We shoot at smaller things and from farther away as we get the hang of it. We practice only with silencers, because we're not training to be cops at the moment, we're studying to be assassins.

We start with a garbage can lid at fifteen paces. I have to hold a cane in my left hand, so we decide I should turn sideways, like an old-fashioned dueler, to make a thinner target. He tries facing forward, with his damaged right hand supporting his left, but he says it hurts like hell when the pistol goes off. He has to stop that method and tries standing sideways, like me, and shooting one-handed.

This goes better. At first, we're just sort of waving our pistols around, and if we hit the trash can lid at all, it's near the outside perimeter. But after we burn up about a thousand rounds, we start to get the hang of it and at least hit the lid with consistency.

Milo lies down and tries out the Barrett. He picks a tree on the other island. The correct method is to apply equal pressure across the trigger with the index finger, slowly, so not even the shooter knows when the rifle will discharge. His index finger won't do this, so he puts the tip of his finger on the trigger and fires by slowly pulling his whole arm backward. Not only does he miss the tree entirely, but the recoil, akin to that of a cannon, jars his damaged wrist so badly that he screams.

He rolls over and tries the process as if he were left-handed, which means he peers through the scope with his left eye. Since he's right-eyed, this proves difficult. At first, he misses the tree again, but after a few rounds his eye adjusts, and he can't shoot any kind of group, but can at least hit the tree.

When we're done, I tell him that we're a couple of buffoons with these weapons and there's no way we can pull this off. I ask him where he intends to shoot from when he assassinates Veikko Saukko. "From the boat," he says.

I start to laugh.

He gets furious. "And what is so fucking funny about that?"

"You can't even hit a fucking tree lying down, and you think you're going to hit a moving target from a rocking boat. It's fucking ludicrous."

His face twists into something like hatred, and it makes me laugh all the more.

He forces himself to stay calm, to maintain his dignity. "I have to go to Helsinki to pick up something I mail-ordered. And tomorrow, you insignificant fuck, I will show you how I'm going to blow his brains out, from a boat, and from several hundred meters away."

"Cool," I say, "I'll look forward to it."

We start back to my place. I catch a couple more fish while he sulks.

38

Back at home, the others are just waking. I show off my catch of the day. Kate wrinkles her nose at it. Like many people not accustomed to country living, hunting or fishing, she prefers such foods from the grocery store, in Styrofoam and plastic wrap. I clean them, put a couple in the fridge for dinner and the others in the freezer chest. To my surprise and delight, I open the lid and find the freezer full of game meat, from rabbits to moose roasts, and vegetables that Arvid and Ritva must have grown last year. Kate doesn't know how to cook game, but I do. It will save a fortune in restaurant bills and give me a pleasurable task to fill my time.

Sweetness tells me that he's had a talk with Jenna. She's bored and wants to go back to Helsinki. He doesn't say it, but I can see he wants to go, too.

"The thing is," he says, "you can't drive. Kate needs to go to her therapy. You need help carrying things and to go places, like the doctor, once in a while. I don't want to leave you in the lurch. You want me to take Jenna to town and then come back here?"

I mull it over. Young love. He'll pine and drink even more without her here. I think they're mostly unhappy because with Mirjami gone and Kate back, the dynamic has changed. We're not living in party central anymore. The people who want us dead have other things to contend with at the moment. Only Jan Pitkänen remains an unknown quantity. Saukko could bring in a killer, but bullets will kill us just as dead in Porvoo as in Helsinki. And with Milo living on his boat, Kate and I would be here more or less alone. We're relatively safe and need that alone time as a family.

"Kate can drive," I say, "and she's in pretty good shape now. We'll rent a car. Go back to Helsinki and have some fun. If we need anything, I'll call. Thank you for all you've done for us."

He nods and smiles, I imagine relieved that he doesn't have to force Jenna to make a choice between going to Helsinki alone, unable to spend every waking moment with him, or staying here with people twice her age or more and boring her to tears. "I'll drop you at a rental place on the way," he says.

They go to pack. I tell Kate they're leaving. She doesn't say she's glad, but it's obvious. She just went off a binge drunk, and watching them get sloshed every night, even if it doesn't make her want to join them, may be conjuring up some bad memories for her.

Ace detective that I am, as Yelena Merkulova pointed out, surely I can find Natasha Polyanova. With the investigative prowess of Sherlock Holmes, I Google "Russian trade delegation" and "rental properties," and it pops right up. They have an office in Eira. Her e-mail address and business phone number are on the website.

Sweetness comes downstairs to grab a beer, and I ask him if he still has all that cash he won cheating at poker. Mirjami never had the chance to take it.

"Yeah," he says, "it's in a paper bag in my backpack. Why?"

"You mind if I borrow a quarter million? I'll transfer it back from my offshore account to yours."

He pops the top of his beer with Kate's new reindeer antler bottle opener. "Sure. What for?"

"Bribes. I don't even know if I really need it."

He brings it to me, I toss it in a desk drawer, and we go to rent a car. Sweetness and Jenna drop us off at the agency on their way. Kate asks what we should get.

I sweep my arm in a semicircle. "This car lot is your oyster." I see her eyeing a new Mercedes SL convertible. I point at it. "I like that one."

"It will cost a fortune."

I shrug. "So? We'll lease it. Drive in style to your heart's content."

She looks at me, appraising. "You're rich now, aren't you?"

"Yeah, but I won't be for long. I like to throw money around and I waste too much of it. Enjoy it while you can." This is true. I never give a damn about money unless I don't have any. My own tastes are expensive, but my wants are few. My salary sufficient. Despite my childhood poverty, money isn't high on my list of priorities. We drive away in the Mercedes.

That evening, we have our first family dinner in months. Kate keeps me company while I cook. Fresh perch in a chanterelle sauce. The mushrooms doubtless gathered in the local forest. New potatoes, sweet and no bigger than my thumbs. I take an excellent chardonnay from Arvid's extensive collection of wine and spirits. The sun is strong outside, but I light candles for ambiance. We don't talk about illness or crimes, sins or forgiveness. I'm happy. I don't remember the last time I could say that.

MILO AND I continue our faux morning fishing. He's still miffed, but at least speaking to me. We approach the islands where we took target practice the day before, he cuts the engine, drops anchor and starts putting things together. A box, some sort of electronic gadget, is on the bottom, then a sheet of plywood, then a small folding boat chair with a cloth seat and backrest, then a tripod with flexible legs. He curves each leg so that they're all on the plywood, but its head is over and to the left of the chair, over the armrest. He screws a Y-shaped mount onto the tripod. It resembles a vise, with two sets of pincers a couple feet apart. He lays the Barrett on it and tightens it, locks it into place.

He pushes the gun around with one finger, to make sure the tripod head allows for fluid movement, both vertically and horizontally. "Sit and look," he says.

He set it up for his height, so I have to hunch over to see through the scope. The boat is rocking, but the gun isn't. It's as steady as if we were on solid ground. He's built a stable gun turret. He surprises me sometimes, but this falls just short of amazing. "How in the hell did you do that?" I ask.

"The same way you watch TV on a boat. Ever wonder how the dish stays focused on the satellite so it's possible? It's done with a fiber-optic gyroscope. Two laser beams are fired through the same fiber in opposite directions. The beam traveling against the rotation has a shorter path delay than the other beam. The differential phase shift is calculated, translating one part of the angular velocity into a shift of the interference pattern, which is measured. It provides precise rotational rate information, largely because of its lack of sensitivity to shock, vibration or acceleration. It has no moving parts and doesn't rely on inertial resistance. They're so reliable that NASA uses them in space projects."

"Jesus, this must have cost a fortune."

"Actually, no. I put this together for very little money."

I stand up. "Let's see it work."

He sits down. "I'll be a little off, because my stock-to-cheek weld is a little different in this position, but I can prove the point. The big advantage is that I can just close my right eye and barely touch the rifle with anything except my index finger."

He fires three rounds, examines his marksmanship through the scope and smiles. "Check it out."

I have a look. The three bullets are in a six-inch group. "OK," I say. "I take back what I said and I shouldn't have laughed at you. This is brilliant."

"I didn't invent the idea. Fiber-optic gyroscopes have been used in fire-control systems for a long time, but apology accepted. Go fish or something. I need to sight in the rifle I stole from the good major and make sure it's worth a shit."

Our pistol practice goes better today. Milo brought disposable pie tins to shoot at, and we hit them at least most of the time from fifteen paces. We go through a thousand rounds again. Today, he asks me to shoot a video of him. He puts on a white paper crime scene suit to keep his DNA from getting on the outer clothing, then puts on camouflage fatigues and a balaclava. We adjust his clothing to hide the white underneath.

"Look at me. Is there anything to give away my identity?" he asks.

I give him a once-over. "Your hand and wrist brace."

"Fuck, I forgot. I've got the shit I stole from Malinen." He takes off his hand brace, slips on a class ring, a watch and a scarf. Subtle and masterful, I think. Small things people forget when disguising themselves.

I make a film for YouTube as he fires the guns he stole from the major: the Barrett—he forces himself not to wince—the automatic rifles and a couple semi-auto pistols. He has to do all this right-handed, and it's hurting him badly. The balaclava masks his pain. I wish another one of us could have done this. Unfortunately, it has to be him because he's about the same size as Roope Malinen, and both Sweetness and I are much too big to be believable in the role.

We start packing up to go, and he sighs. "Shooting left-handed just feels so fucking unnatural."

I start to make a joke about jerking off with his left hand, but don't.

He shakes his head, despondent and dejected. I know how he feels, it's hard to be a crip. I've just been one for much longer than he has and am used to it. I don't offer solace. Everything feels unnatural. There's nothing to say.

On the ride back, I ask him if he thinks he can pick a lock and do a B&E with me.

"What for?"

"The Russian trade delegation rental office. The girls they use as prostitutes live and work in apartments run by them. It's possible they keep all the girls' passports there, too. Best-case scenario: We find the passports, or maybe their identities are on file, either on paper or in an office computer. We find the names of who is in charge of what, just unravel everything and shut down their operation."

"I don't know if I can do it with my lock pick set, but with an electronic pick gun, yeah, we can get in."

I've always wondered how Milo manages to hack anything and everything. "And their computers?"

"Computers are odd little beasts. First, most people don't bother to password-protect their computers. When they do, they usually use a predictable password, so it pays to learn a little about the owner. Their birthdays. The names of their kids and pets. If the passwords are random they're hard to remember, and people often write them down and stick them under their mouse pads or somewhere in the area of the computer. Some computers have default passwords. Some have slots almost never used, for multimedia cards, memory cards, picture cards. I insert one with a virus and it goes unseen. People don't notice when you look over their shoulders as they open their computers. And if all those simple tricks don't work, there are more time-consuming ways to get it. Mostly, though, it's just through people's stupidity."

"My idea is that the day before you carry out the assassinations, we take the info we've gathered there, send it to the police and all the newspapers, and while you're doing your thing, half the force is busy making raids and arrests."

He nods. "Yeah, that's a good idea. Let's do that tomorrow instead of coming out here."

My phone rings. It's Ai. "You asked for regular reports," he says. "We've done thorough investigative work, and I have a comprehensive report for you."

"Do you have dependable encrypted electronic gear?"

"No."

"I'd like to come to your place at five thirty tomorrow morning. Is that acceptable?"

"Yes. That way, I won't be late for school." He rings off.

Now I bring up an uncomfortable but unavoidable subject. "I don't know about killing Jan Pitkänen."

Milo shuts off the engine. "You fucking hypocritical son of a bitch." I'm sitting down. He takes a swing at me—with his bad hand and at my shot jaw—but I move my head and his fist goes by me. He pulls it together and doesn't try again.

"I said something to you once about Sweetness killing a man. You called me a weak sob sister and told me to quit my whining. Pitkänen tried to kill your wife and child, and murdered my cousin—who never hurt a fly—and you're having second thoughts. You're supposed to be in charge here, but I've had to plan everything, do everything, and Sweetness and I are taking most of the risk. You're telling me you can't even do one simple fucking thing?"

He's right, I'm a hypocrite. "Let's just say I'm conflicted about it. I think when the people supporting him are dead, he'll fade into the woodwork and leave us be. I'm thinking about buying him off."

"This is about Kate, isn't it?"

"Yeah, I guess it mostly is."

"Well, I saved her fucking life, not you. You think I don't care about her? As long as that prick lives, she's in danger. Let me put it this way: He's dead. If you don't kill him and I have to, we're through. I'll never speak to you again."

"If I do and Kate finds out, my marriage is over."

"I swear to you, after the fact, we'll never talk about it again, even amongst ourselves. Kate will never know. You seem to keep forgetting that these people want to kill us and your family. Wouldn't you rather lose Kate than see her and Anu murdered? Which course of action demonstrates your love for them more?"

He's right. "I just want out. I don't want any more blood, any more deaths."

He lights one cigarette off the other. "You decided to play this game. You can't just quit when you want to. Grow up."

"And we play for blood."

"That's right. We play for blood."

Milo will do it if I don't, so Pitkänen's dead either way. And Milo saved Kate. And I owe him a debt for that act of true friendship so large that I can never repay it. "You win. I'll do it. But that means I have to know when and where. You should tell me everything about your plan."

"I thought you don't want to know the whole plan so you keep your hands clean, keep the guilt off your conscience, or whatever 'weak sob sister' shit is holding you back."

"I already have a guilty conscience and blood on my hands. Killing Pitkänen doesn't make much difference in that regard. Sweetness will do whatever you tell him. I think it would be good for you to tell me the plan, so I can play devil's advocate and look for holes in it. If you make even the smallest mistake, you'll be caught."

We sit out on deck in the morning sun. It looks to be

another perfect summer day. He begins. "We abduct Roope Malinen and drive him to his summer cottage in his own car . . ."

I stop him. "How will you know the right time? He has to be alone. He might have his family with him or friends visiting. It's vacation season. Even your first move has unpredictable variables in it."

He lights a smoke. I could chain-smoke a pack right now and follow suit.

"Any ideas?" he asks.

I think for a couple minutes. "Yeah. He loves social media. Maybe he'll give you his itinerary. Follow his blog, Facebook and Twitter posts. See what comes of it."

Milo grins. He hasn't done that much lately. "Good idea. Of course, I already have his and his wife's vehicles GPSed."

"When you abduct him," I say, "you can't use restraints that mark him. If his wrists are chafed, it's a dead giveaway that he was set up."

"Good point."

I get a beer from the cooler. I can't remember the last time I had a morning beer. "Continue."

"I go to his cottage as well, to trade boats. He has a Baha Cruisers Fisherman. It's newer, looks different from mine and is bigger and better, plus, you never know who's taking pictures or shooting videos in passing boats. Somebody's waving and saying 'Hi Mom,' and then through bad luck, they capture the serial number on the side of the boat I'm piloting, which obviously isn't his. So I go down the coast to

Saukko's in Malinen's boat and set up from half a kilometer or a little more, like I'm fishing. He comes out to smack golf balls and I blow him away. Even if I miss the first time, sea wind will probably muffle the noise enough that he won't recognize the sound. I can get him."

I finish the beer, crush the can in my hand. "Good so far."

"Then it's just a hop, skip and a jump to the Vuosaari Golf Club. I lined the bottom of Jyri Ivalo's golf bag with Semtex and embedded a cell phone in a way he'll never notice unless he empties the bag completely, and even then, he would have to look close. When I call the phone, it completes the electrical circuit and sets off the plastique. I put an expensive, long-life battery in the phone to make sure it stays charged. The ninth hole is in line of sight, so I can look for innocent bystanders and avoid accidental deaths. The club's docks are just below it. If I have to wait, I can moor there with twenty or thirty other boats and go unnoticed, or if I time it well enough, I can just detonate it as I cruise by and kill Jyri and the minister without even slowing down. They'll be reduced to molecules near the putting green."

I open a second beer. He continues.

"I continue on toward Turku and Malinen's cottage. About this time, you kill Pitkänen. We dress Malinen in the fatigues I wore and leave the stolen guns lying around. We force him through threats to his family to commit his gunshot suicide, then spread the video you just took and the manifesto I'm writing all over the Internet. Plus your skank photo collection of Ivalo and the minister, which places them at two murder scenes and casts, as they say, aspersions on their character. Then Sweetness and I sail to my summer cottage. My car will be parked there. We celebrate having destroyed all our enemies, have a good sauna, and when we feel so inclined, come back to Helsinki."

"Then what?"

"Then, as I said, we pretend like none of it ever happened and go back to our lives. I want to go back to being a cop. Sweetness will get his education, and you do whatever the spirit moves you to do. I hope you choose to keep being a cop. I'd like to keep working with you."

"I see a couple problems. I collected skank at the behest of the prime minister, when he wanted to placate Saukko by starting a hate rag. If you fly it as if it came from Malinen, the trail will come straight to me. Wait a couple days, then if it seems necessary to paint them black, fly the pix on the Net. The other is, I can't drive. Kate wouldn't take it well if I asked her to take me to Helsinki so I can gun down a SUPO captain."

"Hmm, I hadn't thought of that," he says. "When we set the date, make up something to tell Kate, an excuse to take a bus to Helsinki."

A wave of relief goes through me. If I can't bring myself to do it, I can use the public transportation excuse to not kill Pitkänen. Or I can go, but say I couldn't keep up with him, am too crippled up and lost the opportunity, which would likely prove true. Other than these, I can find no holes in

Milo's plan. But the best-laid plans go awry, and if there is even the smallest fuckup or hint that it was a frame-up, the investigation of this multiple murder will be long and thorough, and we, I believe with absolute certainty, will be caught.

W e make an early visit to see Ai. Sweetness was right to recommend him. He has his shit together. He's showered, dressed, made coffee and has *pulla*—sweetbread—frozen, not fresh, but hot from the oven in case we haven't eaten yet. He sits in his throne and chain-smokes. We supplicants pull up chairs near to him. We accept coffee and *pulla*. I notice the coffee is some expensive special blend.

"Everything has been done as per your requests," he says to me, "and since those methods failed, we've gone a step further.

"Cars were tailed to all seventeen houses of prostitution," he says. "All license numbers were taken from the cars, but I realized that the plates could be switched at will, so all the cars were keyed."

I don't know the term. "Keyed?"

"A key was raked just over the gas tank of each car, an inch or two of paint scraped off, to make the vehicles easily identifiable. In addition, although each supposed diplomat was photographed, he was also mugged." He hands me a big pile of wallets and passports. "To make the people you seek even more recognizable, each was assaulted and damage done to his face."

"You're quite thorough," I say.

"The amount you paid us buys thoroughness. Lastly, each and every house of prostitution was searched. The girl you're looking for isn't in any of them. I'm sorry to have failed you. No effort was spared."

I believe him. "You did a good job," I say. "I may call upon you again. Or, if you want or need something, feel free to call me."

"Our business is concluded," he says, and stands, signaling that we're dismissed.

IT SEEMS like a long time since Milo and I pulled a B&E together, although it was really only two or three months ago. We haven't lost the knack. We're in the Russian trade delegation office by six thirty a.m. and out by seven. All my hopes are fulfilled. A cardboard box in the supply room is full of passports in no order, just tossed into it helter-skelter as girls were taken in. We'll take them with us when we leave.

They bother to neither shut down nor password-protect the one computer in the office, I assume because the protection of diplomatic immunity has made the Russians involved lax and careless. It contains names, addresses and phone numbers. I thought a hundred seventy-nine women and only seventeen apartments didn't match up. The records in Sasha's iPad were incomplete because he was only privy to information about their prostitutes in Helsinki, whereas this is a regional office. The network extends to Stockholm, Oslo, Copenhagen, and other cities as well.

The names of which people are responsible for which women are in a list, by country. The Finns who work for the organized-crime group in the Russian diplomatic corps are also listed, along with bookkeeping records of their pay. I ask Milo to do a search and look for any information about Loviise. I hope that they have a record of her, including her current location. If so, we could go and get her right now. There's nothing, my hopes are dashed. Milo just boots it down and takes it with us, power cord and all. The ring can be rolled up at any time now. I'm just waiting on Milo's assassination Go Day to release the info.

The discord between Milo and me is gone, or at least gone to the wayside for the time being. The productive morning pleased him as much as it did me. I spend most of the day reading Ed McBain. Kate bought an e-reader so she can download books. Rather than wait weeks and pay exorbitant shipping rates from the U.S. or UK to Finland, she can have them within minutes at a lower cost. She spends most of the day on the davenport, reading a book about post-traumatic stress disorder. She tells me she doesn't want me to accompany her to therapy today. She feels good, confident enough to travel alone.

This trip really has become a summer vacation, and when I put the coming massacre out of my mind, I feel relaxed and peaceful. It's not hard to do. I can't bring myself to care about the coming demise of the bastards who set out to hurt my family. My main role, it's becoming clear, is that of chief cook and bottle washer. I look at cookbooks, plan a braised rabbit for the evening meal. That night, Kate and I make tentative, rather bungling love, like a couple of shy and inexperienced teenagers.

Quiet living, *sans* a houseful of cops and talk of crime, death and mayhem, brings us together. We quickly develop a pleasant daily routine. I'm wealthy. I start to consider retiring, think about spending my life raising my daughter, start thinking I would like a second child. This is one of the few times in my life that I've felt a sense of harmony.

Then Tuesday comes and blots all this out. Kate leaves for therapy. I play with Anu, and Milo knocks on the door. I won't have to take a bus to Helsinki to murder Jan Pitkänen. Judging by the GPS tracker on his car, he's coming to me.

I ask a stupid question. "How did he find us?"

"Duh. You're on record as owning this house, and my boat has a GPS. He is a fucking secret police detective, after all."

Maybe this was inevitable. It makes me especially angry because I have no choice but to put Anu to bed and leave her alone. I've never done that before. I change clothes fast. Put on my bulletproof vest and a shirt and jacket over it. Milo's not looking. I slip the quarter of a million I borrowed from Sweetness into one jacket pocket in case there's the slightest chance to end this without blood, and my silenced Colt into a holster under it. Milo can follow Pitkänen's car with his iPad. It's synced with his computer.

We have no vehicle, so we just walk, at a snail's pace because it's all I can do, in his general direction. His car comes toward us, he recognizes us, and slows from a distance, I suppose, having lost his element of surprise, considering his best course of action. He pulls up beside us. "Meet me in the cathedral," he says.

Great. The oldest parts of the cathedral—a small church for such a lofty description, it holds about seven hundred and fifty people—dates from the 1300s. It's been at least partially destroyed several times over, the latest being in 2006, when the roof was burned, an act of arson. Still, most of it as it exists is hundreds of years old, and it's a beautiful place, a place where one can feel the presence of God, and we're about to desecrate it.

We see his parked car. He got there well ahead of us. It's either stake out his car and wait, which isn't an option, because I have an untended infant at home, or walk in the front doors and see what happens. A church is supposed to be a place of refuge. I hope he chose it for that reason.

We step in and the doors close behind us. The church is empty except for us. I hear clatter clatter clatter, and see Milo fall. I hear the same sound three more times and feel like Mike Tyson hit me with a combo to the chest, but I stay upright. Pitkänen took a place in a pew about thirty paces into the church and on the left for protection, and with a silenced pistol, shot us both as we walked in. If we hadn't worn bullet-proof vests, we'd both be dead now.

"Goddamn it," I say, "this is the house of God. Can't we kill each other outside?"

"That," he says, "is exactly why we're here."

I say, "Sorry about a few scars on your face. I sympathize, have some of my own. And it's always a damned shame when your wife can't get along with your girlfriend. But this is fucking mental."

He answers. "I am the punishment of God. If you had not committed great sins, he would not have sent a scourge like me upon you."

I get it. He's so crazy that he makes Milo seem level-headed and lucid.

Also, it's evident that he's a crack shot. I see his head disappear as he ducks down. I motion for Milo to go to the left, and I walk down the center aisle.

Pitkänen pops his head up, and I fire. The shot goes high and wild and thunks into a pew far beyond him. But it makes him keep his head down, and he's trapped between Milo and me. I see Milo fire and hear his slide clatter. He stays low and quiet, so I guess he missed but at least kept Pitkänen trapped in place. These silenced weapons make me feel like we're in a silent movie. I'm Tom Mix, here I come. I get to the row he's hiding in. He shoots me in the heart twice more. I see the slide of his pistol is all the way back, so the gun is empty. He has to stop to reload. I don't even try to shoot him. My pistol pointed at him disconcerts him and slows him down. I hop toward him on my good leg and throw myself on top of him instead.

He struggles, but I'm bigger and stronger than he is. I pin him down and reach under his shirt. He's also wearing a bulletproof vest. I pull it up and jam the muzzle of my Colt up and under it, until I feel the underside of his rib cage. I fire four times through his vital organs. He goes slack. Dead-fish eyes stare at me.

I grab my cane, and use it and the pew to push myself up. I call out. "Milo, you alive?"

I can't see him. He's still on the floor. "Yeah, it just hurts like a motherfucker."

"Well, get up and come over here."

He does it, weaving and staggering.

"Would you go through his pockets and find his car keys? We've got to get him out of here, and I have to go home. Anu is there by herself. Kate will shit a brick if she gets home before me."

It's the long way out, but the cathedral has a small and

much less noticeable side door. I feel a sense of the ridiculous as the two of us, both handicapped, and having just taken the equivalent of a vicious beating, grunt, groan and swear as we drag him away. There's no damage to the church, except for some slugs buried in wooden pews and spent brass that will create a legendary mystery, and Pitkänen leaves no blood trail as we drag him away.

We're lucky. Pitkänen is just an average-sized man. And even luckier because Milo isn't strong enough to heft him up with one arm and dump him in the trunk of his own car, but I am. So we drive away and park not too far from my house.

I tell Milo he doesn't have to explain his disappearance to his wife, but I do, so he's in charge of body disposal. I make it home fifteen minutes before Kate. By that time, I'm so stiff I can barely move. I say I took Anu out to Milo's boat. We were getting off and he was about to hand her to me, but I fell and hit my chest hard on an upright support beam. She asks to look at it. The left side of my chest is black and blue and swollen. She asks if I need an X-ray. I say no. Finnish style, she blows on it to make it better, instead of kissing it like an American. She's becoming more of a Finn every day.

40

Kate and I pass the week in quiet solitude. I don't want to touch a gun right now. I tell Kate I'm tired of fishing and sleep late with her in the mornings. We read, watch movies, eat well. There is no talk of the past or future. We live squarely in the present.

On Friday, July 22, we watch the evening news. In Norway, a man named Anders Behring Breivik has gone on a politically motivated killing rampage. About three thirty in the afternoon, he detonated a bomb in Oslo, destroying or damaging government buildings. From there, he went to the island of Utøya, where a gathering of the Workers' Youth

League, affiliated with the Labor Party, was taking place. He went on a shooting spree. The body count is uncertain, but he killed between sixty and eighty people, mostly teenagers.

An hour and a half before embarking on mass murder, he released his manifesto via the Internet, well over a thousand pages, to hundreds if not thousands of e-mail addresses, titled *A European Declaration of Independence*. It explains his political views. Among many other beliefs, he calls for white nationalism and for the deportation or annihilation of Muslims in the Western nations, to preserve European Christendom. He wants to launch a counter-jihad in the spirit of the Knights Templar, and even claims to belong to a neo-Templar organization, Pauperes Commilitones Christi Templique Solomonici, an anti-jihad organization sworn to fight Islam.

Most interesting, from the perspective of our agenda, is that he cites the writings of Roope Malinen as having influenced his own writing and thinking.

There's footage from the destruction of buildings. Several people died in the blast. Some people on Utøya recorded the attack with cell phones and video cameras. Some clips make the news. We watch children being gunned down and dying. It's heartbreaking. Kate cries. I can barely watch it myself.

Milo calls and asks me to come over to his boat. I tell Kate he needs something done that requires a person with two working hands. I give her a hug and kiss good-bye, and suggest she turn off the television and watch no more of this madness. She doesn't.

Milo has a bottle of *kossu* and beers set out for us, in a

cabin with a TV. I think the media is playing them over and over, but he's recorded them. He pours shots. "Tomorrow is Go Day," he says. "You were right—Malinen posted his itinerary in his blog. He's going to his summer cottage to write his magnum opus, something to do with a cultural justification of misanthropy."

"You know," I say, "once you let that first bullet fly, there's no calling it back."

He nods. "I know. Malinen acting tomorrow in sympathy with Breivik will seal the deal. The guns, the video, the manifesto. No one will look further than him. We'll walk away scot-free."

I agree. "Let's drink to your success," I say. We pour them down our necks and light cigarettes.

"If you hadn't tackled him, Pitkänen would have killed us both," he says.

"Yeah, he would have."

Milo pours us another. "Thanks for that."

Brothers in blood, brothers in arms. "What did you do with him?" I ask.

"Drove him out to the countryside, packed his mouth with Semtex to get rid of dental records, then duct-taped his hands to his face to blow off his fingers, the point of course being to destroy his prints. And then, well, you can imagine the result. I walked about ten kilometers through woods until I came to a road with a bus stop, so no one would recall me being in the vicinity."

With practice, we've become quite good criminals.

He points at a cardboard box, taped up, addressed and ready for mailing. "You thought releasing the info on prostitution would take attention away from us. It's too late in the day and a Friday. It has to wait until Monday. I can mail these and plaster all our related documentation on the Internet then. Also, I can fly all the sex- and murder-related recordings of the chief and the minister at the same time."

"Check with me first. The situation has changed. After today, you don't need anything to deflect attention from you. And the bad guys don't have a chance to make any moves before the doors are busted in, and there will be no confusion about who is who. The prostitution ring and murder investigations will drain police manpower and create a media circus. Generate a lot of confusion. Let's choose our moment carefully."

"You'd better go," Milo says. "I have to make some changes to the manifesto. Skim through Breivik's, then make some changes to mine. Claim that Breivik and Malinen were in contact and belonged to the same neo-Templar organization. Little stuff like that."

I stand, and we share a brotherly hug. "You'll make it happen," I say.

He smiles. "From your mouth to God's ear."

41

I wake up, feel immediate fear and trepidation. I force myself to put those things away and ask Kate if she'd like to go out for the day. Maybe antiquing. I don't want to stay in the house. The temptation to stay glued to the television and watch events unfold will be too great.

She agrees. She loves the Mercedes SL we leased, and she finds any excuse to drive it a good idea. We go to a few places, make frequent stops to rest my leg and fortify myself with beer. People around us talk. We hear snippets of conversation about a bomb and disaster. Then, in early evening, I suggest we dine out. We make it home just before the ten o'clock news, and finally, I give myself permission to learn the aftermath of today.

Everything was recorded on security camera tapes. Veikko Saukko's head exploded like a melon slammed against an invisible wall. The chief and the minister got out of their golf cart near the green on the ninth hole. They disappeared into molecules. Where once was a golf cart, there was only a smoking pit. Newspeople quote Malinen's manifesto. Those on the scene at his summer cottage aren't allowed inside, but say police have informed them that Malinen has committed gun suicide, placed a .50 caliber Barrett rifle under his chin and pulled the trigger with his toe. They don't say it, but this means his corpse is headless.

There is no talk of conspiracy or frame-up, only conjecture about why a prominent figure, both a member of parliament and unofficial leader of hate groups, would commit such an act. They show clips of him speaking in public in which he appears unbalanced. Psychologist consultants put their two cents in. I don't have to watch long to know that Milo and Sweetness will walk away from this, that we're all now free, that we and our families are safe.

I thought I might feel remorse because of this drastic and murderous act, but I feel only relief. I feel a sudden urge to make love to my wife.

ON TUESDAY, the shit hits the fan once again. Passports of hordes of women forced into the human slave trade are delivered to the police. Addresses in Finland and abroad accompany them. After orders from me, Milo releases videos of the chief and the minister with apparent murder victims on the Internet. Apartments used as houses of prostitution, under the auspices of Russian diplomats, are raided. Dozens of arrests are made. It's a good day.

I receive a call from the prime minister. "Would it be possible for you to visit me here in my office today?" he asks.

"I'm sorry to decline, but I'm in Porvoo and unable to drive. The bumpy bus ride is hard on my injured knee. I would prefer not to."

I hear the agitation in his voice. "Then may I visit you in Porvoo?"

No way I can get out of that one. "I would be honored."

He arrives an hour later, exchanges pleasantries with Kate. I pour us old and rare single-malt scotch from Arvid's collection, and citing warmth and sunshine, we go out to the backyard for privacy.

"I assume you're responsible for blackening the reputations of the dead," he says.

I don't try to deny it, just say nothing.

"I've seen the dirt you collected, via Jaakko Pahkala."

"The interior minister mandated me with the task of collecting it," I say. "How was it he put it? He had observed that people adroit at one task usually succeed at others. I succeeded." I add, "Beating him was cruel and unnecessary."

"An interesting complaint, coming from you. Fuck Jaakko Pahkala. Osmo gave you the mandate of collecting dirt on my political rivals, not the hierarchy of the National Coalition Party."

"I'm compulsively thorough," I say.

He gets down to business. "What do you want?"

"Nothing," I say. "Or rather, peace and tranquility. I doubt you or anyone can give me those things. They spring from within."

"No, but I can see to your professional well-being."

"I'm thinking of retiring."

He takes a step back, looking me over. "I admit, you look none too well."

"I was shot up badly."

"No more bullshit," he says. "The videos of the minister of the interior and the head of the national police force, both members of my party—although they won't be missed—will lead to an investigation of their cronies and allegations of corruption, which are largely true. If you release the rest of your blackmail material involving the National Coalition Party, it will cause me a hell of a lot of hardship spending my time on damage control instead of furthering governmental agendas. Some officials will be tendering their resignations, including the commissioner of the National Bureau of Investigation. Delete your dirt—and I mean give me your word that it is destroyed, no longer exists—I'll see to it that you get his job."

This is so silly that I guffaw. "You know that even if I swore that I would destroy it, it would never happen."

He can't help himself, gets the giggles and laughs along with me. "You can't blame a guy for trying."

"Tell you what," I say. "I'll get rid of my dirt on you."

He sighs relief. "Good enough."

The irony is great. Jyri Ivalo asked me to head a black-ops unit so he could become the Finnish J. Edgar Hoover. He's dead, and if I wish, power of that magnitude will fall to me.

I drink off the rest of my scotch and offer the prime minister a smoke. He declines. I light up. "A lot of people are in line for that job ahead of me."

"That's my problem, not yours. The public loves you. You're a romantic figure. You solve major cases, get shot to pieces, march on despite it. From my perspective, dirt or no dirt, you're the best choice."

"Were I to take the job, I would take a hands-on approach, investigate cases of my choosing, handpick my staff. I won't be a paper pusher."

"I don't care how you choose to do your job, as long as you get it done. Why should I give a shit if you delegate paper pushing?"

"You asked if I want something. If I take the job, I want punishment of the people trafficking in women, both Finnish citizens and Russian diplomats."

"There were fourteen Russians implicated. How am I supposed to accomplish that?"

"I'll accept five convictions, provided the sentences are lengthy, served in Russian prisons. Of those too well-connected to face prosecution, I want five shot and killed. Call Putin. You have that power. The Finns involved all get prosecuted."

He snorts, exasperated. "It can be done."

"When do you need an answer?" I ask.

"Now. That's obvious, or I wouldn't have come here at your beck and call."

"By the weekend OK?"

"No. A commission has to be formed to investigate this clusterfuck. You have to oversee it."

It just gets better and better. Now I'm investigating my own crimes and those of my accomplices. To ensure that the lone-gunman theory is accepted, and that Milo, Sweetness and I walk free, I have to take the job. If not to protect myself, then them. I owe them that.

"I have to leave," he says. "All this death, mayhem and shit bad publicity is a nightmare for me. What's it going to be?"

"Deal," I say. "Want me to stay in touch so you can be with me for the photo ops?"

"Yeah," he says, "that would be good."

We shake on it, I see him to his car. I go in the house and sit down to rest my knee. Katt takes his customary place on the back of the chair, paws around my neck in choking position, and I go back to reading *Cop Hater*.

Epilogue

October 1, 2011

I sit down at the Hotel Kämp bar. "And for the commissioner?" the bartender asks.

I'm now the commissioner of the National Bureau of Investigation. They put my knee back together well enough so that I can drive again. The pain is and likely always will be constant, but it's bearable, and one learns to live with such things.

"A martini. You know how I like it."

"The commissioner has made an excellent choice."

Loviise Tamm brings clean glasses from the back and puts them in their proper places behind the bar. Since the moment Yelena walked in and found her on her knees in front of Sasha Mikoyan, she has never been in any danger. Yelena demanded Loviise be handed over to her, and her husband, as always, acquiesced. Yelena hid her in Hotel Marski, dropped a credit card, told the staff to cater to her every whim, gave her my phone number and ordered her to remain in her room and live on room service until she saw me on TV. Then she was to call me and tell me her where-abouts. Which she did.

Yelena's faith in me must have been great, to believe I would succeed and be on television because of it. Perhaps, like me, the idea of saving one person caused her to imagine the thundering of hooves and the blaring of trumpets. I hope she heard them as she died. Perhaps she felt her sacrifice would raise her from chattel to savior, a Jeanne d'Arc. If so, in my eyes, she succeeded.

Loviise didn't get her promised secretarial job, but seems happy busing tables and doing menial kitchen tasks here in Kämp.

When I introduced her to Kate, I heard no trumpets or thundering of hooves, but felt satisfaction nonetheless. Sweetness was right, saving Loviise and those other more than a hundred girls didn't cause Kate to come running into my arms, proclaiming all was forgiven, but it certainly didn't hurt my cause either. Slow but sure, our marriage is getting back on track.

It seems we're all healing an inch at a time. Sweetness is attending the police academy. He likes it, although it put a stop to his morning-to-night boozing. It was harder than he thought. Last week, Milo managed to move the tip of his index finger a fraction. That brings hope that he may regain some use of his right hand.

The Finnish recipe for a martini is three parts gin and one part vermouth. It sucks the mop. The vermouth overpowers the gin. The bartender makes a double with Bombay Sapphire and a hint of vermouth, rubs a lemon peel around the edge of the glass, gives the shaker a couple swirls and pours. In addition to two olives in the drink, she puts a few on top of crushed ice in a second martini glass.

The bartender is Kate. This is her first day back at work after maternity leave. She's giving the bartender on duty a break.

"Anything else for the commissioner?" she asks.

I take a sip. Perfect. "Such a well-made drink deserves a generous tip." I slide a gift-wrapped box across the bar to her. She opens it to find diamond earrings and a matching necklace with a diamond pendant.

She gasps. "Kari! Why?" It's all she can get out of her mouth.

"I just felt like it." It's true. I bought them on impulse this afternoon. "Want to stay here after work and have dinner?"

"We need a babysitter for Anu."

"I already took care of it."

"Then yes," she says, "let's have a date. Maybe catch a movie afterward."

"Sounds great," I say, and admire her smile as she serves the next customer.